Coggerton

Coggerton

Jane Wingate

Sampson's Ridge Press
Farmington, NH

Author's web site:
http://janewingate.com/

Cover photograph by Jane Wingate.

First Paper Edition, September 2012
ISBN-13: 978-0-9795043-4-1
Library of Congress Control Number: 2012915416

Published by Sampson's Ridge Press, Farmington, New Hampshire.

For Ruth Doan MacDougall

One

It was a matter of values more than anything else. After three years living in a Boston suburb, Cassie wasn't happy.

Michael Atwood worked for a consulting firm. The pay was good; the commute to work short. The schools and town library were excellent. Boston, with its glut of theaters, museums, and restaurants, was near at hand.

But the landscape was flat. Dirty snow in winter. Oppressive heat in summer. Traffic. Neighbors' dogs barking day and night. Only a scrap of yard for Andy to play in.

She read things like *Living the Good Life*, in which Helen and Scott Nearing told how they had become self-sufficient in the Vermont woods. And she scoured the pages of *The Whole Earth Catalog*, replete with tips on everything from building your own shelter to giving birth in the rough.

While the idea of hatching a baby on a bed of moss didn't appeal to her, certain aspects of The Good Life did: simplifying their needs, growing their own vegetables, simmering hearty stews on a wood stove, and especially, raising their son in the country. She imagined Andy, barefoot, ruddy-faced, shiny-haired, running through the grasses and buttercups of a clearing — their own clearing — in rural New England.

On Sunday mornings she grabbed the real estate section of *The Boston Globe*, going straight to the New Hampshire Properties section, reading to Michael the ads that took her fancy.

At first, when Cassie read him the ads, he had looked up from the sports pages, annoyed, hazel eyes scowling beneath the sweep of brown hair brushed across his forehead. Her mother had always said he looked like a movie star. But finally he started to listen as she read yet another description of an idyllic country property, and soon they were contacting realtors.

One showed them what was advertised as a "handyman's special in need of TLC, with your own farm pond out back." The handyman's special turned out to be a dilapidated, late-nineteenth-century "New Englander" with a rubble foundation, rotten sills all around, weathered clapboards that were, as Michael put it, "goddamn flapping in the wind." And the "farm pond" was a little swamp a stone's throw from the house. "Beavers," the realtor explained.

Cassie imagined the beavers, industrious little fellows, claiming ever more territory, flooding the back yard till, come spring, water still rising, she'd be on tiptoes atop the kitchen table.

Another house they looked at was straight out of a Charles Addams cartoon: slate mansard roof, gingerbread trim, stained-glass sidelights flanking the front door.

The realtor explained, "Lady who lived here — she died about a month ago — kept cats. Last I heard she had twenty-seven of 'em. Loved cats. Never let a stray go hungry. Generous soul, the old lady."

The stench of cat in the house stung Cassie's eyes and burned her throat, reminding her of Jacqueline Kennedy Onassis's dingbat aunt and cousin, Big Edie and Little Edie Beale, holed up in their decaying Long Island estate. Cassie had seen a photo of the crazy ladies, wallowing in filthy, metal-framed beds. And the cats. Cats in the beds with them, cats nosing around in the plates of food. Cats, everywhere.

Finally, Cassie spied the ad: "On 65 unspoiled acres of seclusion, an authentic center-chimney Cape with all the old features: wide floorboards, three fireplaces, gunstock posts, wainscoting. House in need of some repair but basically sound. 10 acres of field, rest woodland. Magnificent view, seasonal brook. Stone walls abound. Fifteen minutes from center of

Coggerton Village. A more private, peaceful location would be hard to secure."

❊   ❊   ❊

Turning into the dirt lane, John Skillin of Countryside Realty said, "For a piece of property this size, and with this much going for it, the price is hard to beat."

Skillin was talking to Michael, who sat in the front seat. In the back with Andy, Cassie strained forward to listen. "Is this driveway passable all year long?" she asked, addressing the back of Skillin's head. He was balding at the crown, and in an apparent effort to conceal the circle of scalp, he had combed his thin, oily-looking straw-colored hair straight back to the nape of his neck, where it disappeared under his jacket collar.

"Oh, mud season you might have a little trouble. But it don't take folks long to learn how to get around in mud season." He nodded to a field on their right. "Been a real open winter. Unusual to have just a few patches of snow left this time of year. Those three days of rain last week's what did it." He snorted. "Hmph! Probably get a blizzard next month. But as I was saying, the price for this place is hard to beat. $37,900 is really dirt-cheap for this property. True, the old place needs a few repairs, a little remodeling, but you folks seem to want to do this sort of thing."

"Where are we going?" Andy asked.

"To look at an old house, honey," Cassie said.

Skillin pulled into the yard. He and Michael got out of the car and headed around the corner of the house.

"*This* house? What *for*?" Andy asked.

Cassie flipped open Andy's seatbelt. "Hurry, Andy. I want to hear what they are saying." Damn them, excluding the little woman.

"But what are we *doing* here?"

"Hurry, Andy!" Cassie snapped, pulling him along by his hand. "Wouldn't you like to live here, in the country?"

Michael and Skillin stood side by side in front of the house, looking through the bare branches of huge maple trees at the hills in the distance. Skillin was saying, "Those three hills over theyah, beyond the village, those are in Wilmot Falls." He paused. "I'd say the view alone is worth a thousand dollars."

Michael asked, "How far is it to town?"

"We're about four, five miles due west of the town center. At night from up here you can see the lights of Coggerton—what we still call the village—twinkling down there in the valley."

"What about the schools?" Michael asked.

Andy tugged at Cassie's sleeve. "Mum, this house is all broken down. It's a broken *down* house."

"Shh."

Andy skipped to the big granite doorstep beneath the front door and sat down.

Skillin said, "There's grades one through twelve, right here in town. And the school bus stops right the end of your lane."

He turned and smiled at Andy, who was busy pulling up clumps of dry grass from between the stone step and the house. "You'd like that, wouldn't you, little fella, riding the bus to school?"

"I don't go to school. I go to kindergarten. Not real school," he said, yanking up another fistful of grass.

"Ah, but you'll be going to real school before you know it, and then you can ride the school bus. Won't that be fun?

"What about the *schools*?" Michael asked.

"Most folks around here are pretty satisfied with 'em. I went to school here—graduated in '58—and I'm doing okay for myself. Own my own business and I can't really complain about that, can I now?"

Cassie sat on the step with Andy.

"Listen, Andy. You can hear the brook. Wouldn't it be *something,* to have a brook in your own back yard?"

"Can I ride the bus to school?"

Cassie laughed. So much for the brook. "We'll see. Maybe."

She looked out at the field to the side of the house, then around Michael and Skillin to the row of four maple trees, and to the hills of Wilmot Falls, far beyond the village in the valley below. Skillin was right: the view alone was worth a thousand dollars. She didn't even need to look at the house to know she wanted to live here forever.

She pulled her gaze from the hills to Skillin's back. He had a big rump for a man. She remembered a guy in the neighborhood where she grew up who had a butt like that. The kids all called him Bum Wobbles.

Skillin said, "Just about everything you need is right here in Coggerton. There's a drugstore, the First National Grocery, a hardware store, a bank, and a library. And we've got churches of just about every faith. There's the Congregational, the Baptist, the Catholic, the Assembly of God, and the Pentecostal."

Skillin paused, looking at Michael, waiting for him to say something, to acknowledge their religion and say, perhaps with relief, "Oh, a Congregational Church. How nice."

"But then, if you folks want the Episcopal, you'll have to go to Barchester, but that's only about ten miles from here. Not far when you're talking country miles."

"I see," Michael said.

"Course, we don't have no Jewish church or like that here in Coggerton." He turned his head to look at Cassie, as if expecting her to answer his unasked question.

"We don't belong to any church."

"Oh. Course, that's okay too. Folks here are mighty tolerant. They believe in 'live and let live.' "

Skillin led them around to the back of the house, and opened a door. "Nobody locks doors in Coggerton. One more nice thing about living in a small town. Fact, generations of Gilmans lived here and never once locked a door."

At the apartment, whenever Cassie went out, she twisted the button in the door knob before closing the door, and, once outside the apartment, turned the key in the deadbolt. She doubted if she could ever break the habit of locking doors, or of wanting to.

The old house was damp inside, and even colder than it was outside. "Dead air," her mother would have called it, going around and throwing open windows.

"Old place hasn't been heated in ages," Skillin explained, sweeping his arm around a large square kitchen with blue and white linoleum, worn to dark gray streaks here and there, and curling around the edges.

Along one wall was an iron sink. On the wall to the left of the sink hung one small, two-door cupboard, royal blue.

Andy had disappeared into the next room. Cassie followed, leaving Michael and Skillin to discuss the water and plumbing and wiring and heating. She wandered through the rooms, trying to get the feel of the house. Large rooms, low ceilings, gray-painted floors. Bare, crumbling plaster in a smaller room, and in a large, sunny corner room, wallpaper with gaudy pink and white flowers on a dark green background. She would get rid of that, and have walls of creamy plaster here, and everywhere throughout the house. Plaster walls set off by woodwork painted in old, authentic Shaker colors: earthy reds, mustardy yellows, steely blues.

"Mum?" Andy called. She heard him running around upstairs.

"Where are you, Andy?"

"Up here."

Cassie stepped into the front hall and looked up the steep

stairway. The steps were covered with droppings. Mice? bats? She shivered.

"Andy?" she called. "What are you doing?"

"I'm just looking around up here in this old attic. Isn't that neat, the way the stairway goes around?"

"Yes. Come down here now."

Andy picked his way down the steep steps, baby-fashion, leading with his right foot, dropping his left to catch up. Cheeks rosy against the gray paint of the stairwell paneling. She helped him down the last high step and closed the door to the stairway just as Skillin and Michael stepped into the hall.

Michael looked at her, his eyebrows raised.

"Yes."

As they were leaving, Skillin said, "You'll find this a very friendly neighborhood. Lots of old families live out here."

At the end of the lane Skillin stopped before turning onto the road to town. He nodded at a farmhouse across the road. "That big farmhouse? Thurlows live there. Been here gener-ations, since the first Thurlows settled on that same land in 1800."

Tradition, Cassie thought. Roots.

"Matter of fact, this road is called Thurlow Hill, after those same Thurlows."

The car nosed into the road and headed down the hill.

"Everybody knows Thurlow Hill. Whenever you tell folks where you live you just say, 'Thurlow Hill' and everybody knows exactly where you mean."

Cassie liked the idea of being able to say her address was simply "Thurlow Hill." Their apartment, 430 Patton Street, Apt. 6A, was no place to throw down roots. Shouldn't she and Michael want to create roots for Andy? After all, both she and Michael were themselves rootless, in a way. Her parents and Michael's father were dead, and his mother, from a trailer park in Englewood, Florida, wrote them frequent letters describing the progress of the oranges in the tree outside her kitchen window.

With no grandparents for Andy to visit on Sundays and holidays, didn't they owe it to him to help him plant roots? Then, in later years, Andy could say to his friends, "Well, I grew up in the country. It was a good life." Or he might say to his own children, "Let's go visit the folks at the old place."

Soon, perhaps within a month or so, she would be saying, "Oh, we live out on Thurlow Hill."

"Ah," people would nod in recognition. "Yes, of course. Thurlow Hill."

Cassie dragged the damp rag along the shelf under the bathroom mirror, lifting as she came to them Andy's plastic canoe, the Crest, the dental floss, her hairbrush, Michael's comb, the tube of Vaseline standing on its lid, the Pond's Creamy Peach Facial Moisturizer and, at the end of the shelf, the Keri-Lotion bottle.

There, she thought. The last time I have to clean that shelf.

She closed the bathroom door to shut out the hockey game Michael was watching on television. A sports fanatic, he didn't miss a hockey, football, or basketball game, or a boxing match.

Sometimes she wondered why they got married. She hated sports. Hated the violence, hated the hysterical sportscasters' reporting down to the last bloodletting play of every game.

Lately Michael had taken to watching the cop shows. *Starsky and Hutch, Kojak,* even *Charlie's Angels.* Honest to God, she thought. There's a streak of redneck in him.

At times they seemed to have little in common. But Cassie would never think of divorce—no woman in her family had ever been divorced—and now, surely this move to the country would revitalize their marriage. As the move would bring them back to basics, would bring them closer to the earth, to what really matters, so would it bring them closer together.

She pulled a fistful of Kleenex from the box on the counter, dribbled a little water on them, and rubbed the spots on the mirror.

Still holding the tissues, she leaned over the sink, her face only inches away from the mirror. More gray hairs. Christ, what do you expect when you hit thirty-two. She sneered at her reflection. "You ain't no spring *chicken* anymore, you know," mimicking the way her mother used to say it, as she glanced up from the navy or maroon mittens she was always knitting while watching TV. "That Lena Horne's no spring chicken, you know."

Cassie lifted the toilet seat and said, "And the last time I have to clean you, too."

She hated cleaning the toilet. Hated even more knowing the toilet was probably never really clean. Who knew who rented the place before they moved in here, and what careless man's piddle had lodged, and caked, in that crack under the tank? It was impossible to get the toilet really clean.

In the bathroom of the Coggerton house they would, of course, have a new, sleek toilet with an oval bowl. She yanked out more tissues, wet them, and ran them over the rim of the bowl. Fuck it. Good enough. At least there *was* a toilet in the new place. It would be awful to have to use an outhouse.

Once, waiting with Andy in the pediatrician's office, she had leafed through a medical magazine, coming across a feature titled "Medical Quips and Quotes."

One Quip told of woman in the south somewhere who was doing her business in an outhouse. It seems a chicken, lurking in the bowels of the outhouse, bit the woman right on the butt. Or rather, pecked her hemorrhoid. Not long after the peck, the woman croaked, having contracted septicemia from that chicken bite.

For days after reading that, whenever she used the toilet at night, Cassie looked into the bowl first, always turning on the overhead light and peering in before sitting down.

Not that she expected to see a chicken in there. But weren't there other things? What about those stories of people in the cities flushing baby alligators down the toilets? Alligators that paddle around in the pipes below the city, thriving and growing to full size among the raw sewage. What if one of those baby alligators didn't get flushed all the way to the sewer pipes? If, instead, one of them got hung up in the trap just below the toilet and every time the toilet flushed, it hung on, wedging its hideous little elbows against the sides of the trap, resisting the downward suck of the water. And then, what if, just what *if*, some night that baby alligator worked its way back up into the toilet bowl and lay in wait there, ready to leap up and deliver a savage nip?

At least there would have been no baby alligators flushed down the toilet in their Shaker house.

Two

By the end of February they were settled in the old Cape. Or rather, they had moved into the four downstairs rooms they could quickly get clean enough to live in. There was the large square kitchen, the green room for their bedroom, the room with crumbling plaster for Andy, and the bathroom with the usable toilet and tub.

Cassie and Michael had talked about buying a small house trailer and setting that up next to the house and living in it while they were working on the house, but she feared it might become too easy to just stay in the trailer in the shadow of the old house, while the house itself rotted from within, till there was nothing left but a fragile, weatherbeaten frame with icy winds whistling through it.

At least, actually living in the house, they would be compelled to keep working at it till they had a proper home.

They would start off on the right foot by hiring local people to do the work because, as Michael reasoned, they had a reputation to maintain, and if something went wrong, they were unlikely to skip town.

Still, Cassie was the one who ended up doing much of the grimy work. She ripped out old plaster with a crowbar, never knowing what was between the old split laths and the exterior sheathing. Corn cobs, nut shells, and filthy squirrel nests spilled out.

Once a small battered water-stained book fell out of a ceiling she was ripping down. She opened the cover and read the penciled, crudely-formed words: "This Math Book belongs to Eliza Gilman. October 16, 1823."

Eliza Gilman! Well, the place was known as "the Gilman place." Cassie thought of the frail farm girls of the nineteenth century. Frail, but nonetheless hardworking girls who, if they were lucky, survived childhood, and if they were luckier still, survived childbearing. Girls like Eliza Gilman, who turned the venison roast on the spit on the fireplace hearth by day, and huddled under quilts in her low-posted rope bed up attic by night, working out a few sums in her math book — this very same math book — by the light of her sputtering candle, while the house creaked and snapped in the cold and the frost formed on the sharp points of the roofing nails only inches from her head.

She showed Andy the math book, pointing to the ceiling where it came from. When she enthusiastically explained to him that the book was more than a hundred years old and that a little girl, maybe only a couple of years older than he, owned the book ("Maybe her only book in the whole *world*, Andy. Not like you, with a whole bookcase full"), Andy shrugged and said, "The book came from up there? But why would anybody put a book up there? That's *dumb*."

The old horse-hair plaster sifted into everything, covering every surface with gritty dust. Cassie's hair was sticky with it, and for all she knew they were eating it. Worst of all, on damp days the old plaster smelled like horse manure.

Evenings, Michael would come home from his new consulting job in Bourne, thirty miles from Coggerton, to find Cassie exhausted and grimy, and Andrew red-cheeked and chipper after his days of mucking around in the last of the slushy snow, and in the sand pile the mason had dumped in the yard for his work.

However worn out Cassie was from working on the house, she was determined not to gripe to Michael. Besides, her exhaustion was colored by her exhilaration at being there, and there wasn't a day that passed since they'd moved in that she didn't have some ecstatic comment about the place for Michael when he got home from work. Living there, she said, was like being on vacation all year round.

She chattered away about the afternoon light on the hill that rose behind the brook at the edge of the field, and about the red fox she'd seen in the field at dusk one afternoon — how it walked straight toward the house and then, the very minute Cassie realized it wasn't a dog and was ready to savor the sight of it, it seemed to sense that it was discovered, and abruptly changed direction, zig-zagging over the patches of snow at the edge of the field and into the woods. And one day, Cassie was startled to see, in a wild snow squall, a red-winged blackbird, buffeted by the wind, side-stepping on the lawn before taking flight.

Throughout every day, she was aware of the change of light. The sun rose over the hill and flooded Andy's bedroom, casting a rosiness on his bedroom walls, the floor, his sleeping body. And as the day wore on, the late-winter sun swept a low arc across the sky, leaving Andy's bedroom to shine, by noon, into the bathroom, and by late afternoon, coming into the kitchen to spread its slanting rays along the counters, floor and table.

She thrilled to the loveliness around her. Mornings were especially glorious. She often sat up in bed as the light grew, watching the lights of the village lose their nighttime sparkle, then dim, then go out. In the kitchen one morning, making Michael's lunch, she watched fog at the end of the field give way to dense rolls of pink dawn clouds that cast a fluorescent glow over the field.

Where they lived before, all she saw from her kitchen window, mornings, was the flat face of the other wing of the apartment block. She never saw the sun until it was well above the tiny yard between the two wings.

Cassie made all the calls necessary to settle themselves into the town. She called the post office to make sure they had the address right. She called the library, amused to hear it was open only twenty hours a week. From the hardware store she got the names of a local plumber and heating contractor, a carpenter, and a well-driller.

Getting a well drilled was at the top of Cassie's list. When he showed them the house, Skillin pointed out the old dug well, mentioning that in a dry spell at the end of the summer, they might "run a mite shy of water."

Consulting the Yellow Pages, she found a well-driller, Myron Ricker. "Ricker's Artesian wells. Myron Ricker, Prop. Need Water? Our Business is Going in the Hole."

She dialed the number.

"Ricker's Artesian."

"Hello. This is Cassie Atwood. We live out on Thurlow Hill. In the old Gilman place?"

"Ayup, I know the place. You the new folks from Massachusetts just moved in."

"Yes." What a difference from living in the city, where neighbors hardly cared if you even existed.

"The reason I'm calling, Mr. Ricker — excuse me, this is Mr. Ricker, isn't it?"

"Yup. Myron Rickah."

"We need a well drilled, and—"

"Well, I guess we can do that for you. Have a pretty tight schedule right now, though. Busy time of year, right now. Lots of folks wantin' wells drilled."

"When do you think you'd be free to do ours?"

"Well, hate to say I could be out your way before end of May, middle of June."

"Oh! That is a while. You see, we've only got a dug well and—"

"Oh yuh."

"— and we've been told it might go dry in the summer. Can you recommend any other well-driller around who could do it sooner than that?"

"Well, Mrs. Atwood, you can try. They're all right theyah in the phone book. Nearest one next to here's twenty-five, thirty miles. You just suit yourself. Just maybe you'll be lucky and find yourself a driller 'fore I can get theyah."

Jesus, don't make him mad. Keep friendly with the locals, Michael said.

"Oh no, Mr. Ricker," she gushed. "You come so well-recommended from Gilsum's that we'd just as soon wait till you're free. If that's all right." What the hell did I add that for, she wondered. Jesus, *I'm* hiring *him*.

"That'll do, I guess. I'll figure to be at your place last of May or so."

"Okay. great. And what do you charge for—"

"Seven dollars a foot. Flat seven."

"That sounds fine. Thank you, Mr. Ricker." She had no idea if seven dollars a foot was fine.

As soon as she hung up the phone, it rang, right in her face, and she jumped back. She waited to be sure it was her ring: one long, two short, and not the ring of the other party on the line.

"Hello?"

"Mrs. Atwood? This is Emma Thurlow. Your neighbor just up the road?"

"Oh, yes, hello."

"Well, we've known for some time from John Skillin that you folks'd come in, but I thought I'd give you a while to get settled before I called you. Movin' in's a mighty tiresome business, 'specially when a body's movin' into a place that's been empty so long."

"Well, yes it is. But how nice of you to call, Mrs. Thurlow. I was hoping we'd get to meet soon."

"Goodness, least I can do is be sociable. What do you say I stop by sometime soon so's we can meet. Can't really get to know one another on these cussed telephones."

"Why yes, that would be nice, Mrs. Thurlow. Why don't you come by tomorrow afternoon. For coffee?

"Tomorrow afternoon'd be just fine. And now don't you fuss. Out here we don't any of us feel we have to put on fancy airs."

Cassie plugged in the coffee pot. Andy was reading, lying on his stomach on his parents' bed.

While she waited for Emma Thurlow, Cassie folded clothes she'd just taken in from the lines Michael had hastily put up the previous weekend.

Heaped on the end of the bed, the clothes were cold from the late-winter wind. She buried her face in a towel. It smelled sweet. It was true: the air was cleaner here. She glanced out the window at the head of the bed, looking through the bare branches of the maple trees at the blue hills in the distance. And the views are lovelier here. And the dawns and sunsets more glorious. She stood up and walked to the window. And that flock of evening grosbeaks feeding on the ground beneath that maple tree just now.

She felt smug, recognizing the grosbeaks. But then, how could she miss? After all, an evening grosbeak was pictured right on the cover of the Peterson's *Bird Guide* she had bought just the other day in the Waldenbooks in neighboring Wyndham.

The grosbeaks flew up, chittering, into the branches of one of the maples, and Cassie returned to the clothes. "Andy, smell Daddy's t-shirt. See how nice it smells, just off the clothesline."

Andy buried his face in the t-shirt. "Ooh! Just like McDonald's after they just cooked a big bunch of French fries."

Cassie rumpled his hair, laughing.

What a time-waster, folding clothes. Once she tried stuffing Michael's t-shirts and drawers into his bureau unfolded, figuring he knew the difference between an undershirt and underpants. He was indignant, as if calling her virtue into question.

She remembered the way his mother fussed over laundry when she came to help when Andy was born. She spent a long time hanging laundry just so on the clothes lines, even buttoning Michael's shirts as she hung them, telling Cassie, "They last much longer this way." When the clothes were dry, she folded Andy's diapers in perfect thirds, and Michael's t-shirts in perfect quarters, with the sleeves neatly and mysteriously tucked inside the neat white squares. And shirts. As Cassie watched Michael's mother fold his shirts before putting them in the ironing basket, and then after ironing them, hang them on hangers with the buttons facing right, Cassie understood why Michael, in the first years of their marriage, complained about the way she hung his shirts on hangers. She hung them with the buttons facing left. He all but said it: That's not the way my mother does it.

But now she might as well take her time folding clothes, because whenever she expected anyone, she was never able to start a project. She envied people who could be up to their necks in paperhanging or furniture refinishing when they expected callers, refusing to let the important business of their day be interrupted by people stopping by. Whenever she expected anyone even for a quick visit, the day was shot. The most she could manage was to clean the bathroom sink, maybe, or put away dishes, perhaps, or as she was doing now, fold clothes.

Andy looked up from his book. He'd been reading for a year and a half, since he was almost four. Cassie was grateful he could read; it gave her hours to herself.

She'd read to him since he was ten months old, starting with cloth books that hung limp in her hand and frayed at the edges, and books with thick cardboard pages and titles like *Things That Go*. That one, Cassie remembered now, was a dreadful thing that had gaudy color photos of stuffed animals riding, stiffly posed, in all manner of things like a toy scooter, a wagon, a car and a motorboat, which was photographed on phony paper waves, the boat tilted at an angle to suggest great speed. Andy loved all the books, and was indiscriminate in his choices, sometimes sitting on the floor, turning the pages of a trading stamp catalog.

Now he was reading *Charlie and the Great Glass Elevator*. He said, "Hey Mum. You know what?"

"What."

"Charlie and everybody in the elevator are oh*bert*ing in space."

"What do you mean, 'oh*bert*ing?' "

"*You* know. Like spinning around and around."

"Oh. I think you mean 'orbiting'. That's *orbiting*, honey."

"Well," Andy said, exasperated. "You know anyway what I mean."

Emma Thurlow, tall, square-shouldered, square-boned, got out of her pickup truck and walked toward the house, smiling broadly. Her short gray hair was parted in the middle and pinned back on one side with a gray bobby pin, on the other with a red plastic barrette. She wore a brown-flowered cotton dress under a quilted black jacket, and faded black sneakers. Cassie noticed her left big toe sticking out, and remembered what Emma had said when she called yesterday: "And now don't you fuss. Out here we don't any of us feel we have to put on fancy airs."

"Mrs. Thurlow," Cassie said, holding the door open. "Here, let me help you with that," she added, taking a jar of pickles Mrs. Thurlow was holding out toward her. "Thank you."

Mrs. Thurlow stepped inside. "Well now, dear, first thing you must do is call me Emma. Heavens, no one calls me Mrs. Thurlow."

"All right, then. Emma. And I'm Cassie." She indicated a chair at the kitchen table. "Please, do sit."

Cassie poured coffee and sat at the table opposite Emma.

Andy came into the kitchen with his book, staring at Emma.

Cassie said, "Andy, this is Mrs. Thurlow. She lives in the big house up the lane. The one with the sheep in the field. Andrew, say hello to Mrs. Thurlow."

"Hi."

"Hello there, Andrew. My, what a big fella you are. How old are you, dear?"

"Five and a half."

"Five and a half. Well. You must come play with my grandson Dennis. He's six years old. I imagine you'll be going to school next year, won't you dear?"

"I'm going to ride the bus. I used to go to kindergarten but then we moved and now I don't go anymore." Andy opened his book on the table and began reading.

"Oh? Kindergarten?"

"Yes. Where we lived before." Cassie said. "But when we heard there was no public kindergarten here, we decided there'd be no harm keeping Andy home till he starts first grade next September."

"Ahh," Emma nodded. Leaning across the table toward Cassie, she said, confidentially, "Course, if you want him to go to kindergarten, we have two really nice ones right here in Coggerton. Reasonable, too."

"I see."

"They don't either of them charge more than twenty-five dollars for a whole month. My grandson Dennis now — he's in first grade this year?" He went to kindergarten last year. He went to Tyme for Tykes. They spell that T-Y-M-E, to go with the 'y' in Tykes."

Cassie nodded.

"And you know, Dennis did just fine there. They teach

them a lot of creativity there. Wouldn't hardly a day go by but Dennis would bring home some little project or other. Some days it'd just be a picture colored real neat. But *other* times, he'd bring home something different. The two young women who run it, you know? They're Coggerton girls themselves, and they have lots of imagination." Her eyes widened. "Why *one* day, Dennis brought home a finger painting—done, if you can just imagine, in chocolate pudding."

Cassie smiled, nodding.

"Course, it wasn't really much to look at, no masterpiece or anything," Emma said. "But Dennis had fun doing it."

"I can imagine."

"And it's not all play there. I should say *not*. They teach them what they need to enter first grade. My Dennis learned all his letters and numbers by the end of last year, and he could print them all, too." Then, to Andy, "My, are you *reading* that book?" She looked at Cassie. "Reading, already?"

Cassie shrugged.

"Well!" Emma said to Andy. "You *are* a smart little fella, aren't you?"

Engrossed in his book, Andy didn't answer.

Then Emma asked, "Do you have any more, Cassie?"

Cassie looked across the table at Emma's coffee cup. It was still full.

"Yes, there's a whole pot. Has yours gone cold?"

"No, I meant, Do you have any more children?"

"Oh!" Cassie laughed. "No."

"Almost a shame to bring up a child all by himself out here in the country. Good thing Will and I had our two. We didn't have but a handful of neighbors when our kids were young, and we were mighty glad our Vernon and Esther had each other to play with."

"I see."

"Course, some people *can't* have any more children."

"That's true."

"Why, my sister Blanche, over to Bridgton way — that's Bridgton, Maine, you know?"

Cassie nodded.

"Well, my sister Blanche had just one daughter and, course, Blanche had always said she wanted a large family. But seems no matter what she and Clary did — Clary's her husband — no matter how hard they tried, they just *couldn't* have any more children. All they had was little Eleanor. Course, some people feel they can't afford to have more children." She paused, waiting for Cassie to take the cue.

Cassie said, "Well, I suppose with the cost of everything nowadays, they —"

"But you know, Will and I felt we could always find room for another baby."

Cassie imagined a house full of babies. Babies in cribs, in carriages, in pulled-out dresser drawers, in the bathtub, in cartons on the kitchen table, propped up in corners of couches. Babies everywhere in Thurlows' farmhouse, with still more being brought in the doors and windows, lowered in slings down the chimneys. And Emma calling out cheerfully, "Right over here: always room for another baby!"

Emma went on, "Course, it weren't always easy. Fact, there were times when we were downright — well, *poor*, that's the only way to say it," she said. "Why, when Will went off to war and my Vernon was a baby — why he weren't nothin' but a little shaver, Vern weren't — well, at one time he had fourteen patches on his little coat. I can still see them now. Most of 'em red, cut from an old dress of mine. *Fourteen.*"

"Goodness!"

"Yes. But then, we didn't let a few hard times keep us from havin' our Esther. As Will always says, 'Every baby kind of makes its own place.' Course, if folks want to have only one child, that's *their* business, and I'd be the *last* person to —"

Loud enough for Andy to hear, Cassie said, "Well, with a son as perfect as Andy, who could ever want any more kids?"

Eager to change the subject, she said, "Michael was at the First National the other day and he saw a sign in the window about the town meeting."

"Oh yes. They're required by law to advertise for town meetin' in at least three public places. Course, there's really no need to advertise for town meetin'. Everybody knows it's held first Tuesday of every March. And, far as I recall, there's never been a town meetin' cancelled. Not for snow, not for anything. Are you and your husband figurin' to go?"

"Michael said he'd like to go, but to tell you the truth, we don't know who we could get to babysit for Andy. Would you know anyone who—"

"Heavens, I'll be glad to sit with Andrew. Why I know just how you feel, not knowin' any of the girls around, and to tell you the truth, there aren't more than one or two do any sittin' in the neighborhood."

"I really couldn't think of imposing."

"Nonsense. Besides, I think it's you young people ought to go to town meetin', ought to be involved in town affairs. After all, we older folks have had our say. Not that we don't still take an interest. But mostly, we think it's you young folk ought to be involved. Course, you can't vote till you've been here six months, but that don't keep you from goin' to town meetin' and listenin'."

"Well, thank you. Are you sure?"

"Course I'm sure. Now don't you think anything more about it. Meetin' begins at seven-thirty, and you'll want to be there on time. Sometimes things can get mighty lively, and I shouldn't think you'll want to miss any of the fireworks."

Emma looked at the clock over the table. "Heavens! Is that the time? I've got to run. My Will'll be expectin' his supper." She put on her jacket. At the door, she said, "Goodness, we didn't hardly get a chance to get to know one another. But never mind. We'll have plenty of time for that, now that we're neighbors."

Three

The village of Coggerton, with stores on the ground floors and apartments over them, was still new to Cassie and this was the first time she had seen it at night.

Michael slowed up under the overhead yellow blinker. Straight ahead was a drugstore, its front a bright yellow square against the darkness. Also in the town center was a laundromat, a First National grocery store, Helene's Dress Shop, Gilsum's Hardware, the bank, the library, the First Congregational Church, and Mary Ellen's Lunch.

Michael turned onto Main Street. The stores petered out and then there was the town hall, and beyond it, nineteenth-century clapboard houses lined the street.

The town hall was brick, with neo-classical pilasters (the pediment with the date 1877 in raised cream-colored numerals), and a flagpole hanging over the granite steps. Heavy doors painted shiny dark green opened into the building.

On the right was a ticket booth, its window boarded and the whole booth varnished over, indicating it had not been used in ages.

Past the ticket booth were two doors, both with opaque glass windows. On one, in black letters: "COURT," and on the other, "TOWN CLERK," and the hours the town clerk was open for business. On the opposite wall, a door saying "SELECTMEN" and next to that, an open door with a sign tacked to the doorframe: "BEANO, MONDAY, 6:30," and "REST ROOMS," and an arrow pointing down a flight of steps.

Straight ahead were two sets of double doors, propped open. Inside, people were removing coats and putting them on backs of chairs.

Not wanting to appear conspicuous by going into the near-empty hall, Cassie and Michael lingered next to the town clerk's office.

The outside doors opened and slammed shut, letting in clutches of people, and blasts of cold March air. Once inside, most of the men removed their hats; a few pushed their caps to the back of their heads. Most hesitated just inside the green doors, wiping their feet, a gesture which struck Cassie as self-conscious rather than necessary, since the floor was all wood, worn bare, without so much as a trace of varnish remaining.

Some of the people went directly into the hall; others sucked a few last drags on their cigarettes before snuffing them in the bucket of sand just inside the doors. Others nodded curtly, almost shyly, to people they recognized. The more outgoing greeted one another with grins and loud talk, mostly about the weather.

Cassie and Michael picked up two copies of *The Annual Report of the Town of Coggerton* from a carton on a card table just inside the hall.

After the smoke-filled foyer, the hall seemed blindingly bright from the rows of pearly incandescent globes suspended from the high ceiling.

At the front of the hall was a small stage. Pulled across the stage opening was a faded maroon curtain, threadbare on the folds which undulated out toward the hall. Over the stage, a basketball hoop, and on the wall to the left of the stage, a schoolroom clock with a white face and black numerals. Sepia prints of Washington and Lincoln flanked the clock.

Emma had told Cassie that in the 1890's the town hall used to be an "opera theater." Cassie was taken with the idea that little Coggerton had such a thing, and wondered just what sort of "opera" Coggerton enjoyed in those days.

In front of the stage, in what would have been the orchestra pit, were two tables. At each were seated three men. Tribunals.

Rows of wooden chairs were set up on both sides of the

center aisle. Along the left and right walls of the hall, stretches of bleachers ascended, their blond newness looking out of place with the century-old worn floor and the dark patina of the wooden chairs.

In the aisle between the first two rows of chairs stood a tall man who looked about sixty. He wore a gray flannel suit, a narrow red plaid tie, and brown penny loafers. Cassie figured he must be the moderator, Judge Parker.

Emma had said, "Just about everybody in town's done business with Judge Parker, for one thing or another, because he's also the only lawyer we have. Most people think the Judge is too easy on kids who get hauled in for speedin' and things like that. Fact, folks call him 'Suspended Sentence Parker' because no matter what you get hauled in for, seems like that's all you get, a suspended sentence. Hardly nobody ever goes to jail if Judge Parker's sittin' court."

Arms folded across his chest, Judge Parker kept his eye on the back of the hall, squinting behind his horn-rimmed glasses, watching to see when the people arriving had thinned to stragglers so he could open the meeting. Nodding and chuckling, he chatted with people as they took their seats.

At last, he said, "Looks like just about everybody's here." Smiling amiably, glancing at the banks of bleachers on either side of the hall, he added, "Seems like there's more of you out tonight than usual. Guess this open winter we've had has got spring fever started early."

The townfolk laughed good-naturedly.

Cassie was already enjoying this town meeting, this group of people come together to make their own rules for their own lives. The last time she and Michael voted, they did so by pulling the levers of a machine in the city ward they lived in. She'd read and heard so many times about small-town New Englanders cherishing their town meeting tradition. Here tonight, perhaps, she and Michael would see why. Surely *here* was true democracy in action.

"Let's get started," Parker said. "I'll read the articles, and selectmen chair, Roger Stiles, will explain them as we go along."

The three men seated at the table on the left shifted to life, shuffling papers. The selectmen. The selectman in the middle, busily sorting and blocking papers, looked like a country and western singer, with his beige western-style shirt with brown piping along the collar, yoke, and cuffs, and a string tie. His thick brown hair, meticulously groomed, was parted on the side. Beneath his drooping eyelids, expressionless eyes swept back and forth over the people.

Judge Parker said, "Roger?"

Roger began. "Let's go through the warrant, article by article. If you have any questions, feel free to ask us, or Winfred Gilsum on the budget committee." (He nodded at the three men at the other table). "The warrant articles begin on page five, and the breakdown starts on page nine, so it'll help if we all stay together on this thing." He looked out over the heads of the people. "Seems to me next year we ought to print this thing so we don't have to keep turning back and forth from the articles to the breakdown."

People fussed with their warrants, inserting index fingers between pages nine and ten.

Stiles nodded at the moderator. "Any time you're ready, Judge."

For a while everything went quickly. Judge Parker read the articles, explaining them; the people riffled through their warrants, following along. Occasionally Stiles called upon Winfred Gilsum, the Chair of the budget committee, to explain a proposed expenditure. Cassie whispered to Michael, "Of Gilsum's Hardware. The guy who recommended the well driller."

Whenever discussion of an article appeared over, Judge Parker—bemused, doing his slow-motion shuffle, arms folded across his chest, or sometimes with his hands clasped behind his back—asked, "What is your pleasure on this?"

Cassie was wondering what Emma had meant when she said there would be fireworks at the meeting, when Judge Parker came to Article 15.

He read, "Article 15. To see what sum of money the town will vote to raise and appropriate for the Police Department."

Until now, the people had been making motions and voting with a kind of rhythmic plodding. Now they stirred, talking among themselves, as if the real meeting was about to begin.

"Last year," Parker began, "The Police Department spent $36,269. This year the Department is asking us to appropriate $42,000. Perhaps we'll let Chief Paulin explain the increase. Chief? Where's the Chief?"

Heads and shoulders swiveled left and right, then toward the back of the hall.

At the back of the hall, framed in the doorway, was a heavy-set cop, with thick gray hair, and deeply creased forehead and cheeks. He stood as if at attention, his legs straight, his feet splayed.

"Well," he said. "Course, salaries are the biggest item in our budget. We have to hire two new specials on account of all the people movin' into some of the outlyin' areas. And this year we're askin' for five hundred more to meet personnel expenses. And if you take and add to them salaries the new muffler system we need on the cruiser and the expenses of runnin' the office, then you got your $42,000."

Parker asked, "Is there any discussion on the article?" He nodded at a man sitting in the last row of bleachers on his left. "Vic?"

Stocky, clad in green work pants, a green work shirt, tan leather work boots and a red plaid wool jacket, Vic remained seated, legs spread, feet braced on the row of bleachers below, hands propped on his outspread knees, elbows flared.

"Now don't get me wrong. I'm for adequate police protection same's everybody else. But if you ask me, we got enough police protection already in Coggerton."

A man next to him stood, and without waiting to be recognized, he said, "Name's Ern, as most of you know. I have to agree with Vic here. We don't have no crimes in this town to speak of. Sure, few kids downtown drinkin', but that ain't no harm. We all did that. Just a few kids havin' fun. But that ain't no reason to pay the police more money. 'Sides, no matter what you pay 'em, seems all they do's spend the mornin' drinkin' coffee down to Mary Ellen's."

At this, there was good-natured laughter and much agitated chatter; heads bobbed up and down in agreement. Someone said, "Makes sense, no need to have more police protection," and someone else shouted, "That's right, what Ern just said."

All eyes turned to Chief Paulin. He put his cap on, slowly shaking his head left to right, then turned abruptly and left the hall.

Judge Parker called out, "All right, order please. We have more business to cover. Is there any discussion on this article?" He looked around the hall, nodded and started to ask, "Well then, what is your pleasure on—?"

"Mr. Moderator," a woman called. And again, louder, "Mr. Moderator!"

Parker said, "Ah. Yes, Mary. Do you want to make a motion?"

"Well, I don't know about that, Judge. But there's one thing more I want to say about this police business."

"All right, Mary."

"Well, I been listenin' to all these opinions back and forth about this police business. Now, I'm for law and order same's most people in Coggerton. But seems to me we been gettin' by all these years without all these specials on the police force, and I don't see no reason to add any now. So I think we ought to 'propriate 'nough money to fix the cruiser, 'cause after all, the chief can't very well do without that. And then, I think we ought to 'propriate a one hundred dollar salary raise for the chief, to show him we appreciate what he does for the town."

The townfolk applauded. Mary, emboldened, continued, "'Cause these are hard times for all of us. Isn't hardly anyone here hasn't been affected one way or 'nother by inflation, and that includes the police department. But Chief Paulin and his two regular officers might just consider tightenin' their belts along with the rest of us. After all, it's for the good of the town."

Mary sat down. The people applauded again, then voted to raise $200 to fix the cruiser and $100 to increase Chief Paulin's salary.

Parker said, "Article 16. To see if the town will vote to maintain the access road to Lilac Lane Estates." I think we ought to let Myron explain this one. Myron? Myron Ricker?"

A man across the aisle from Cassie and Michael raised his index finger as if making an auction bid.

Cassie poked Michael. "Hey, that's Ricker, the guy I called to do the well."

Ricker was slight, gray-haired, and dressed all in gray: dark gray overcoat, gray suit visible under the overcoat, gray bow tie. His eyeglasses were thick-framed gray plastic. On his lap, a gray Fedora. Even his face, with its bulbous nose and thick fleshy lips, looked gray.

From talking with him on the phone, she would never have expected Ricker to look like that. She wasn't sure what she expected. Someone younger or at least more rugged-looking, perhaps. A laborer. But this guy, this gray man, looked like an undertaker.

Ricker said, "Right heeyah, Judge Parker. What we're askin' the people to do is vote to maintain the road we're buildin' for some lots up on the old Province Road, the cross road between Coggerton and Marston Corners. We're puttin' in twelve, maybe fifteen homes up in theyah, on nice-size lots too, some's big as 90,000 square feet, not too expensive either."

From the back of the hall, someone called out, "Myron Ricker, just what have you got up your sleeve now?"

Ricker ignored the question. "Now we have a lot of young people here in town that's growin' up, gettin' married, startin' families of their own. They're wantin' a place to live. Place of their own, not too expensive, somethin' they can afford to pay for in a reasonable space of time. They're just workin' folks same's the rest of us, but they're entitled to a little place they can call their own, a little plot of land nobody can tell them what to do with, nice little place where they can raise their kids."

Ricker's voice neither rose nor fell, and there was no break between words and sentences, as if he never took a breath anywhere in the middle of what he was saying.

Was there no thrill, no catastrophe, that would cause Ricker to speak faster, with even a hint of expression? Cassie pictured him droning on, sitting in a chair on a beach, water rising up over his legs, his chest, past his bow tie to his chin, inching up over his mouth, nose and eyeglasses, and finally closing in over his thinning gray hair and still, still he would be droning on, his voice a watery rumble. Now, his gray words floated heavily up over the sea of heads, settling above them, a flat leaden canopy.

"Now what we're proposin' is this. Once we get them lots in and the road built and get a start on some nice little homes for our young people we'd like to see the town help out up theyah by maintainin' that road. We figure the town'll get some tax revenues on those properties and least it can do is maintain the road. So that's what we're askin' for a vote on here tonight."

When Ricker stopped talking, people straightened in their seats and rustled to life again, as if the heavy pall that had lulled and numbed them into a stupor was suddenly lifted.

"Norm?" Parker said, nodding at a man already standing.

"What Myron's said makes a deal of sense. Too many of our

young people are leavin' town or talkin' about it. If people like Myron are willin' to give our kids a decent place to live, seems that'd be encouragement for them to stay right here, where we'd like to see them settle. Now what I'd like to do is, I'd like to just ask the Budget Committee if we got sufficient money enough in our budget to take on Myron's road. Seems tax revenues we stand to get from them new homes he's buildin' would more'n make up what it'd cost us to maintain that little strip of road up in there. Winfred, how do we stand in the budget for somethin' like Myron's road?"

Winfred Gilsum, pipe in mouth, riffled through a stack of papers, pulling several out, taking his time, as if he were browsing through the Sunday paper. At last he looked up, took out the pipe and stuck it in the other corner of his mouth.

"Well, Highway Department's workin' on a pretty tight budget, but then so're all the rest of our town departments. Course, my own feelin' is, folks like Myron ought to be encouraged. We have a fair number of people out of work here in town, and we all know Myron employs buildin' crews made up of some of our own people. So as I say, seems to me Myron's doin' us a favor all around, and it's my feelin' the least we can do is help him out by maintainin' his road."

Ahead of her, Cassie noticed a man with his hand raised.

"Yes, Jim?" the moderator said.

Jim stood and turned to face the people. He was tall, slender, white-haired, clean-shaven. He had the bluest eyes Cassie had ever seen, and they stood out sharply against the slight ruddiness of his high, broad cheekbones. Under a blue plaid flannel shirt he wore a navy turtleneck jersey.

He looked young, though judging from his white hair and the thin lines fanning out from the corners of his eyes, Cassie figured he must be about sixty. He stood with his hands in his pockets, and when he spoke, he spoke plainly, without the elaborate prefaces with which the other townspeople began their rants.

He said, "We ought to think carefully before we start taking over private roads for every developer that comes along. There hasn't been any talk here tonight about how many new schoolchildren are coming into Coggerton. As it is, we have the first and second grades in the basement of the Congregational Church because we don't have room for them at the elementary school. And what about our fire department? They're just barely equipped to handle what we've got in town now, without having to protect all these new houses. The police have all they can do, too. "So I say we ought to let Myron Ricker maintain his own road."

There was a commotion in the bleachers, and as heads turned to see what it was all about, Parker called out, "Vic? Do you have something to say?"

Vic and several men were talking among themselves. Cassie couldn't make out the words, but it was clear from their tone and from Vic's agitated gesticulations that they were angry.

"You bet me and a lot of others have somethin' to say. And that's that here we have Myron Ricker, wantin' to do somethin' for the town and our young people. Now, lots of us are tired of people like Jim there, tryin' to fog up the issue by talkin' about schools and police and fire. Them things ain't got nothin' to do with what we're talkin' about now. And I for one am gettin' sick of it. What we're talkin' about is progress, and there's always *someone* tryin' to stand in the way of progress." He snorted. "Now, everybody in town knows Myron, knows he's honest. Ain't like we're talkin' here about some big-time developer comin' up from Massachusetts. We're talkin' here about someone who's been here all his life, been in business here for years. And before Myron, his father had the business."

Vic became increasingly impassioned. He had a captive audience and he knew it. Anyone who felt as strongly as Vic felt must really care about the town. He lowered his voice, which had the effect of forcing the people to listen even more intently.

They strained to hear as he continued cozily, confidentially, "So let's cut out all this foolishness and take on Myron's road. We all know Myron ain't goin' nowhere, ain't gonna skip town like some slick operator." The people laughed genially. "So let's get behind Myron, and forget all this jealousy that comes up sometimes when someone tries to do something good for the town."

The people applauded, deafeningly, until even Vic became red-faced, as if he could handle only so much attention.

Almost unanimously, the people voted to foot the expense of maintaining Myron Ricker's road.

Judge Parker read the last article on the warrant. "Article 17—ought to be an easy one, folks. To see if the town will vote to raise and appropriate $125 for the Bicentennial Celebration. This article was put in the warrant by a petition from the Women's Club. So perhaps we ought to let them explain it. Julia? Is Julia Eggers here tonight?"

"Here, Judge."

"Go ahead, Julia."

Julia Eggers was a short, square, corseted woman in a shiny flowered dress. Her white hair was parted in the middle and done up in rows of tight, flat curls. Cassie imagined her at Women's Club meetings, leading the flag salute, her back rigid, her hand placed just so on her blocky, patriotic bosom.

She said, "As you all know, every year the Women's Club plants petunias in the waterin' trough on Elm Street and around the flagpole in Hansen Park. And that comes out of the Women's Club's own funds." She tipped her head down, peering out over her bifocals. "Now we have a Bicentennial Celebration comin' up this July. We have talked with most of our businessmen here in town and they've said they'd like to cooperate with us on this. Some of them have already begun prettyin' up their store fronts. Right at this very moment Winfred Gilsum is remodelin' the front of his hardware store."

Winfred, the Budget Committee Chairman, nodded and smiled.

Julia continued, "Now Winfred's store will look very nice for the Bicentennial. He's puttin' in windows with those little panes. He's going to paint them white, real colonial-lookin'. As soon as he gets that done, we'll plant petunias in window boxes for him. And as other businesses in town get their places freshened up, we'll plant petunias for them, too." Julia looked around the hall, smiling benevolently. "So the $125 we're asking for is not for our usual plantings in the watering trough on Elm or around the flagpole in Hansen Park, but for the flowers we're going to plant in the window boxes around town."

The selectman seated next to Stiles raised his hand. "Excuse me, Judge?"

"Go ahead, Ronnie."

"Well, we all know what a fine job the Women's Club does, with all their charities and good deeds. And somehow I think it's only right—fittin' you might say—that these good ladies be in charge of our Bicentennial Celebration. I think we all want to do somethin' to preserve our heritage, and these ladies seem to be on the right track. So I move to appropriate $125 for the Bicentennial Celebration."

There was agreeable, good-natured applause throughout the hall, and from the back a voice called, "I second the motion."

"Ayes" rang throughout the hall, and Judge Parker's question, "All those opposed?" was lost in the racket of people getting up, putting on their coats, chattering, commenting on the way things went.

Cassie said to Michael, "Hurry up. I want to talk with that man."

"What?"

"Come *on*. Before he goes." She angled across the aisle and touched the man named Jim, whose back was to her, on the elbow.

"Excuse me," Cassie said. He turned and she said, "My name is Cassie Atwood. And this is my husband Michael."

The man nodded.

"And you are Mr. —?"

"Brackett. Jim Brackett."

"Mr. Brackett," Cassie said. She hesitated, thinking, Cripes, what do I say now? Why did I even want to talk with this man?

"I — we — were listening to what you were saying about the development going on in town. I just wanted to — I mean, is there a problem with development?" Up close, he didn't look sixty.

"Kind of depends on who you talk to, as you can see here tonight." He turned his head and nodded at the people who were walking out of the hall. "Are you new in town?"

Cassie said, "We just moved into the old Gilman place out on Thurlow Hill." How handsome he was.

"Sam Gilman's place."

"Yes." She looked at Michael. He was scowling, looking past Brackett, chewing on the inside of his mouth. Damn him, always off in his own little world. "We love it out there."

"John Skillin had that property, didn't he?"

"You know Skillin?"

Brackett nodded. "Oh, I know John Skillin all right. It's Skillin and Ricker who are —" He stopped.

"Where do you live, Mr. Brackett?"

"Out on the Wilmot Falls Road, with my brother."

"Oh! We can see the Wilmot Falls hills from our house."

Brackett smiled, intensely blue eyes twinkling.

"But what were you saying about Skillin and the other guy?"

"Ricker." Brackett shrugged. "It's Ricker and Skillin who are doing most of the —"

"Well, Cassie," Michael interrupted. "Don't you think we ought to be going?" He said to Brackett, "We left our son with a sitter. Nice meeting you, Mr. Bracken."

Cassie glared at Michael. *"Brackett."*

Brackett looked at Cassie, then at Michael, then at Cassie again, nodded, turned and walked from the hall into the raw March night.

"Goddamnit, Michael," Cassie said, drawing the shoulder harness of her seatbelt over her chest and snapping it shut. "Did you have to be so rude to that man?"

"What the hell are you talking about?"

"To Brackett. Not listening to him. Cutting him off like that. Not even getting his name right."

Silence.

"Jesus, not even getting his name right," Cassie repeated.

"Oh, I heard you, for Chrissake. Who the hell is he, anyway, that you wanted to talk to him? Honest to God, you and your old ladies and old men."

Cassie looked at him, seething. *"What?"*

"Shit. You know — that big deal every Christmas, making those cookies for all the old farts. All those old maid schoolteachers and what you call lonely old men. You collect them like shit collects flies."

Cassie's eyes stung. But no. Not this time. Damned if she'd get into this with him again.

"Christ, you ought to pay half as much attention to Andy and me as you pay to all those old duffs. Why don't you bake us some cookies once in a while?"

"Michael, I just don't get it. What's it to you, anyway, that I send out those cookies?"

But then, they were home, and because they were about to go inside where Emma Thurlow was sitting with Andy, the argument was left, as were most of their arguments, unfinished.

❁   ❁   ❁

Emma was sitting in front of the television, knitting a pink and purple afghan.

"How did it go? Were they all wound up tonight? Oh — and Andrew's just fine. He was just as good as gold. And such a smart little tyke!"

"It was sort of hard not knowing any of the people there," Michael said.

"Oh, after a while you'll get to know pret' near everybody in town."

"Emma," Cassie said. "What about Myron Ricker? What else does he do besides drill wells? There was a big fuss tonight about some development of his."

Emma stuffed her knitting into a flowered cloth bag with brown plastic handles. "Well, Myron has his hands in a lot of things. We went to school together, Myron and I. Graduated in the same class, though he never was much of a student. Kind of a plodder, if you know what I mean."

"Yes, and God, that droning."

Emma laughed. "That's right. That's Myron, all right. But never mind about that Myron. People say — here she mimicked Ricker's monotone — 'Now don't you worry none about the Rickers. They'll get by.'"

"But what does Ricker do, besides the well business?" Michael asked.

"Well, I guess you could say he's a builder," Emma said, shrugging. "Guess you could say he's into real estate in a way, too. His family's been in Coggerton for generations — just about forever. They own hundreds of acres. They do a lot of timberin'. I suppose that's where he gets the lumber for his houses. Then he sells lots from the land once he cuts off the timber. That's one thing you have to give the Rickers credit for. They don't hardly *waste* anythin', that's for sure." She laughed, and added, again imitating Ricker perfectly, "Don't you worry none about the Rickers. They'll get by."

Cassie said, "Emma, there was a man there tonight, a Jim Brackett, and—"

"Yes, Jim," Emma nodded.

"—and after we met him—"

"Or rather, after Cassie introduced herself to him," Michael interrupted. "Cassie'd be in her glory working in an old folks' home. Or in a place like Florida. She'd be in heaven there, the way she latches onto the geriatric crowd."

Emma threw back her head and laughed, loud and cackling. It was clear she found Michael charming.

Cassie ignored him. "Brackett said Ricker is overdeveloping the town."

"Oh, that Jim Brackett. He's always the noisiest one. Take someone like Myron who's at least *doin'* something for the town, and Jim Brackett will always find fault."

"He lives on the road to Wilmot Falls?"

"Yes. Over beyond Hog Hollow."

"Hog Hollow?"

"That's right, Hog Hollow. That's over the other side of town, just this side of Wilmot Falls. There used to be a pig farm over theyah. That's why it's called Hog Hollow. But now there's just a row of little houses where the pig farm was. Well, actually, they're no better than camps."

"Jim Brackett," Cassie prompted.

"Oh, yes. Jim Brackett lives out beyond Hog Holler. Lives alone with his oldest brother Woodbury in a run-down farmhouse that's been in the family for generations." She paused, "Course, Jim Brackett's had his troubles, no denyin' that."

"Like what?"

"Well, there were five of them Bracketts, not countin' their mother and father. Woodbury, he's the one still livin' with Jim, you know? He's older than Jim by about twenty years, because Woodbury had a different mother. So Woodbury's the oldest, and Jim the youngest. Then there were two sisters, Leona and Margaret, who married two boys who were cousins, and they all went off to live out west somewhere. And then there was one more son, Levi, and that's where the tragedy comes in."

Emma shifted in her chair, searching for a more comfortable position. "One year, they were gettin' in hay in the middle of a thunderstorm—a late August crop it was. The three boys and their father were all workin'. As I heard tell it, Jim was on the lower floor of the barn, haulin' the bales out of the wagon while Levi, Woodbury, and the old man were all up in the barn chamber, stackin' the bales. And, well, there, you can almost guess the rest. There was an awful bolt of lightnin' come down. Story was that bolt just run right along the ridge pole of that tin-roofed barn and lit it up like a Christmas tree. The old man and Levi were killed right off, and Woodbury, he was touched—knocked unconscious and thrown to the floor. They said it was a miracle he ever lived to tell it."

"God."

"Yes, it was an *awful* thing. That's why Jim dropped out of school to—"

"School? Where was he in school?"

"Oh, he'd been two years or so up to the college in Hanover. Dartmouth. But when his father and Levi got killed, there was just him and Woodbury left to run the farm and take care of the old lady — actually, Jim's mother — so he quit school." Emma scowled. "Course, probably those couple years at the college is what makes Jim act like he's just a little better than the rest of us. And now that he spends most of his time takin' care of Woodbury, I guess he's got nothin' much else to do besides complain. He's always wantin' to run down the town, it seems." She shook her head wearily. "Always get a few people wantin' to run down the town."

Glancing sideways at Michael, Cassie said, "He is a good-*looking* man, that Brackett."

Emma's eyebrows shot up and she nodded. "My, I guess

so. Nobody'd argue with that. Why, he's had such a string of women chase after him through the years — he could have had his pick of any of 'em, but, well there, I still say 'twas those two years up at Hanover what made Jim Brackett think he was just a bit too good for the rest of us." Emma blushed, and Cassie wondered if she had been one of Jim Brackett's rejected admirers.

"But he did have a point about Ricker's development, any-way," Cassie persisted. "He was the only one who pointed out that more houses mean more taxes for schools and other things."

"Well," Emma said. "I suppose. I suppose Jim Brackett don't mean any harm."

The next day Cassie made a batch of chocolate chip cookies and mailed a dozen of them to Jim Brackett on the Wilmot Falls Road.

Four

Cassie tugged at pieces of old roof shingles and brittle clapboards tangled up in the dead grass of the old lawn. She leaned her rake in a notch of the ancient lilac bush in the corner where the main part of the house joined the kitchen ell, and walked around to the front of the house to check on Andy, swinging on his rope swing in one of the old maples. She sat on the granite front step. Its coldness startled her, reminding her that despite the warmth of the April day, the chill of winter still lingered.

The softness in the air and the absolute stillness save for Andy's feet dragging through last year's leaves was intoxicating. The people who settled here picked the perfect spot to build this house.

The old Cape was at one end of a field which once was farmed but, as Cassie would discover with delight as the seasons passed, was now gone wild with—each in turn—dandelions, wild strawberries, hawkweeds, black-eyed Susans, iron bushes, blueberry bushes, wild raspberries, milkweeds.

In front of the house were four ancient maple trees which both dwarfed and sheltered the house. Beyond the maples, the land sloped to drifts of junipers and high-bush blueberries. Emma had told Cassie farmers were death on junipers, but Cassie loved the bowl-like shape their prickly branches made, and the dust-blue berries nestled in the branches.

Beyond the blueberries and the junipers was a stone wall, one of many criss-crossing the land. On the other side of the wall was an ancient orchard of twisted, dying apple trees.

In the distance was the village of Coggerton. At night, Cassie sometimes knelt up in bed to look out at the lights in the valley—blue sparklers in the clear air.

Now Cassie looked beyond the village of Coggerton to the three hills of Wilmot Falls, wondering if one of those tiny houses on those hills might be where he lived, and if he ever got the cookies she'd sent.

Cassie turned her gaze to the hill at the end of the field, where maples against the banks of evergreens were beginning to show red buds, and here and there, new chartreuse leaves. The air was clear and fresh, full of promise.

Skirting the edge of the field was a brook, noisy when Cassie listened for it, unobtrusive when she listened to other sounds, like Andy scuffing through the crackly leaves under the swing. Deep in the woods, a partridge was beating its wings, drumming like a one-cylinder motor cranking up, gaining momentum, then levelling off to a brief, steady whirring.

Cassie returned to her work, loading into the wheelbarrow armloads of trash mixed with hay. When she tugged with the rake at a clapboard that had sunk into the ground, a fat-bellied spider scooted up the rake handle. Used to gray, anemic-looking citified spiders, Cassie shuddered at this one's size and dark brown color. With her gloved hand, she flicked the spider onto the ground and watched it scurry under the dried grass. A wasp flew down and lit on the handle of the wheelbarrow, then floated up to the peak of the house, where other wasps, brought to life by the unusual warmth of the day, were drifting around.

Cassie heard a car rattling down the lane, and stepped around the side of the house just as Emma Thurlow was turning her pickup around and heading it out the driveway.

"Out here, Emma," Cassie called.

As Emma walked toward her, Cassie noticed she was limping.

With effort, Emma lowered herself onto the round granite slab covering the old well, saying, "Ah, feels so good to be sittin' down. When I'm on my feet all day, I have a lot of trouble with these very coarse veins of mine."

"Your what?"

"My veins. My very coarse veins. I've been troubled with them ever since my Esther was born."

Cassie realized: Emma meant varicose veins. She sat on the well rock next to Emma and said, "What a gorgeous day."

"It's simply beautiful. There isn't hardly a day goes by I don't thank Heaven for this clean air we breathe. I can't imagine how people in the city stand it, all that pollution."

"I know."

"Will and I were talkin' about you folks just last night. Will said it was about time you folks took an afternoon off from all this work to do a little socializin'. And he said, 'Emma, why not just ask those young folks to dinner Sunday?'" She paused, embarrassed. "If that's all right."

"Well, that sounds very nice. We'd love to."

"Fine, then. Will'll be pleased. He's been sayin' it's about time we all got more neighborly."

Andy came up the slope from the maple trees, practicing his skipping. He settled himself by the sand pile, where his Matchbox cars and Tiny Tonka trucks were where he left them: on roads, hillsides, under bridges, one truck filled with sand, its body tipped up, ready to dump its load.

Emma looked at the house. "How is the work going?"

"All right, I guess," Cassie said. "The insulation's in, downstairs, anyway, and except for this side, the new clapboards are on. The heating and plumbing are started. But it's slow."

"Oh?"

"Yeah. All these workmen give you a date when they're going to show up. You count on them and get all ready for them, then they don't come. And when they finally do get here, there's not a word of apology, or even any explanation about why they are late. Sometimes I wonder if we'll ever get the place finished."

"But they do come, don't they?"

"So far, anyway, but usually later rather than sooner." She

frowned at Emma. "But that's not the point. They don't come until weeks — *weeks* — after they say they'll be here. Like Gilsum's Hardware. They told us they'd be here the first of the month and here it is almost May and they just came to start the new plumbing two days ago."

"Well, one thing you'll come to see is that country people are different from city people. They're not so much in a hurry to do everythin'. Out here in the country we're much more, well — *relaxed*, you might say. Not like city folks. I imagine that's why we don't have so many ulcers, don't you?"

"That's one way of looking at it, I guess. I never thought of it quite that —"

Nodding at the wheelbarrow full of junk, Emma said, "You seem to take to this kind of work yourself."

"I like it. It's a good change from ripping out old plaster. That's one reason we came here, really — to be outside as much as possible, enjoying the land."

"Funny," Emma said. "When I was in my next to last year of high school, I thought I'd like to go to the city. Matter of fact, I wanted to go to school down to Boston, but my folks said it'd be the state teachers' college or nothin'. So I was just stubborn enough to say, 'Well, then, it'll be nothin'.' Course, can't say I ever regretted my decision. Will and I got married fresh out of high school — in a proper June weddin', too, and it weren't more'n a year after that our Vernon was born, and ever since then I've been too busy to ever have any regrets."

Andy looked up from the sand pile.

Emma said, "How's my little friend, Andrew? You remember your Auntie Emma, don't you, love?"

Andy nodded.

"But I guess when it come down to it, I always knew I'd settle right here in Coggerton. My family moved here from Vermont when I was too young to remember, but Will's people've been here on that same farm for generations now."

Cassie said, "Andy, leave the sand in the pile. Don't drag it all over the yard. Sorry, Emma, you were saying?"

"Nice place to live, Coggerton is. Nice place to bring up kids. We have good neighbors, helpful but not nosy. We're all interested in each other, if you know what I mean, but we respect each other's privacy, too." Emma looked at the house, shaking her head. "My, but wouldn't Old Man Gilman be surprised to see what you've done to this old place."

"You mean Sam Gilman?"

"Yes, Old Samuel. He was the last Gilman to live here. Matter of fact, up till when you folks came, only ones ever lived here were Gilmans."

"When I was ripping out some of the old plaster, a book fell out of the ceiling with the name Eliza Gilman in it."

Emma nodded. "She would have been one of 'em. Fact, Will's mother had an old book I once saw which told the history of this area. It said a Gilman and a Thurlow — same ones what settled these two farms — were present at Coggerton's first town meetin' in 1796. So that gives you some idea about how old the place must be."

"How long did Samuel Gilman live here?"

"Old Sam? Well, he was still living here in 1970, I think." She shifted her weight on the well rock, trying to get comfortable on the cold granite.

"Where is he now, the old man?"

"I was comin' to that." She rubbed her leg as she spoke. "Course, Sam was old, real old. Eighty-one years old, and he had arthritis real bad. So when John Skillin come along and asked old man Gilman what he'd sell the place for, old Sam said 'For just what it'd cost me to go the County Farm.' That's just what old Sam said. He said, 'All I want is to go to the County Farm to die in peace.' So the old man got $2500 which was more money than he'd ever seen in his entire life. And John Skillin got what he wanted, this house and the 120 acres that come with it. So everybody come out of that arrangement real satisfied. Old Sam got to go to the County Farm. Lived there almost two years before he died. And John Skillin got himself this property to make a little profit on."

"I don't understand. You say there were 120 acres to this place? We bought sixty-five. What happened to the rest?"

"Oh. Well, when John Skillin bought the place from Sam Gilman, he kept a goodly amount of land to go with the old farmhouse here, and he held back the rest for house lots. Nice big lots, too. Each one has at least five acres. I must say John believes in doin' things right. It would've been just as easy for him to divide this land into one-acre, two-acre lots. He would've made a lot more money doin' it that way, too. But John says he believes in keepin' good relations in the neighborhood. Says he doesn't think it's right to pack in the houses the way some of those big-time developers do."

Dumbfounded, Cassie said, "Where is the rest of the land? The lots, I mean."

Emma turned and indicated with an outstretched arm the woods behind the house. "Up that way," she said. "Oh, not anywhere on that hillside you can see. John Skillin believes in maintainin' people's privacy. The lots are over the brow of that hill. Up Thurlow Hill a ways. Higher up than this place here. Fact, there's an even better view of the Wilmot Falls hills from up there. But then, you can't have everything, can you? You might not have quite the view that folks who buy those lots will have, but then, they won't have this pretty house and all this land, will they?"

Though flabbergasted, Cassie decided not to pursue the subject, sensing that it would be imprudent to question Skillin's motives.

Instead, she said, "Emma, where can I buy eggs? Does anyone sell fresh eggs around here?"

"Matter of fact, you know that place just above ours, on the flat, where the hill levels off? Just before you come into the Otis Corner Road?"

Cassie nodded.

"Sally Wilkins lives there and she keeps chickens. She and her husband don't have much money, so Sally sells the extra eggs to buy grain. She's happy if she makes just enough to break even."

"Thanks. I'll get in touch with her."

With effort, Emma heaved herself up off the well rock, panting, "Matter of fact, Sally was tellin' me and Esther just the other day — Esther's my daughter, you know? — that she'd like to meet you."

They walked toward the pickup, Emma limping heavily, Andy skipping along behind.

"Yes, and, well, you won't find any fresher eggs than Sally's, that's for sure."

"I don't see what you're so pissed about," Michael said. "We got half the 120 acres with the house. You'd think sixty-five acres'd be enough for you. For anybody."

"You sound like Emma."

"Christ, what do you want, anyway?"

"There's just something shady about Skillin, that's all. Emma said he paid Sam Gilman $2,500 for the house and the whole 120 acres. He got $38,000 from us. What do you suppose he'll get for those lots he's going to sell?"

"Who gives a shit? We still got a good deal. The guy's got a right to make a profit. Besides, maybe he'll have trouble selling those lots."

"Oh sure. We'll see how much trouble he has. Remember what he told us? 'The view alone is worth a thousand dollars.' "

"I still don't see why you're so goddamn riled."

"Goddamnit, the dishonesty. Implying there was just us

and the Thurlows and a few others in the whole area. Now it sounds like it'll be suburbia if he sells all those lots."

"For Christ's sake, don't borrow trouble. He hasn't sold any yet."

"He will, the fatass."

"The fat—what?"

"Fatass. Didn't you notice how big and fat his butt was?"

"Jesus, that's typical of your logic. No I didn't notice how fat his butt is. Now *tell* me, what's that got to do with—"

"Well, it is. And there's just something slippery about the bastard, that's all."

The next day Cassie left Andy with three hours of Saturday morning cartoons, and Michael putting up a bathroom mirror, and went to buy eggs.

She had learned that here in the country there were more than four seasons. Not only were there summer, fall, winter, and spring, but "mud season" and "black fly season"—"The likes of which you ain't *never* seen!" Emma had warned, with more than a little glee.

Cassie's boots made a sucking sound as she trudged up the soggy lane, but the ridges between the car tire ruts were beginning to dry out, and the strips of water in the ruts themselves were thinner, not so deep-looking.

Their lane passed through one of Thurlows' fields, a field that once belonged to the Gilmans, but was sold to the Thurlows, Emma had told Cassie, "Back along, when Will's father had intentions of puttin' the whole field into squashes." The sixty-five acres the Atwoods bought was what Skillin had called land-locked, but with a deeded right-of-way through the field.

Partway up the lane, Cassie stopped to look back at the house. At the end of Thurlows' field, along the stone wall which divided Thurlows' land from Atwoods', was a row of birches and poplars. Through the budding branches, Cassie could see the end of the Cape with its clapboards stained brown and its new, still unpainted six-over-six windows. Anyone driving by on the road had to be looking just right to see the house. In another month the leafed-out trees would completely hide it.

She shifted her gaze to the top of the field above their lane. A row of pines along a stone wall marked the end of Thurlows' field. Skillin's first house lot would be there. Likely Skillin will tell whoever buys that lot that the view from there is worth two thousand dollars.

At the end of the lane, she turned onto the street and started up the hill. On her right, close to the road, was Thurlows' house. Connected to the house by a row of low sheds was a big barn with a rusting corrugated tin roof. And beyond the barn, a field, opposite the one the Thurlows had bought from the Gilmans. Except for where it rose gently at the upper end, the field was fairly level. In it were a dozen or so sheep, grazing almost motionless, rooting among the brown grasses for new green shoots.

On each side of the road, defining the fields, were stone walls—fine walls with only an occasional boulder fallen onto the strip of grass on the road side of the wall.

Beyond the crest of the hill, the road dipped and then leveled off. On her left, Skillin's lots began. Strips of shiny red surveyor's tape were attached to trees every 150 feet or so. Cassie didn't understand how they could be five-acre lots. They looked like lots set out for tract housing.

She heard water rushing through a culvert beneath the road. The brook, channeled under the road, snaked off into Skillin's lots. Dogs were barking somewhere ahead of her. It occurred to Cassie that the brook must be the same brook that runs through their land.

She counted the lots as she walked. On the right side of the road, opposite the sixth lot, she came to an aluminum mailbox with "LES" stenciled on one side in big black letters. On the other side, in smaller letters: "Lester Wilkins."

Heading up Wilkinses' driveway, she passed a pile of sand and a few big Tonka Toy trucks, rusting and bent. Propped against the sand pile was a plastic boat-shaped sled, once red, but now faded to a dusty pink from being left out in the weather. Next to the house, chickens pecked around in a fenced enclosure, at one end of which was a coop with a tarpaper roof.

Wilkinses' house was a double-wide trailer, sided in white, trimmed out with royal blue shutters, corner posts, gutters, and a drainpipe running down one corner. In the yard was a bright blue station wagon, and, marooned on the brown grass near the chicken coop, a snowmobile peeked out from under a blue plastic tarp.

Cassie wondered what else they had to match the blue house trim. Snowmobile suits? Bathroom towels and bed linens? Smoke curled from the chimney which, she noticed with some disappointment, was made of red bricks.

Ever since Cassie had crossed the brook where it ran under the road, dogs had been barking and now, as she followed Wilkins' driveway around to the right of the house, she saw the dogs. They were hitched to a dog house, pulling on the ropes that bound them. One, its tail curled downward between its rear legs, looked savage. Both barked and growled and strained toward Cassie.

A door flew open and a woman yelled, "Goddamn sons o' bitches, shut up! Racer! General! Shut up!"

The dogs barked a few more times, their growls turning to whimpers and whines and they settled themselves on the ground by the dog house.

"Damn fool dogs. Don't know why I put up with 'em."

Cassie said, "I'm Cassie Atwood, from the old Gilman place, and—"

"I know. Come in." She held the door open for Cassie, who sidestepped by her into the house. The storm door rattled shut.

Cassie said, "And you're Sally?"

"That's right. Emma said you'd be comin' for eggs. Take a seat. Want some coffee?"

"No thanks. I just had breakfast."

Sally sat opposite Cassie, her coffee cup in front of her (brown horizontal rings around the inside of the cup), alongside a shell-shaped turquoise ashtray filled with butts—butts without filters, smoked down to the last inch, and Parliament filter tips, snuffed out at various lengths, some with pink lipstick stains.

Sally reached for a package of cigarettes, took one out, put it in her mouth, and reached for a silver lighter next to the ashtray. She looked at Cassie, took her unlit cigarette out of her mouth and said, "You smoke? Want a cigarette?"

"No thanks."

Sally was thin, with pallid skin and straw-colored, straight hair. On one side of her head were two big pink plastic rollers. Her eyes were hazel, lusterless, and when she spoke, she kept her lower lip pressed stiffly against her bottom teeth. Only when she opened her mouth to take a cigarette did Cassie see why: there were at least four teeth missing in front. Her blue terrycloth bathrobe sprung snagged threads.

The Formica-topped kitchen table separated the narrow kitchen from the living room with its picture window looking out on the front yard and street. Over the table in its rectangular gold cage a Shell No-Pest Strip hung next to a wagon wheel lamp, with bulbs in the shape of candle flames.

A sandy-haired boy with a crew cut was sitting on the floor in front of the TV. The cuffs of his too-small pajamas were half way to his elbows; the top hiked up to show a half-moon of his back above the waistband of the pants.

Sally lit her cigarette, taking a long drag to get it going. Her back to her son, she said, "Lance, this here lady is Mrs. Atwood. Say hello to Mrs. Atwood."

Lance turned around.

"Hello, Lance."

Lance stared at her, his blue eyes expressionless.

"Lance! You mind your manners, now. You say hello to Mrs. Atwood."

"Hi," he said, and turned back to the television.

"How old is Lance?"

"Seven. Owen is my other one. He's almost two. Full of the devil, that one. He's over town today with his grandmother. Les's mother. Isn't your boy about Lance's age?"

"Andy? He's five."

"You oughta bring him up sometime. Let him play with my boys. Ain't too many kids close by they can play with. I imagine your boy must get pretty lonesome, down there all by himself."

"Actually, he—"

Sally crushed out her cigarette. Her pink nail polish was chipped and there was dirt under her nails. "Emma tells me you was a schoolteacher, down to Boston."

"Actually, in a town near Boston."

"My Lance here's havin' an awful hard time of it in school. Fact, he never did learn to read last year, so they're havin' him repeat first grade." She leaned back, coughed, took out another cigarette, and lit it. "We tried everthin' to get him to do better last year—punishin' him, takin' away his TV. We even beat him, but none of it done any good. He's stubborn, that one."

It didn't seem to matter to Sally that Lance was hearing all this.

"Have you talked with Lance's teacher?"

"Me and Les both talked to her. But you don't get nowhere down to that school. All she said was he was actin' up and didn't seem to be innerested in nothin'. We tol' her, as long as

Lance is in her room, she's 'sponsible for him, and she could do whatever she wants with him. Keep him after school, beat him real good if she has to. I tol' her Lance better improve or I'll know why he don't."

About halfway through Sally's harangue, Lance turned from the television to stare at Cassie, who smiled at him.

Sally turned around in her chair. "You mind ya own business, you. What we're sayin' ain't none of your goddamn business." She snuffed her cigarette, and lit another.

"Me and his father tell him all the time that nowadays you got to get an education. We tell him he don't want to quit school at sixteen to get married or nothin' like his father and me did."

Cassie calculated: the kid is seven. That means she's probably not more than twenty-five years old. She looked ten years older.

"Not that Lance should be ashamed of his father or nothin'. He makes a good livin' and works hard. But we tell Lance he ain't never gonna get nowhere if he don't finish high school. We tell him that all the time."

"How long have you lived out here, Sally?"

"Three years. Both me and Les grew up downtown. But we got tired of livin' in apartments, tired of rentin'. So just about the time we started lookin' for a little land we heard Will Thurlow had a piece to sell, so we didn't waste no time gettin' ourselves up here to see them—Will and Emma I mean—and it's a good thing we did too, because just the Sunday before we come to see Will some rich people from Massachusetts been here and was about to buy this land from them."

"I didn't know this used to be the Thurlows' land."

"Yeah. And once Will heard we was innerested he said he'd just as soon sell to us as to that Massachusetts couple. 'Just as soon keep it in the family' was what Will said."

"Family? Are you related to the Thurlows?"

"Nah. That's just the way Will put it. What he meant was

he'd rather sell to someone from Coggerton rather than some outsiders."

"How much land do you have, Sally?"

"Nine acres. It's shaped like a piece of pie. Long piece of frontage, then it skinnies up at the back. Will said that way no one could build too close to us on either side. And no one'll be buildin' back of us neither, long as Will and Emma own all around us. Will's real considerate that way, makin' sure everybody has enough land for privacy. Course, he ain't sold no more lots yet, neither. And I bet when he does he ain't gonna be so generous as he was to us. We got all this land for only $4,000. Will says 'fore you know it, goin' rate for land'll be a thousand an acre. And I bet anybody up from Massachusetts from now on wantin' to buy land from Will'll have to pay that too."

"That's a lot of money," Cassie said.

Sally shrugged. "They got it, them Massachusetts people. But I bet you're glad to be out here in the country, where it's clean and healthy."

"Yes, we are."

"Out here in the fresh air. Must be some change from the city."

"Yes, it is," Cassie said, amused that Sally would go on about clean air and healthy country living, considering her house stinks of cigarette smoke. And God knows what that that No-Pest Strip overhead is giving out. "But I really must be going, Sally."

Sally went to the refrigerator and took out a carton of eggs. "These are yesterday's eggs. Hope you don't mind."

"I'm sure they'll be fresher than any I can buy in the supermarket. How much do I owe you?"

"Seventy-five — no, seventy cents'll be okay. Now, you come up again sometime, and bring your boy."

"Thank you," Cassie said.

When Cassie got to the sandpile, Sally called after her, "By the way, you like dirty books?"

Cassie turned. "Excuse me?

"Dirty books. You know. Me and my friends buy 'em, and when we get through with 'em we swap 'em back and forth." Sally was grinning, and with her lower lip pressed against where her teeth were missing and her upper lip drawn back to show her nicotine-stained upper teeth, her grin was appropriately lewd. "Cause you know, if you got any to swap, I got lots I already read. Some are real good, real dirty."

"Gee, Sally, thanks, but I really don't get much time to read, not with the work on the house and all."

"You sure?"

"I guess not right now, anyway."

"Well, you just let me know if you change your mind."

Walking down the road, Cassie heard crows. She looked up and watched them as they angled across Thurlows' field on her right, over her own house, toward the hill that rose in the east beyond the house until, no more than three black dots, they disappeared against the green-black pines on the hillside.

Watching them, Cassie wondered what sort of dirty books Sally relished, and she pictured her, up there with the crows, pale against the spring sky, curled up on a drifting cloud, legs tucked up under her terrycloth bathrobe, hair in rollers, cigarette in one hand, a dog-eared paperback in the other, the turquoise shell ashtray in her lap. Grinning, her lower lip stretched taut over the gap in her lower jaw.

Five

At noon on the last day in April, Cassie, Michael and Andy walked up the lane for Sunday dinner at Thurlows'.

They passed through the opening in the stone wall that separated their land from Thurlows'. The right side of the lane was lined with blackberry vines, their thorny leafless branches red now in the spring. Behind the row of blackberries were scrubby white pines with old, dying apple trees here and there among them, almost obscured by the dense evergreens. On the power line running alongside the lane perched a row of starlings, their chubby bodies squatting in groups along the wire. As Andy, skipping along ahead of Cassie and Michael, passed them, the starlings took flight all at once, swirling, their beating wings audible on the soft spring air. Then they descended in a cloud, disappearing into the grasses of the field.

When the Atwoods reached the end of the lane, dogs in Thurlows' yard began barking. Agitated, Sally Wilkins's dogs, further up the hill, chimed in.

Thurlows' large, two-story farmhouse was weathered to a paintless gray. Plastic sheeting was stapled to the lowest clapboards and weighted down against the foundation every two or three feet with split logs. Where the brittle plastic was torn, it crackled in the light wind.

They followed the lane to the kitchen door at the back of the house. On the right side of the lane, opposite the house, was a rusting red gas pump, the old kind with a round face. Behind the house was a purple car with fins. Along its side were painted bright green lightning bolts, outlined in black. Below the lightning bolts, also in black, was written, "Give 'em Hell, Vern!"

The wheels were off; the car was up on blocks. Its wind-shield was broken; glass shards on the hood glinted in the sun.

To either side of the muddy lane, the grass was littered with dog bones and here and there, dog messes—some fresh, some white and dried out. In a pile of sand just outside the kitchen door were some faded cardboard A&P frozen orange juice containers, a yellow plastic shovel, plastic containers with Cool Whip labels still on them. Andy headed for the sand pile but Cassie called him back, not sure where the sand pile left off and the dog shit began.

Two dogs poked around the corner of the house, barking, but keeping their distance. At the door, Emma yelled, "Bonnie! *Bonnie*! Hush up! Jebbie—*Be nice!*" Then, to the Atwoods, "Come in, come in." The dogs quieted, disappearing around the side of the house.

They stepped into a small hall, and Emma shut the door behind them. They squeezed together to make room for her while they took off their coats and thrashed with their boots.

Emma backed into the kitchen, saying, "Heavens, don't fuss about your boots. Nobody ever takes off their boots here. Nothin' you can hurt in this house."

The kitchen was square, with a sink next to the door from the hall. Beyond the sink was an electric stove with a second oven over the cook top. Opposite the kitchen door a big rect-angular table was against the wall beneath a picture window which framed part of the barn and beyond the barn, the sheep field.

A massive fieldstone fireplace separated the kitchen from the living room. Its raised hearth was a huge granite slab with the numbers "1969" carved on the front face of the slab. The hearth, itself a foot high, had brass fireplace tools in a holder on one end and on the other, a chipped bowl with the words "Our Pet" on the front.

The sides of the fireplace went up straight for five feet or so, then angled in sharply to fit between two hand-hewn beams in the low ceiling.

The firebox was open to the living room as well as the kitchen. A log was smoldering in the fireplace and a screen to catch sparks was set up on the hearth on the living room side. Through the opening, Cassie spied a maroon couch with round arms, just like the one in Cassie's grandmother's house. It was upholstered in stiff wool that itched — hurt even — when she rubbed against it. It reminded Cassie of the cars of the late forties and fifties. She called it the Studebaker.

Amid the confusion of Michael and Emma greeting one another and Cassie and Michael being introduced to Will, Emma said, "Come see my fireplace."

Everyone turned to the fireplace, admiring it in silence.

Emma said, "I've always wanted a fireplace exactly like this one. And Will said when we redid the kitchen I should *have* my fireplace."

Cassie said, "It certainly is impressive. I've never seen one like it."

"Thank you," Emma smiled.

Michael said, "Gee, where did you get all those big stones?"

"Here and there. On our own land. Mostly we got them from the stone walls. Took us a while to get just the right ones," Emma said.

"I can imagine," Michael said.

Throughout all this, Will Thurlow was standing at the end of the fireplace, one foot up on the hearth next to the "Our Pet" dish. He was slender and — except for a Friar Tuck fringe of reddish hair — bald, with perfectly round blue eyes, a small nose and mouth. He was wearing a pair of moccasins, gray wool slacks with cuffs, and a white shirt open at the neck, revealing a thatch of red hair below his Adam's apple. He was smoking a pipe, looking from Emma to Cassie to Michael and to the fireplace while they spoke.

While Cassie stood there staring at it, murmuring compliments, she was thinking of the original fireplaces that must have been in the house. Lovely, shallow fireplaces with their wafer-thin bands of cream-colored mortar binding the courses of bricks to one another. She said, "The work you must have put into this. Did you build it yourselves?"

Will said, "Well, uh, yes. Least Vern—that's our boy—and me, we did most of the real heavy work, haulin' the stones and mixin' the mortar."

Emma said, "But we did hire out Wendell Boudreau — he's a mason by trade — to help with the plannin' and all. Because Will always says—don't you Will—Will always says somethin' we waited for so long had to be just right."

Will nodded and said, "Wendell knows his business."

Andy reached around Will's legs for the "Our Pet" dish.

"Andy honey, don't play with the dog's dish," Cassie said. "You might break it."

"It says 'Our Pet' on it," Andy said.

"And isn't that cute, huh? But don't *play* with it, Andy. Come on off there now and look at this gigantic log in the fireplace."

Andy pulled himself off the hearth and stood beside Cassie, who said, "I imagine that really heats the whole area." Actually the log in the fireplace was smoldering and now and then gray smoke curled out into the kitchen, stinging her eyes.

"I should say," Emma said. "Why some days the oil furnace never once comes on."

Will knocked his pipe against the inside of the fireplace opening, and tucked it in his shirt pocket.

Emma said, "Well. You folks must be pret' near starved. Why don't we all sit down?" Emma indicated where they should sit at the table. Cassie and Andy sat on the side of the table that faced the fireplace, Michael sat across from them, and two places were set for Emma and Will opposite the picture window framing the barn and the field where the sheep pastured.

Will stood with his hands on the back of his chair and for a moment Cassie thought he was going to say grace. Then she realized he was waiting for Emma, who was bringing bowls and plates of food from the stove to the table.

Cassie asked, "Emma, may I help?"

"Heavens, no! Everythin's ready. Now you just stay put and relax."

Cassie watched Emma as she trudged from the stove to the table, and from the refrigerator to the table, eager to help in case Emma changed her mind. She glanced at Michael and Will. Not their role to watch, ready to help. They were to be served, waited on.

Cassie looked around the kitchen. The cupboard doors were painted a shiny yellow. In the lower corner of each door was painted a black quarter-circle. The same black quarter-circles were painted on the upper corners of the cupboard doors under the counters.

Cassie stared at the marks, thinking they must be some sort of decoration but couldn't figure why only one corner of each door had the quarter-circles.

Emma put a loaf of Nissen's white bread on the table. She said to Cassie, "I see you're noticin' Will's idea."

"What?"

"Will's idea. He painted those on there so's the smudges wouldn't show."

"Smudges?"

"You know, finger smudges. Will says you always notice on kitchen cupboard doors finger smudges and grease marks where the doors get opened and shut so much. So Will painted the corners black so the smudges wouldn't show."

"Ah. I see."

"Course, I haven't got my handles on the doors yet. They're already bought, nice hammered copper ones, but Will just simply hasn't had the time, with all his other work." She sighed. "But it's coming. Can't do everythin' all at once." She looked up at the ceiling. "It really *is* coming. Would you believe, looking at this ceiling, that only a year ago we didn't even have these beams showing? Knew they were there, of course, and we always wanted to show 'em, but pullin' down all that plaster and puttin' up the sheet rock is such a messy job."

Cassie and Michael and Will and Andy were all looking with Emma at the ceiling. The beams had been scrubbed of the dirt and now were tan-colored. Between the beams was sheet rock, nailed up but not finished off and painted. It was yellowed, almost as yellow as the beams.

Will looked embarrassed.

Michael said, "A lot of work, isn't it, Will?"

"I *guess* so." Everybody looked down from the ceiling and Will continued, "There was a man up from the University last summer. Not here to see us or anythin' but he stopped in for directions to a place over on Otis Corner Road. He took a look at these beams and said he never seen any so big nor so close together. Remember that, Emma?"

Emma nodded. "And he said too he never seen a house built so overall sturdy as this one, goin' by the framin' and all." She sat down, and looked over the table. "There, I guess we're all set." And then, looking up at the ceiling again, she said, "But it's comin'. Little by little."

The table was covered with a yellow plastic tablecloth. At each place were unmatched heavy plates, cutlery with little stars on the handles, and water-filled glasses with silver flowers on them. Next to Andy's smaller plate was a teaspoon and a red plastic cup. Paper napkins stood vertical in a plastic holder in the center of the table.

Will carved the roast and passed the platter of meat to Michael. Emma stacked fistfuls of bread on a plate in front of her, unscrewed the cap from a jar of homemade bread and butter pickles, and put a fork in it. She passed around a bowl of wax beans—home-canned, she said—cut into small pieces.

Will passed to Michael a bowl of potatoes cut in halves, boiled with their skins on.

When the serving and spooning and passing and clanking were over, Emma mashed her potato with her fork and put a piece of bread on her plate, ladled gravy over both the bread and the potato and asked, "Would anyone like me to serve gravy? Here, Andrew, let me give you some bread and gravy."

Emma took Andy's plate, put a piece of bread on it and poured a ladle of gravy over it, smearing the gravy over the bread with the bottom of the ladle. Andy stared; he'd never had bread and gravy before. He ate bread only two ways: with butter on it, or with peanut butter and Marshmallow Fluff between two slices.

Emma returned Andy's plate and asked, "Cassie?"

Cassie passed her plate to Emma, who took a piece of bread and put it next to Cassie's potato. She hesitated. Cassie hadn't mashed her potato.

"Oh, just on the bread will be fine, please, Emma."

Emma nodded and poured the gravy over the bread, spreading it to the edges with the ladle.

Emma served Michael and Will gravy and bread, looked around and, as a signal for everyone to begin eating, said, "There, now. I guess we have everything."

There was no conversation for a while as they busied themselves eating.

Andy tried the meat, then went on to the bread and gravy, which Cassie had cut up for him. Cassie watched as he gobbled up the bread and then moved on to the pickles and devoured them. He knew what a potato was and had no intention of touching his. He looked at the plate of bread.

Emma said, "Oh. Would you like more bread and gravy, dear?"

"Yes."

"Yes, *please*, Andy," Michael said.

"Yes, please."

Emma gave Andy another piece of bread and gravy, Cassie cut it, and Andy attacked it.

"Anyone else?" Emma asked, smiling.

"Gee, that's good, Emma. I'd like some more," Michael said, holding his plate out to Emma.

Cassie couldn't believe it: her kid and her husband, crazy about the bread and gravy. She had been avoiding hers, concentrating instead on the meat and potato. What she was missing? The gravy was caramel-colored, shiny, thick, glossy-smooth. It sat on the bread like one of those joke-store plastic pools of beer or vomitus. "Fool Your Guests! Give 'Em a Barrel of Laughs!"

She cut a piece of the bread and gravy with her fork and tasted it. The gravy bore no resemblance to meat of any kind. All Cassie could taste was salt. Flour and salt. It must be the salt that Andy and Michael were after. Poor darlings, victims of her bland meals. Maybe she should get a few salt licks and lay them around near their beds. "I see you put up those beans and pickles yourself, Emma. Do you do a lot of canning?"

"Oh my yes. I put up whatever we have left in the garden after we eat all the fresh we want."

"It must be a lot of work."

Emma beamed. "Well, when you've lived practically all your life in the country, it becomes second nature to you, all the work. Besides, we have to watch our pennies, you know, and every little bit helps."

After dinner Emma said, "Now, wouldn't Andrew like to see the new baby lambs in the barn?"

Will slid the big double doors open and they stepped inside, hesitating a moment to let their eyes adjust to the darkness.

Cassie looked up. Overhead a square of the ceiling was cut out and she could see all the way to the high peaked roof. In the dimness of the upper chamber, some boards tossed in a heap. Bales of hay, stacked in the shape of a Mayan temple. A ladderback chair without a seat, an old oak commode with a door missing, both spattered with guano. Instead of the sweet smell of hay, or the stringent smell of cow manure, Cassie smelled grease (motor oil?) and the acrid odor of cat.

On the floor of the barn just inside the door was a coil of oily-looking, thick rope, and along the wall was a bookcase filled with coffee cans holding nails, rusting nuts and bolts, paint brushes. Everywhere, cobwebs—thick strings of ancient dust hanging in streamers from the beams, and draped in flowing bands along the walls which at one time probably had a fresh coat of whitewash every year but which now were as gray as the webs festooning them.

Cassie shivered; it was chilly in the barn. When she was little she used to imagine with delicious masochistic delight being in haunted houses, dark places where lacy cobwebs stretched from corner to corner in every room, and from baluster to baluster of the stairs leading round and round and up, disappearing into the black upstairs where hideous monsters lay waiting to get her.

But in her fantasies, the stairways were always shiny dark wood, and the cobwebs spun by artistic spiders into shimmery delicate magical patterns, scary but beautiful—*Charlotte's Web* masterpieces—not these dirty strands and mats.

Will walked ahead into the gloom with Michael, who held Andy's hand, while Cassie and Emma stopped between the rows of stanchions with their rusting drinking bowls.

Cassie asked, "I see you used to have cows here?"

"Oh my, yes. I should say," Emma said. "Back when Vern was in high school. Ten, twelve years ago, we were milkin' up to forty head."

"Why did you stop farming?"

"Well, like everythin' else, I suppose. Wasn't hardly 'nough money in it to make a decent livin'. Back when our Vern and

Esther were babies we could get by all right. But by the time they got to high school, the price we were gettin' for the milk just wasn't goin' up like the price of everythin' else, and Will just couldn't see the sense in it any more.

"Seems too bad."

"For a while Vern thought he'd like to keep up the farm. Got the cows down to about twenty, where he figured he could manage it alone, and for a little while he was doin' pretty good. Gettin' by, anyway. But then he got himself married and when other opportunities come his way, he decided it was time to quit strugglin' so hard, so he sold the cattle, and I can't say he or Will was sorry about it, either."

Cassie crossed her arms, tucking her icy fingers in her armpits.

"What does Vern do now?"

"Vern? Well, I don't know exactly *what* you'd call him." She frowned. "He has his own dump truck. He hauls gravel and crushed stone, and sometimes hot top for some of the new driveways in town. Then he's got his new bulldozer. Lately he's been usin' that over to Wilmot Falls, where there's a lot of new buildin' goin' on. State says anybody puttin' in a new home has to meet certain requirements for septic tanks and leach fields. Vern says the quantity of crushed stone and the pipe and what not the state requires is foolish, but he says who's he to complain. Just that much more work for him, he says. That Vern—always did see the practical side of things."

From the darkness of the barn ahead of them, Andy called, "Hey Mum, come see what's in here."

"In a minute Andy. We'll be right along."

"Hey *Mum.* Come *here!*"

"In a minute, honey! Sorry, Emma. Please go on."

"Then in the winter, when there's no hot toppin' or much buildin' goin' on, Vern hauls lumber and even lends a hand with the loggin' end of it, too."

"Who is it he works for?"

"Why, anybody needin' him. Works at anything, that boy will, if he can make a decent wage at it. Right now he's workin' for Myron Ricker, clearin' some land for some house lots over beyond Hog Hollow."

Cassie remembered. Hog Hollow, on the way to Wilmot Falls, where Jim Brackett lives. And ah, how that name Myron Ricker keeps coming up.

"Myron's got all kinds of work for Vern, and treats Vern real good, too. Vern helps out first with the loggin' — that clears the land — then hauls gravel for any roads Myron might be puttin' in. Then after Myron gets his houses all built Vern gets to put in their septic systems."

"Does Ricker have many developments around town?"

"Well, I don't know's you'd call them *that*, exactly. It's not like Myron's some big developer from out of state. He builds a few houses here and there, sometimes as many as eight, ten at a time. No more than that. And what Myron builds are good little houses. Nothin' too fancy, but we're not a wealthy town, you know, and what houses Myron does build, people can afford."

"I see."

As Cassie and Emma walked on, Cassie noticed dark shapes in the stalls at the end of the barn. Funny-looking cows. She remembered a line from Robert Frost's "Mending Wall": "But here there are no cows."

She squinted: snowmobiles. Half a dozen, in the cow stalls, their bullet noses pointed toward the stanchions, their blunt behinds facing the manure troughs. Two were draped in green covers with "Ski-Roule" written across their sides.

Cassie wriggled her numb toes inside her boots. "Are all these yours, Emma?"

"Heavens, no! Only the Ski-Roules are ours. The rest people bring after the season's over, and Will works on them, doing tune-ups and repairs. Another month or so, machines'll pret' near fill this barn. Will loves to fool with them. Comes by it naturally, you might say, after all those years of workin' on farm equipment, fixin' tractors and the baler." She shook her head. "That hay baler of ours. Why, I think it was bein' fixed more often than it was bein' used. Will always did say the cussed thing weren't hardly any good ever since the day we bought it."

"Snowmobiling's big around here?"

"Well, I guess. I guess you could say it's just about the biggest sport there is. I'm not one to brag, but we had one of the first machines around, a whole winter before they caught on. Now, seems like pret' near everybody we know's got one. Snowmobilin's the best thing ever happened around here. Before these machines come along, most folks never left their houses in winter, never left their TV screens. Now seems like just about anybody can get out and enjoy nature."

Andy shouted, "Mum! Hey Mum—come see these baby sheep."

Cassie and Emma walked down a ramp into a shed built onto the side of the barn, joining Michael, Andy and Will next to a row of pens.

The shed had never been whitewashed; its walls and slanted roof were the warm rich brown of old rough lumber. The light coming in the row of tiny dirty windows behind the pens fell pale upon the wood, the hay littered with pebbles of sheep manure, the gray-brown backs of the ewes and their young. Everything was bathed in gold, as if lit by candle-light.

In each of the pens were a ewe and a lamb. Two of the lambs looked newly born, and were clattering about, the patter of their tiny hooves on the wooden floor of the pen sounding like corn popping. Their mothers chewed their cuds while the babies frisked about them.

There was a calm in the sheep shed. Cassie felt it, and assumed Will and Michael felt it because they were speaking in hushed voices. Cassie felt encapsulated by the quiet and the cocoon of the golden glow, thrust into a dreamy world of birthing and tending and peace. "Away in a manger . . ."

Her own little lamb was half-hanging by his armpits over one of a pen's slats, scuffling his feet on the wooden ramp to maintain his hold on the rail. "Hey Mum! Look at *this* one. This is a brand *new* one."

"That's right, Andrew," Emma said. "He was born just this morning."

The new lamb was unsteady on its feet. As it kept trying to nurse, its mother was determined to clean it. Just as it seemed it had a good hold on her teat, she gave it a lick which unhitched it from her and sent it stumbling to the side. Both were equally determined: the lamb to suckle, the mother to clean.

Cassie, Andy, and Emma stepped over to another pen, where Michael and Will were standing. In the pen was a young ram.

Andy asked Emma, "What's that big thing between its legs?"

"That's his bag, dear. That means he's a little boy, just like you."

Andy scowled. "His *bag*? What does he need a bag there for?"

Cassie stared at the ram, waiting till it moved into a position so she could see between its hind legs. God, what enormous balls—the size of a small grapefruit.

"Well," Emma said, embarrassed.

Andy looked at his mother. So did Michael and Will. So she was to be the instrument of enlightenment.

"That's a boy-sheep, Andy. A male. Just like you. And—"

"Are those his *ballikins*?"

"That's right. His ballikins."

Andy's eyes opened wide, his interest increasing tenfold.

Cassie smiled. Michael smiled. Will chewed on his lip, reaching for his pipe in his shirt pocket.

❀   ❀   ❀

They came out of the barn into the daylight, squinting. Cassie looked up Thurlow Hill to the end of the field across the road. She could see the first of the red tapes which marked off Skillin's lots.

"Emma, remember you were telling me about John Skillin's house lots above your field there?"

Emma nodded. "They begin just over the brow of the hill. Nice view from up theyah."

"Yeah, I know. What I don't understand is, if Skillin is dividing the land into five-acre lots, why are all his red flags so close together?"

Emma said, "Will, can you explain?"

After a couple of pulls on his pipe, Will said, "Sure, that's easy enough to explain. Skillin sets his frontage at 150 feet or so to give everyone who buys a lot from him some frontage on the road. That way everybody can build close to the road so's to be able to pick up power and phone lines. Course, school bus stops along the road here too."

Cassie still didn't understand. "But how does he get the five acres in each lot?"

"Well, he just makes 'em skinny-shaped, is all. Some of those lots go back as much as 1,500 feet."

"But what good is a piece of land 150 by 1,500 feet?"

Will said, "Well, there's no law says what shape a piece of land has to be. Five acres is five acres, no matter what it looks like."

"*Really?* Seems a house lot shaped like a bowling alley isn't anything I'd want to buy. I know I wouldn't want to be packed in there like sardines."

Will said, "Course, lot of people don't feel that way. Far as that goes, lot of city people'd pay top dollar to get five acres out here in the country."

Cassie looked at Michael, knowing he was waiting to see if she'd "flip out and cause a stink," as he put it whenever, as *she* put it, she "refused to buy shit like that."

Michael said, "Well, probably time we got going. All set, Cassie?"

Cassie glared at him. *"Sure."* Then, "Emma, thanks very much. It was nice of you to have us over."

Michael held out his hand to Will, who seemed embarrassed by the unexpected gesture. Flustered, he took his pipe from his mouth with his right hand, quickly shifted it to his left hand, and took Michael's hand which was pointed, waiting, at him.

"Welcome, I'm sure," Will said, nodding.

Cassie said, "Thanks again, Emma. And Will, thanks a lot."

"Pleasure," Will said, blushing.

As Cassie and Michael crossed the road, Emma called out, "You all come again now. And Cassie, you come up any time. The coffee's always on."

Six

Cassie turned the garden rake over and smoothed the ground the way Emma had demonstrated.

When Cassie had read "Prepare the seed bed" on the vegetable seed packets, she imagined getting out fresh sheets, blankets and pillows to cover the area where she was about to plant lettuce seed. Why couldn't they simply say, "Get the dirt ready"? As she pulled the rake toward her, bending frequently to pick out still more rocks, she remembered what Emma had said: "You'll work this same garden plot for years and never clear it of rocks. Seems rocks grow faster in these hills than vegetables." On Emma's advice, the garden plot they'd had tilled was near the house, "To discourage 'coons and other critters."

Andy was playing with a bow and arrows Michael had made for him out of willow branches. He had lately been watching *Robin Hood* reruns and was obsessed with playing his current hero. Now and then he would climb atop his sand pile, string an arrow in his bow and shout into the air, "Stop in the name of the poor!" Or, on his way to other adventures in the name of the poor, he would sing or hum phrases from the program's theme song: "Oh don't deceive me, Oh never leave me. How could you use a poor maiden so?"

A car rattled down the lane. Cassie peered around the corner of the house, startled to see an old dusty-blue pickup truck, the kind with round fenders covering the wheels.

Jittery, Cassie squinted to see who it was. After all, she and Andy were alone all day at the end of a dead-end lane. Now and then she imagined leather-jacketed Hells Angels roaring into the yard, plundering and vandalizing, raping her and snatching Andy.

Then she recognized the man climbing out of the truck. Jim Brackett.

"I've been meaning to stop by to thank you for the cookies. I don't have a telephone or I would have called." His dark red turtleneck jersey was lovely against his rosy cheeks and blue eyes.

He handed her a dark green wine bottle. On it a sticker: "June 1975."

"Dandelion wine. Last year's. This year's isn't racked up yet."

"Racked up?"

"Racking is siphoning wine off to get rid of sediment. I usually rack mine twice before I bottle it. It's fine to drink now, though some people save theirs till winter, when they say it's like taking a draught of summer sunshine." Nodding at Andy, "Your son?"

"Yes. Andy, this is Mr. Brackett. You know those hills we can see from the front yard?"

Andy nodded.

"Mr. Brackett lives over there."

"Hi, Andy. And please call me Jim."

"Would you like to sit down?" Cassie asked. "I have a couple of lawn chairs that I could —"

"Thank you, but I won't be staying."

Andy wandered over to the old lilac bush in the corner of the house, where chickadees were gorging themselves at the feeder. He inched closer, staring up into the branches, watching the birds as they flitted from the feeder to branches of the lilac, where they hammered out the kernels of the seeds. Now and then above the whirring of the chickadees' wings came the scolding notes of varying pitches: "Chick-dee-dee-dee." Andy raised his bow, lined up the arrow, aimed at the lilac bush, and pulling hard on the bow string, let the arrow fly up into the branches. The arrow went straight for about two feet, then veered off, hit the house and landed on the ground behind the bush. The chickadees went about their business, unaware of this Nimrod in their midst.

Jim said, "Hunting, huh?"

Andy turned, smiling sheepishly. He retrieved his arrow from behind the lilac bush and ran off to play on the rope swing in the maple tree.

"Sweet child," Jim said.

"Yes." Michael didn't like it when she called Andy "sweet." Just last night, he had said to her, "The kid needs to get out of that fantasy world of his and begin to see what life is really all about. You ought to get him to start pulling his weight around the house."

Cassie sat the wine in the grass next to the house, leaning the neck of the bottle against the lowest clapboard, wiggling it, making sure it was stable.

"Sam Gilman would be mighty surprised to see how much work you've done on this old place."

"That's what Emma Thurlow said. Say, is he buried in that old cemetery? We've been there but so many of the old stones are fallen over it's hard to tell how many graves are actually there."

"You mean the old Gilman plot at the end of the field?"

"Yes."

"No. When Sam died at the County Farm, some cousins had him buried in the town cemetery in Coggerton. Nowadays very few people are buried in the old family plots. I guess undertakers have sold them a bill of goods about embalming and vaults, and lawn-mowing over the graves. When I was a boy of ten or so, I watched my grandfather make his own coffin — planing and sanding that thing on the long trestle table in the kitchen, working on it by night in the light of the kerosene lamps. Then he put it up attic and when he died, my father and uncle put him in that coffin and we all walked up the hill to our family plot and buried him, and that was that."

He paused, looking in the direction of the Gilman cemetery, hidden in the woods at the far end of the field. "Sam had a sad life."

"How is that?"

"His brother Jonathan — his only living relative after his parents died — got killed in the First World War, and that left the place pretty much to Sam. He never married and mostly kept to himself down here."

Cassie wondered if Jim had ever married, and if by chance he had a son who just happened to look like him, only younger.

"Did he farm the place?"

"Not much more than a vegetable garden. Before the war, the Gilmans had cows, and used to make cheese here and store it over the winter. After mud season they'd bring it by horse and wagon into town to sell it. Then the war came, and soon after that Sam's mother and father died."

"How did Sam earn a living?"

"Doing odd jobs here and there." He looked up at the house. "Does your husband like working on the place?"

Cassie shrugged. "Sometimes. Once in a while. But because I was the one who really pushed to buy it, I'm the one who's responsible for getting most of the work done." Feeling disloyal, she quickly added, "Of course, his job is in Bourne and he works long hours. Sometimes I hardly see him except on weekends." Half of which he spends in front of the goddamn boob tube.

"What does he do for work?"

"He's an engineer." Cassie glanced up at him, realizing he'd been looking directly at her, that his eyes were right there, ready to meet hers. "Emma Thurlow said you were at Dartmouth."

"Ah, Emma. Yes, I was."

"What did you study?"

"History. But at the beginning of my third year, I returned to the farm."

Looking out over the field, Cassie said, softly, "Because of the accident with your father and brother."

In the corner of her eye she saw Jim looking at her. She said, "Emma again."

Jim's blue eyes matched the sweep of blue sky behind him. She felt him looking through her, and at the same time, deep into her.

"It must have been awful, the accident."

"Yes. It was."

Were he a child, Cassie thought, I would reach out and touch him, to offer small comfort. Instinct would have me pat his arm, caress his cheek. Or were he a woman I could reach out. Human beings connecting. But he was neither child nor woman, and there were rules about touching men.

Jim bent over, snapped off a dandelion, and straightened again. "Have you tried dandelion greens?"

"I have. Emma showed me how to pick them." She noticed how clean his nails were.

"Do you like them?"

"I love them. Andy tried a few and turned up his nose, declaring that he wasn't going to eat grass."

Jim smiled, his blue eyes twinkling.

"But my husband wouldn't even try them." She shrugged. "But that's typical. He's so damn clap-trap minded about some things." Then, "Sorry, I didn't mean to—"

Jim was silent. She tried to read something in his face, but there was nothing. Eyes clear, expressionless.

"Another month, that field will be ablaze with yellow and red hawkweeds. It's a pretty sight."

Cassie liked his long graceful fingers, and the way his thumb angled out sharply from his wrist. Liked the way the joints of his thumb were clearly defined. She always noticed men's hands. What a man's hands were like could turn her on or off, no matter what the rest of him looked like.

But what am I doing, looking at this man's hands. He's old enough to be my father. My son's grandfather.

There was a twittering overhead and they both looked up.

"Goldfinches," Jim said. "Males have their summer colors now."

Tiny birds, the females olive, the males bright yellow and black and white, dipped and rose against the blue sky as, in a flock, they sped around the house and into one of the maple trees.

"I must be going. My brother Woodbury will be expecting me."

At his truck, Jim said, "It was nice seeing you, Mrs. —"

"*Please—Cassie.*"

He nodded.

Cassie extended her hand. Hesitating a moment, Jim took it, his grasp strong, warm.

It was the first time Cassie had gone by herself for a walk in the woods, though she and Andy often walked to the old stone bridge over the brook at the edge of the field. At the bridge, Andy had formed crude balls from the last of the icy snow and tossed them into the brook, delighting in watching them bob along on the rushing water.

Weekends, she occasionally managed to pull Michael away from watching sports, and the three of them would trudge into the woods.

Cassie had imagined that these walks, these family walks, would be the highlight of their life there. Imagined the three of them, walking abreast, hand in hand, discussing this tree or that leaf, stopping to hear that bird or to notice those wild-flowers.

Instead what she got was an unpleasant attack on the woods that often left her wishing they'd never gone.

Michael would charge on ahead — head erect, hands in pockets, branches sliding and snapping across his red windbreaker — forging ahead as if he were blazing a trail, or as if he wanted to cover as much land as he could in one foray. Once, in his big black work boots with the heavy lug soles, he trampled over a carpet of foamflowers, not even noticing them underfoot.

Cassie preferred to amble along, stopping often to savor the sights and smells around her, which frequently elicited a scornful stare from Michael, who would turn and scowl, as if to ask why she was lagging behind. You'd think they were shooting the rapids and she wasn't pulling her weight.

And walks in the woods meant one thing to Andy: playing good guys and bad guys, which entailed running from tree to tree, hiding, assuming, like the ostrich in the sand, that if his eyes were hidden behind the tree, then the whole of him was invisible. Then he would jump out with a yell that would make Cassie want to strangle him.

Sometimes Cassie would try to interest him in a bird, thinking he might stop and shut up for a moment, anyway. She'd say, "Listen, Andy, hear that? That's an oven bird." There'd be silence for a minute while Andy listened. More often than not, the bird didn't deliver, and Cassie would attempt to further entice Andy by gripping his arm and imitating the oven bird — "Teecha teecha teecha!" — hoping the bird would take the cue. Usually it didn't and Andy would get fidgety, eager to get on with his rampaging.

Once they had come to a stone wall and when she helped Andy over it, wary of the loose boulders on top, Michael complained, as he so often did, that she "candy-assed the kid." Or he fussed that she was "turning him into a hypochondriac."

Helping Andy jump down off the wall, it occurred to her that she'd never once heard Michael say "I love you" to Andy. And she remembered how at Christmas, when they were wrapping presents for Andy, she would write elaborate notes for him and stick them on the packages, while Michael would write on a plain tag in block letters just one word: ANDREW.

But on this spring Sunday, armed with a can of Off and a bug hat, Cassie headed straight out behind the house, through a dense pine grove, and into a clump of swamp maples, where the spongy ground squeaked under her sneakers.

Just beyond the maples, a stone wall, and over the wall, the brook. Bunchberries — dainty white flowers against fresh green leaves — sprinkled the mossy edge of the brook. She was glad Michael was not here to trample them, and remembered how gently Jim Brackett had snapped off a dandelion the day he'd come with the wine. He would not mash down bunchberries.

Cassie balanced the can of Off between two rocks on the wall, wiggled some top rocks to find a stable place where she could cross, and climbed over. She looked up the brook to where it angled out of sight, then down the brook, where it ran straight, rushing over mossy rocks in miniature, tinkling waterfalls.

A black fly was under her bug hat. Cassie had tried to ignore it, but now its high-pitched whine annoyed her. She pulled the elastic of the hat away from her neck and stretched it over her forehead, just below the hair line, letting the hat trail behind her, an olive-drab wimple.

She sprayed Off onto her hand and lightly wiped her forehead, her nose, her cheeks, her chin, under her bottom lip, her neck.

She decided to follow the brook downstream, toward the stone bridge.

By now, gangs of black flies had found her. A week ago, they were just beginning to appear. What few there were didn't bother Cassie, and she couldn't see what the fuss over black flies was all about. But now she knew.

Cassie remembered from her college days a folk song called "Black Flies," sung by folk singer Jackie Washington. The song told of a work crew building a dam in North Ontario. Hearing that amusing song in that smoky Boston coffee house in the '60s, she had no idea that black flies were every bit as vicious as the song said.

Now, with a cloud of them following her, she remembered the chorus of the song:

> And those black flies, little black flies
> Always the black flies no matter where you go
> Die with the black flies picking my bones ...

Cassie swiped at the cloud in front of her. For about two seconds they dispersed, then reassembled.

At the bridge, the brook rushed and foamed where it narrowed to flow between the two cut-granite abutments, then turned inky in the dark shadow of the stone slabs of the bridge itself.

Cassie scrambled onto the bridge and sat down, hanging her legs over the edge. Her wrist stung. A black fly was firmly entrenched, its rear legs churning the air like the legs of a dog digging frantically for a bone. She flicked it off. Little bastard.

Where the fly had been, there was a tiny hole in the center of a purple dot. Around it, a pink circle was blooming into the size of a dime: a tiny boob. What could these flies do to you if you weren't protected by clothing and repellent? She thought of *The African Queen*, in which Humphrey Bogart, after tugging the boat through chest-high muck, trying to get out of the endless swamp, crawls on board the boat. He is covered with bloodsucking leeches. He pleads, "Argh! Get them *off*, get them *off*!" He and Katherine Hepburn pick and claw frantically at the leeches while he shudders, in horror and disgust, "Filthy little devils!"

Cassie dosed her wrists and ankles with more Off, singing:

> Black flies, black flies everywhere
> Crawlin' in your whiskers and

Crawlin' in your hair.
They're swimmin' in the soup
Swimmin' in the tea
The devil take the black flies
Let me be ...

She pointed the can of Off at the cloud of flies and jabbed spray at them. Briefly, barely noticeably, the flies scattered, instantly regrouping as if they'd never broken formation. She breathed deeply, through her nose, fearing that if she opened her mouth a knot of the little bastards might attack her tongue, then charge down her throat and devour her from within.

Along both banks of the brook grew still-young skunk cabbages, and clutches of fiddlehead ferns whose stems arched like the backs of proper ladies at a tea party, their tight fuzzy coils unwinding, yielding to the warmth of the day.

Everything shimmered chartreuse: the skunk cabbages and fiddleheads, the young leaves of the hardwoods overhead, and their reflection in the pools of the brook. Cassie lay on the bridge, looking up through the lace of the leaves at the pale blue sky, feeling the chill granite beneath her spine. The moist air hinted at the coming summer.

The flies, left behind by her sudden act of lying back on the bridge, found her again, seeming even more frantic. *Jesus Christ!*

Leaving the bridge, Cassie followed the brook to where the land dropped off sharply. Here the brook quit its gentle gurglings and glassy sliding noises, churning and foaming over a giant's staircase of boulders and ledges.

She squatted on a flat rock on the bank, overlooking the ravine. At the top of the bank was the old Gilman cemetery, enclosed by a wall of granite slabs. A few of the slabs were tipping out from the wall, looking as if a touch would send them crashing down the bank onto her.

She climbed the steep slope, picking her way over and

around small boulders, rubble dumped there by the farmers who cleared the fields of larger rocks, using those to build walls marking off pastures. The rocks made the climb difficult. Grabbing onto saplings that grew up out of the bank, she pulled herself up the slope, her legs and back aching with the strain.

When she was almost at the top of the slope and could see the tops of some of the gravestones, she twisted her ankle and fell onto a pile of rocks, hurting her leg and hip as she fell. She settled herself on the rocks, massaging her ankle, fretting: God, what if I'd broken a leg in this ravine? Who would hear my cries over the roar of the brook? And when my can of Off ran out? Had anyone ever been completely sucked to death by black flies? And—!—hypothermia? Even though it was May, nights were still frosty. She'd never survive in her jeans and corduroy jacket. And even if the bugs didn't get her and the night stayed balmy, there was starvation. Nothing to eat. No berries yet, no acorns within reach. Only gray rubble and last year's brown leaves. She couldn't even eat her sneakers, which were rubber and canvas. Not a piece of edible leather on her body.

The ravine below now looked ominous. No underbrush grew in the twilight down there. The trees, mostly thin white birch, shot way up, reaching skyward, their foliage all at their tops where it found light. Directly below her a huge rotten tree had fallen across the brook. Bear country.

Cassie pushed herself up off the rocks and picked her way to the opening in the cemetery wall. Once, surely, the cemetery itself had been a walled-off section of field, in the sunlight, the loved ones' gravestones visible from the house. Now woods surrounded the cemetery. The part of the wall barely visible from the house could almost be mistaken for just another stone wall marking off a pasture, except for the fact that the cemetery wall was not boulders piled in a long irregular mound, but great oblong blocks of granite, carefully chosen and fitted together.

The cemetery was round, or nearly so. At the highest spot, in the center, were the stones marking the graves of James and Lydia Gilman, the couple who had settled the place. The rest of the stones, marking the graves of the next generations, were placed all around, further down the gentle slope.

Cassie came to a stone she hadn't bothered to read before, because it was bent over, its letters facing the ground. Now she kneeled down, dragging the black flies with her, and twisted her head up under the stone to read: "Eliza Gilman."

Eliza? The same Eliza—frail farm girl—whose math book fell out of the ceiling?

She squinted at the second line on the slate stone: "Daught. of," and then the third line: "James and Lydia Gilman." Cassie rubbed her fingers over the lichen-filled letters of the next line. "Born—" Damn. Eighteen *something*. And then: "Died 1845. Ae 36 y. 2m. 17d."

Eliza Gilman. A Gilman in 1823 when she wrote her name in her math book. (She would have been fourteen in 1823.) A Gilman still in 1845 when she died. A spinster. So childbirth didn't carry her off after all. What, then? Smallpox? pneumonia? Or something mundane, like foul well water—water from the same well they were using now?

Eliza Gilman, dead at thirty-six. Cassie, thirty-two, could not imagine herself dead in four years.

She stood, brushing the pine needles from her knees, and looked out over the gravestones at the house beyond the long sweep of field. She remembered Jim telling her how they brought his grandfather to the family burying ground, in the coffin he made himself. And she imagined Eliza's solemn funeral procession coming down across this field. Mourners in black walking slowly from the house, heads bent in sorrow, the Gilman men in stovepipe hats carrying the honey-pine coffin over the waving grasses, the women walking to the side, faltering, children clutching their trailing black dresses.

Or did they haul Eliza by wagon, wrapped in a simple

winding sheet, her waxy-blue bare legs hanging over the end of the wagon. "They brought Bill home in a hurry-up wagon / Oh Lord, his feet was a-draggin' ..."

A dog barked. She limped from the darkness of the cemetery into the golden warmth of the field, tipping her face to the sun which now, in the late afternoon, was beginning to set behind the house.

The same dog (deep-throated — haroomp haroomp haroomp) was just below the field, toward Coggerton. Set off by that dog, another dog chimed in, its bark a high-voiced yipping that, unlike the steady, paced barking of Deepthroat, came in short frenetic bursts.

Michael was sitting up in bed, shaking Cassie.

"You must have been having one hell of a dream," he said. "You've been yelling about leather and acorns. Jesus."

Cassie struggled to remember. Something about a plane. An accident. The plane went down (Was it shot down?!) into the ravine by the brook. She was the only one in it. She was injured, couldn't move, facing starvation. "Leather," Michael said she'd said in her sleep.

She told Michael how when she was climbing up from the brook that afternoon, she'd twisted her ankle and fallen, and and how she'd sat there imagining what it would be like being stranded in the ravine, with no one able to hear her cries over the roar of the brook.

He said, "Well, you're all right now, aren't you?"

"Yes, but *then* — this afternoon I mean — it was frightening."

Michael yawned and lay back down. "Oh go to sleep."

God, what if she'd told him she'd been raped and mugged? Would he dismiss her with, "But you're all right *now*, aren't you?"

She whispered, "Michael?" She paused. "Michael?" She touched his shoulder, then quickly drew back her hand.

Michael's deep breathing told her he was asleep. Lonely, she kneeled up in bed and looked out the window. The full-moon light fell blue and cold around the house, its brightness reaching far beyond the maple trees.

She wondered where on those dark hills Jim Brackett lived, and she wished, absurdly, that he were next to her now. Would he understand her fear of being stranded in the ravine?

She looked down at Michael and pictured Jim there instead, moonlight falling on his white hair, on his ruddy cheeks. Annoyed with herself, she hissed through clenched teeth, "*Christ!*"

She stretched over the headboard of the bed, pressing her cheek against the window glass, squinting toward the end of the field to about where she guessed the cemetery to be, hoping to see the gray wall marking it.

Instead, only the field, a calm sea in the moonlight, with here and there black clumps of junipers. The moonlight did not penetrate the black woods at the end of the field.

Seven

"Mr. Ricker?"

"Ayup, Rickah heeyah."

"This is Cassie Atwood. Out at the old Gilman place?"

"Ayup."

"I—we—were wondering if you're still planning to drill our well, since it's the middle of June."

Silence.

"Mr. Ricker? Are you—?"

"I'm heeyah. Lookin' at my schedule. Been a busy spring. Lots of folks ahead of you wantin' water, and it wouldn't do for me to take anyone out of turn, now, would it?"

"Of course not, but could you give us some idea when you—"

"Well, got three, maybe four wells over to Wilmot Falls to do, then couple right here in town, then seems I ought to be 'bout ready to have my boy Erlon move my rig over your way."

His unflappable indifference to the possibility of their well running dry was infuriating. But knowing it was too late to line up another driller, Cassie said, "Well thanks, Mr. Ricker. We'll see you when you get here."

"Ayup. Just as soon's we can free up our rig from the other places."

With Ricker's monotone still droning in her head, Cassie stepped outside, walking barefoot through the cool grass to the garden, where rows of young green plants against the brown soil looked, as the seed catalogs put it, "well-established." She imagined the soil drying, baking hard, finally cracking, begging water they'd be unable to give it because they had barely enough for themselves. Bastard, that Ricker.

To the side of the garden Andy was playing in the sand-box Michael finally got around to building for him. The late morning sun fell shiny on his brown hair. Settled well down in the sandbox, hunched over, his back curved, his face involved in whatever his hands were busy doing down in the box, he looked like a Peanuts character.

Cassie brushed sand from one of the triangular corner seats and sat down.

"Hi, old boy." She riffled her hand through his hair, slightly damp with sweat.

"Look, Mum. I'm making all these roads, and they all lead to different camps, and my trucks bring supplies over the roads to the people in the camps to fight off the bad guys."

"Ah." There was nothing she could identify as roads. There were wheel marks of Andy's Tiny Tonkas in the sand, and here and there were little mounds patted into cone shapes, some showing imprints of Andy's whole hand. Atop all the mounds (Andy's "camps," Cassie figured) were wooden Fisher Price people—no more than two inches tall—faded from being left out in the weather. No arms or legs. Perfectly round heads. One was a little girl with a plastic yellow Dutch-cut wig glued onto her head. A second was the grumpy gas-pump boy that came with a Fisher Price garage they'd bought Andy for his second birthday. Down-turned mouth and frown marks, a red baseball cap with the visor turned sideways in a gesture of defiance. A third was an airline pilot. Blue limbless body, blue cap, confident smile.

Scooping up fistfuls of sand and sifting them through her fingers, Cassie looked out over the field. Drifts of yellow and red hawkweeds bent on their tall stalks in the light breezes—breezes seen more than felt. Jim had said June would bring the hawkweeds to the field. He'd also said the Gilman field was a pretty field. That was an understatement. But then, everything about Jim seems understated.

Among the hawkweeds, lush purple clover grew closer to

the ground. And here and there, beneath the taller hawkweeds and daisies and milkweed shoots, ethereal sprinkles of bluets arranged themselves in ready-made bouquets among the new green grasses of the field.

The air was full of bird songs, some identifiable, like the ceaseless upbeat song of the robin ("cheerup cheerilee cheerup cheerilee") and the rising metallic spiral song of the bobolink as it rose up out of the field, flashing yellow and black and white in the sun before settling down onto a still-green ironbush, its song ending as it descended with a slower, high-pitched "pink pink pink." And then, birds Cassie could not identify added their voices to the general chorus regaling the June day.

Andy was humming tunelessly, absentmindedly, stopping now and then when the business beneath him in the box got especially interesting or demanded his full attention. His thin forearms were beginning to color from the summer sun. She was grateful he was content to play alone most of the time. Occasionally she felt guilty that he had no playmates, telling herself, to lessen her guilt, that come September, he'd be in school, would make friends, and wouldn't be lonely.

With the still-dimpled hands of babyhood, Andy patted a new mound into shape. Cassie resisted an aching temptation to scoop him up, hold his head in the crook of her arm, his body in her lap, where she could look down into his face and feel him tight against her, the way she held him when he was a baby.

She leaned over and kissed the top of his head, warm and moist on her lips, then returned to the garden to thin the new carrots.

After supper, Cassie walked up to Wilkinses' for eggs. The black flies had gone; now mosquitoes hummed about her as she walked. Somehow, outside at least, they didn't seem quite as insidious as the black flies. Slower moving, easily slapped as they lazily settled on her hand or arm or cheek, getting ready to bite. And mosquitoes could be killed in the air, smacked between the hands.

But in the house, what nasty little fuckers they could be. When she was young, at her family's summer camp, a single mosquito in the house could send her mother into a frenzy. Cassie could never understand why. She loved to lie in the dark and hear one humming about her head. She would wait and wait and wait, patiently, until the humming stopped. Then she knew it was about to bite, and all she had to do was wait until she felt a sting, then slap it where it stung. It was not important to get to sleep those summer nights. Waiting out the mosquito was just another idle game of childhood.

Now, though, she went into a tizzy over a mosquito in the bedroom. Now she turned on the lights and kept them on till the offending mosquito landed and was killed. Maddening, the midnight hunt. While Michael lay there, she stood teetering on the bed, spotting the little fucker against the plaster wall, the next instant losing it against the honey-colored beams overhead.

Now there was an alarm clock to face in the morning, a husband to get off to work, Andy to tend, house and garden work to do, and she understood why one little mosquito drove her mother batty.

In Wilkinses' yard Lance and his younger brother, Owen, were playing in the dirt pile near the corner of the house.

"Hi, kids."

The little one, Owen, whose right arm was wrapped in a dirty bandage, looked up expressionless, green snot on his upper lip. He went back to his digging. Lance watched her as she went around the side of the house to the kitchen door.

She and Sally had fallen into a routine. Sally would greet her at the door, invite her in, indicate the chair she was to sit in, offer her coffee which Cassie refused. They would chat for a few minutes and always it would be Cassie who would say something like, "Well, guess I'd better be going. Left my two fellas back there by themselves. No telling what mischief they're getting into." She didn't know how to say, when Sally opened the door, "I don't want to stop, I don't want to gossip, I just want to get my eggs and beat it. So fork 'em over and here's your dough." Gutless, afraid to alienate the neighbors. Gutless, dumbing down her language, using words like "menfolk," pretending to be just like Sally, saying she had to be home, "bein', course, only one able to keep my menfolk outa mischief."

Sally had a lot to say about snobs — "people who think they're better'n the rest of us" — and Cassie did her best, at least in conversation where hypocrisy came easy, to be just like the rest of them. And all for a dozen eggs.

Now Sally was sitting across from her, dragging on a Parliament, her hair in rollers, asking Cassie if she'd like to come to a Boontonware party.

"A what?"

"Boontonware. One person opens up her home, and the lady from the company comes round with all the things and shows 'em — you know, demmastrates 'em — and people buy 'em. Course, only if they really *want* 'em, and, course, person who opens her home gets a prize, too."

Cassie pictured a giant woman leaning over Sally's house, kneeling on the slanted roof for leverage, prying off the roof with a giant beer can opener.

"Well gee, Sally, to tell you the truth, I never go to Tupperware parties."

"Tupperware? This ain't no *Tupperware* party. It's *Boontonware.* Glasses, real nice. Nice enough to use for best, even." Sally snuffed her cigarette. "Ain't no *Tupperware* party."

"Thanks, Sally, but I really don't need anything, and —"

"Well, you just let me know if you change your mind. You might change your mind, you know. Most everyone's gonna be here. Ain't hardly no one yet says she won't come. There'll be Midge Fecteau and Stacey Dalpey and her mother from over town. And course, Emma and her Esther."

"Pretty good crowd, huh?"

"You met Esther yet?"

"Not yet."

"She's real nice, Esther. Our kids play together a lot."

There was a commotion in the yard. Lance was pulling a stick away from Owen, who was sitting in the dirt, howling, holding on, inching along on his bottom each time Lance tugged on the branch.

Sally spun around in her chair. "Goddamn kids." She stood up, her chair scraping on the linoleum floor. She yanked the screen door open, stepped outside, slammed the door shut, and yanked the stick away from Lance, shouting, "Ya want this stick do ya, ya goddamn little bastards? I'll give ya this stick. I'll give it ya both good!" She flailed away at Lance, striking him across his chest. Lance stood rigid, arms straight by his side, head jerking back, and eyes snapping shut with each blow.

Cassie counted: six blows.

Sally said, "And you, ya little bastard." She struck Owen across his chest and bandaged arm. Thwack thwack thwack.

Owen sat in the dirt, whimpering, eyes following his mother, cheeks shiny with tears. He began to rock, back and forth, holding his bandaged arm close to his body, its hand curled inward against his chest. Lance stood motionless, his mouth hanging open, his eyes narrow slits.

Sally came inside, sat down, and reached for a cigarette. She struck a match, her cigarette flapping up and down between her lips as she said, "That'll teach 'em. Never share nothin', those two. Always pesterin' each other over one thing or 'nother."

Drenched in sweat, tense, Cassie asked, "What did Owen do to his arm?"

"Oh, that. He got what he deserved. Don't know how many times I tol' him leave my coffee cup alone. Well, yesterday the phone rung and my coffee cup was right here on the edge of the table. Right like this. I tol' Owen, I said to him, 'Don't you dare touch that coffee cup.' Course, he don't *mind*, that one, and next thing I see he's pullin' that cup all over himself. Burned his arm and hollered and bawled, but I tol' him it's his own fault and maybe now he'll listen."

Cassie wiped her sweating hands on her jeans.

"He got just what he was lookin' for. Me 'n' Les, we didn't feel sorry for him one bit. They gotta learn somehow. And you know what else? You can bet he don't touch my cigarettes no more, neither."

"What do you mean?"

"My cigarettes. He kept reachin' for 'em and reachin' for 'em and finely I tol' him it was time he learned to leave 'em alone, so you know what I did? I took and held onto his hand real good, and then I pressed a goin' cigarette right into his hand, right here, right like this." With her left hand she pushed an unlit cigarette against the open upright palm of her right hand.

Holy shit. "You *what*? The cigarette was *lit*?" Fucking Christ.

Sally frowned, the fact of Cassie's disapproval gradually registering on her face. With an air of finality, indicating the end of the conversation, she said, "Anyway, he learned. He learned real good. He don't touch my cigarettes no more."

For a moment she and Cassie stared into each other's eyes. Then Cassie said, "Well, I'd better be going. Do you have the eggs, or—?"

"Sure, I got eggs. Plenty. I'll just go get 'em from the coop."

While Sally went for the eggs, Cassie looked out at Lance and Owen. Owen was still sitting in the dirt, his mouth down-turned, his eyes blank.

Lance was on his knees, hitting a rock with the stick Sally

had used on him. Up came his arm, way above his head, and down it came, hard, rhythmically, over and over again, his face expressionless, rigid, except for his eyes, which blinked with each blow, the way they had when the same stick had fallen across his body.

The next morning, Cassie opened the carton of eggs Sally had sold her the night before. Three of the eggs were cracked.

"Goddamnit."

"What's the matter?" Michael asked.

"These eggs I bought last night. Three are cracked."

"So?"

"So maybe Sally's mad at me because I'm not going to her Boontonware party."

"Jesus. How paranoid can you get?"

"You weren't there last night. She was really pissed off because I'm not going to her Boonton party."

"Boonton*ware*."

She glared at him.

"Well, you said it was Boontonware, didn't you?"

"That's not the point, what the party is. The point is I think Sally hates me. Jesus, I know she does after she saw it made me sick, burning the kid with the cigarette."

"That's a little weird, all right. But listen, that's got nothing to do with the eggs. You really are paranoid. Why would she give you broken eggs? It wouldn't be smart. She'd lose customers if she passed out broken eggs."

"She's not smart. She's dumb. And creepy."

"So what the hell. No one's forcing you to buy eggs there."

Cassie wished Michael were a little more concerned about the eggs, and a lot more concerned about Sally Wilkins beating her kids.

Eight

Emma Thurlow met Cassie and Andy as they were picking up the mail at the end of their lane. "Have you got a few minutes?"

"Well, I guess—"

"Come up to the house. I'd like you to meet my Esther."

In Thurlows' back yard was a rusting metal swing set, not there when the Atwoods had been to Sunday dinner. Two swings, their seats worn to bare, splintery wood, hung from rusty metal chains.

A boy was swinging by his arms from the cross bar between the two upright end supports that formed an A. In the sand pile next to the door a little girl was spooning sand into an orange juice can.

"Andrew, come meet my Dennis." Emma took Andy by the hand and led him to the swing set. "Dennis?"

Dennis stopped swinging and dropped his feet to the ground, but still held onto the crossbar with both arms.

"Andrew," Emma said. "This is Dennis. Dennis, Andrew lives across the road, down the lane. Wouldn't you like to play with him while his mother talks with your Nana and your Auntie Esther?"

Dennis went back to his swinging, this time showing off, looking over his shoulder to see if Andy was watching him.

Emma said to Cassie, "My Vernon's boy. I watch him most days while Vern and his wife work."

Cassie said, "I'll be in the house with Dennis's grandmother for a few minutes, Andy. You stay out here with Dennis and—" Cassie looked at the little girl on the sandpile.

"April," Emma said. "April Dawn. Esther's girl."

"With Dennis and April," Cassie said. "And I'll be out soon. Okay?"

Andy's pleading eyes told her that it was not okay, but he didn't protest as he watched his mother walk into the house with Emma.

In the kitchen stood a young woman wbith a baby on her hip. She wore a tight, short-sleeved, pink pullover sweater, the kind that was fashionable in Cassie's high school days, worn with a matching cardigan, and often with a silk neckerchief. Sweater sets. The woman's legs below her blue shorts were pale, and covered with tiny bumps. Her bare feet were dirty. Her orange, dry-looking, brittle hair hung to her shoulders.

Emma said, "Cassie, this is my daughter, Esther. Course, I've told her all about you." She held her index finger out toward the baby, who grasped it in his hand. "And this tyke here," she said, jiggling his arm, "is my youngest grandchild, Gordon Lessard, Jr., named after his daddy."

Cassie said, "My, he's a sturdy little fellow, isn't he?"

Esther said, "Oh yes, he's quite the big bowie. And we have something to brag about too, don't we, Gordy?" Esther paused, as if waiting for Gordy to chime in, then announced, "We went all day yesterday without a diaper!"

"Goodness! How old is he?"

"Eight months," Esther said, bouncing the baby up and down on her hip. His round little head bobbed backward, forward, left and right.

Cassie shook her head. "My!"

Emma said, "Both my Esther and Vernon were completely trained by their first birthdays. But I must say, the way our Gordy's going, he might be trained even sooner than that."

Esther said, "Course, we have our little accidents now and then, but we are doing very well, mostly."

Either one could be the other's mother, either one the mother of the baby. Their voices, their inflections were the same; Esther looked, Cassie figured, the way Emma must have looked twenty-five years ago.

What would they think if she told them, "And Andy and me, *we* were in diapers—still pissing and shitting our pants—till we were *two*!"

Emma carried the three coffee mugs to the table. On the table was sugar bowl fashioned like a milk pail, with a lid and a wire handle for carrying it.

Emma set a half gallon carton of milk on the table and put a spoon in the milkpail sugar bowl. She opened a cupboard over the sink, and as she stretched, her cotton housedress hiked up above her knees, revealing white thighs of dimpled fat. She took down a box of graham crackers.

Esther sat the baby on the table, his legs dangling over the edge. Emma handed him a graham cracker.

The baby, white-skinned, with plump thighs and forearms that bulged above his pudgy hands, was dressed in an undershirt, a diaper, and yellowed plastic pants that crackled as he kicked his feet straight out, his spastic kicks bouncing him up and down on the table. On his feet were yellow and white booties, crocheted with big needles.

Cassie glanced out the window to check on Andy.

Emma said, "Now don't you worry about him. He'll be just fine out there with Dennis. Nothin' out there for him to get hurt on."

Dennis was still hanging by his arms from the cross bar of the swing set, kicking up dirt as he pushed himself off the ground.

Andy was swinging, earnestly, working his mouth. Except for glancing at Dennis now and then, he could have been playing alone, swinging on his own rope swing.

The baby threw his graham cracker onto the floor. Emma picked it up, swiped it on her apron, and passed it back to the baby, who resumed chewing on it.

"I've been meanin' to talk to you about somethin'," Emma said. "Every year, first two weeks of July, they hold Bible School at the Otis Corner Road Community Church."

From somewhere in the middle of the house a washing machine vibrated and hummed.

Emma went on, "Doesn't matter what your religion is. Our regular church is the Advent Christian, but when our Vern and Esther were children, they both went to Bible School. Didn't you, Esther."

"Uh huh. Vern and me, we always said Bible School was the best two weeks of the summer. We always said we'd take Bible School any day if it meant we could get out of doin' chores!"

Emma said, "Course, if you got any special opinions about any particular religion—"

"We don't belong to any church," Cassie said.

The washing machine squealed to a stop.

"Well, we *know that*," Emma said. Then, embarrassed, she quickly added, "Course, what a body does, whether he goes to church regular or not is nobody else's concern. Some mighty fine people we know aren't churchgoers—at least, not regular churchgoers."

How did Emma knew they weren't churchgoers? Oh. Skillin. The day he showed them the house, he had fished around, trying to make them name their church.

Emma continued, "I was thinkin' that Bible School would be good for Andy, where he's alone much of the time."

"Where is the school held?"

"Otis Corner Road Community Church. You go ovah to the corner, up past Wilkinses', and go left about four miles or so."

"Okay, I know where you mean. What time does it start?"

"Nine o'clock—right, Esther?"

"Yup. Nine to eleven."

"Only two hours? Gee, I don't know if it's worth it, dropping Andy off and coming back and then having to run back to get him again."

"You could stay there. Maybe bring a magazine. When I brought Vern and Esther, I didn't have any trouble fillin' my time for two hours. I'd just sit in that church and do my knittin'. Shouldn't think a body'd have any trouble fillin' up the time."

"Who else goes from around here?"

"Well, there's Stacy Dalpey's girls, and little Jimmy Fecteau's goin' this year. Right, Esther—Midge's boy?"

"Yup."

"Emma continued, "And I think my Vernon's planning to send his Dennis again. He had *such* a good time last year."

Esther stuck her finger in the leg of the baby's plastic pants, then wiped her finger on her shorts. "Well, Gordy, looks like you have something for Mama." She stood up, swinging the baby onto her hip. "Mama's fault, Gordy. She should've set you on the potty and let you try. Guess we better get some dry pants on us." Then, to Cassie, "Real nice meetin' you."

As Cassie was leaving, Emma said, "You're comin' to Sally's Boontonware party, aren't you?"

"Actually no, I'm not."

"You're *not*? Have you something else planned?"

"No, I just prefer not to go."

"Oh. Well. I see," Emma said, her face reddening.

They stepped outside. April Dawn was still playing in the sand pile. Andy, still sitting on the swing, but no longer swinging, grinned when he saw his mother. Dennis was running back and forth from the swing set to a tree behind the swing set, making squealing-brakes noises as he skidded into the dirt beneath the swing set.

Cassie blurted, "Emma, does Sally Wilkins abuse her kids? I mean, I was up there last night and—"

"You mean Owen's arm? That was a burn, an accident."

"Well yes, that, but also the cigarette—"

"Course, I don't always approve of what Sally does," Emma said. "But deep down, she's a good girl and—"

"And?"

"Well, when it comes to their kids, seems folks have a right to raise 'em whatever way they see fit, includin' how to discipline them."

Andy ran to his mother. Cassie took his hand. "Ready to go, honey? Say goodbye to Dennis."

"Goodbye."

Dennis slid into the dirt beneath the swing set, his brakes screeching.

The sun was at their backs as they walked hand in hand down the lane.

"Did you have a good time with Dennis?"

Andy was humming. No answer.

"Andy, did you have fun with Dennis?"

"I guess so. Except he didn't want to play, and he wouldn't talk to me. Just kept running and yelling."

Mosquitoes found them. Cassie brushed one from Andy's hair.

Scratching an old bite on his arm, Andy said, "These mosquitoes make me itch!" He dropped Cassie's hand and ran ahead, stopped, bent over, picked up a stone, and tossed it into the woods.

As she looked at her boy, small and fragile in the distance, she thought of Sally Wilkins whipping Lance with the stick. She imagined herself standing over Andy, stick raised. She shuddered, forcing the thought from her mind, pushing away the sound the stick had made as Sally brought it down on her son.

Andy skipped toward her. He stopped, looked up at her and said, "Hey, you know what?"

"What."

"You know what the opposite of itching is?"

"What."

Andy held his arm straight out in front of him, the back of his hand against Cassie's stomach, digging at the old bite with his other hand. "Scratching," he said.

The first day of Bible School was already warm when Michael left for work early in the morning, so Cassie knew it was going to be hot.

She had called Stacey Dalpey and Midge Fecteau, offering to take their kids. Both accepted her offer, Midge Fecteau saying, "We 'preciate it, since both me and Stacey have more little ones at home to tend." And Cassie told Emma she'd take her grandson.

Dennis was standing at the end of Thurlows' lane. His face was shiny, his wet hair parted and slicked down, comb marks fresh. When Cassie buckled him in next to Andy in the back seat, she noticed his fingernails were dirty.

Turning onto the washboard gravel of the Otis Corner Road, Cassie saw clouds of brown dust roiling and swirling in her rear view mirror. Bushes on the side of the road were coated with dust. Almost three weeks with no rain, and none in sight.

In the front yard of Dalpeys' small mint-green house was a post with an electric lantern on top. Below the lantern hung a sign which said, "Dalpey's." Dalpey's what? Cassie wondered. Dalpey's house? Dalpey's signpost? Maybe Dalpey's sign? Dalpey's family lives here? Dalpey's got rhythm?

Coming out of Dalpeys' house were two girls and, Cassie guessed, their mother, Stacey.

Except for a slight difference in height and the fact that one was blond and the other brown-haired, the Dalpey girls could be twins, miniatures of their mother.

In her sleeveless scoop-neck jersey and tight short shorts, with her pert, upturned boobs and legs that made up two thirds of her height, her long wavy brown hair, parted in the middle, and her round brown eyes, small nose and small mouth, Stacey Dalpey reminded Cassie of a Barbie Doll.

She strapped the two Dalpey girls in the front seat. They sat there shyly, staring straight ahead, unused to the touch of this woman who was not their mother. She said, "Don't you worry about your girls, Mrs. Dalpey. I'll take good care of them."

"Oh, I ain't worried," Stacey said. She leaned into the car window. "You mind the lady now, Laura Ann and Heather Jo—hear? You behave now."

The Fecteaus' trailer perched precariously on cement blocks, the yard behind it sloping steeply.

Midge Fecteau filled the narrow doorway of the trailer. As Cassie was getting out of the car, a boy squeezed by Midge and jumped down the three cement-block steps, smiling, friendly-looking. His round head, his black hair an almost-shaved wiffle cut, made him look like a tiny convict. He was dark-skinned, and his eyes were so dark the pupils were not distinguishable from the nearly-black irises. He wore a faded brown short-sleeved cotton shirt, buttoned up to the neck, a pair of dark brown shiny pants, and brown oxfords, scuffed on the toes.

Cassie got out of the car and walked around to let Jimmy in next to Andy. When she pulled out the belt to strap him in, his smile vanished and he became panicky, wiggling his legs and grabbing at the belt.

From the doorway of the trailer, Midge called, "Oh, he ain't used to them belts. It don't matter none if he don't wear one."

Cassie patted the boy's arm. "Okay, Jimmy, but you must sit very still all the way, okay?"

Jimmy nodded, grinning again, his teeth bright against his brown skin.

❀   ❀   ❀

The small, white-clapboarded church could have passed for a schoolhouse or a grange hall, were it not for the sign on the side which said, in faded black letters, "Otis Corner Community Church. Reverend Merlon Weekes."

Cars were pulling into the dusty parking lot, wheels chattering on the coarse gravel. Older children piled out of cars, sought out their friends, congregating in clutches, affecting nonchalance, shifting from foot to foot and leaning against the side of the building, shrugging, boys with hands in their pockets, girls with arms crossed.

A few of the younger kids played tag, but most eyed one another warily, since this was only the first day, and more time was needed for self-consciousness to dissolve into easy friendship.

On the small patch of brown lawn between the building and the road, two teenage girls were playing ring-around-the-rosy with a group of the youngest kids, some still in diapers. A third teenager was standing outside the ring. As each car arrived, she called, "All the kids in the nursery ovah heeyah. All little kids over heeyah." She jerked her head left, right, left, right, her long blond hair sailing.

One mother, her hair in blue plastic rollers, pulled a little girl by the upper arm toward the group of toddlers. The child was screaming, holding back, stiffened legs dragging in the gravel.

The flouncing teenager knelt in front of the little girl. "Whatsa matter, honey?"

The mother said, "Don't for the life of me know what's got into her. She'll be all right after a while. Maybeth, you *stop* that now. You go with this nice girl and Mama will see you after Bible School."

The teenager said, "Maybeth? Wanna come with me? Wanna come with Tracey and play with the other kids?"

The mother released her grip on Maybeth's arm. Tracey swung the child up in the air by her arms. Wincing, Cassie could almost hear the child's shoulders wrench loose in their sockets.

Without a glance back at her child, Maybeth's mother drove off, her wheels churning up dust.

At the door of the church stood a large woman in a flowered dress. Hot sun flaring on her white hair, glinting on her sequined gray eyeglasses.

She stood with her legs together, ankles touching. On her feet, navy blue cloth shoes, reminding Cassie of what in junior high school girls called "flats": oval-toed shoes that came in pastel colors to match pastel shirtwaist dresses puffed out with crinolines. Every girl who wore flats thought she looked like Cinderella.

The woman, arms outstretched, made beckoning motions with her hands. In a high voice that rose above the strains of ring-around-the-rosy she called out, "Children, time for Bible School to begin. Line up in your age groups." The kids shuffled about, forming lines.

Tracey and the other two teenage girls herded the toddlers onto the steps, first in line.

Cassie led Andy to the line, leaving him with the ones his size, telling him she'd wait at the back of the church and see him when school was over.

"Now let's see," the woman said, looking down into the faces below. "Who would like to hold the plates this first day of Bible School?" When no one volunteered, she said, smiling, "Come now, wouldn't *someone* like to hold the plates?"

The blond Dalpey girl raised her hand.

"Why, thank you, Heather Jo. The Dalpey girls will hold the plates today. Come up here, girls."

So, Cassie thought, the blond one is Heather Jo. When they got into the car she wasn't sure which was which. The other one, Laura Ann, walked up the steps and stood before the woman, who reached around inside the door, picked up two collection plates, and handed them to the Dalpey girls.

Cassie fished in her purse for a quarter, tapped Andy on the arm and whispered, "See those bowls the girls are holding? You put this money in one of them when you walk by. Okay?"

Andy took the quarter, looked at it, frowned, nodded.

The woman began to sing, her voice piercing:

> Come let me tell
> Great things the Lord has done
> Come let me tell
> Great things the Lord has done
> He made us all
> And loves us everyone ...

As the woman sang, the children marched up the steps in two lines, dropping their coins into the plates. A few of the older children recognized the song and were singing along.

Cassie brought up the rear, smiling at Heather Jo, who smiled back, looking important. In the foyer, she waited till the lines disappeared up the left and right aisles of the church. She sat in the last pew on the right side, trying to find the back of Andy's head in the center section. It was as hot inside the church as it was outside.

In the last rows were older kids, their heads and shoulders sticking up above the backs of the oak pews. Then the lines of heads descended like steps to the front where Andy's group sat, only the tops of a few heads visible. The toddlers, Cassie decided, must be in the very front row, invisible little Bible scholars, tended by the three teenagers who sat with them in the pew, two on one end, Tracey on the other, all three now and then looking down and talking to their charges.

Up front, facing the children, stood the woman who had led the children in.

"Hello, boys and girls. My! So many new faces! Now for those of you who don't know me from last year, my name is

Mrs. Weekes. You all know Reverend Weekes." She looked toward the back of the church.

A short, slight man stood up in the last row on the other side of the aisle, nodding several times, as if modestly acknowledging sustained applause.

"Now, Reverend Weekes is going to have the juniors this year," Mrs. Weekes explained. "Mrs. Trafton is going to have the middlers. Beginners will go with Mrs. Balch. And this year Tracey Balch is in charge of nursery Bible class, so all you little ones go with her each day after we have our service. So. The first thing we ought to do is learn our song we march in by." She held up a white poster card with words printed in blue magic marker. She read the card, pointing to the words.

> Come let me tell
> Great things the Lord has done
> Come let me tell
> Great things the Lord has done

"Now boys and girls, shall we try that much?" She nodded to a woman at a small organ near a window on the side of the church. The woman watched Mrs. Weekes, waiting for her uplifted hand to drop. Mrs. Weekes sang, holding the card in front of her with her left hand, beating every syllable in the air with her right. A few children joined in, hesitantly, then, as she repeated the first few lines twice, then three times, more sang, gaining courage and volume with each repetition.

She said, "That's very good," while the organist started another round, not aware yet that Mrs. Weekes had stopped. Mrs. Weekes looked over and laughed and the organist giggled and shrugged in apology.

Mrs. Weekes held up a second card. "Now we have another song to learn. It's called 'He Has Me Singing a Happy Song.' Are we ready?" She nodded at the organist, who leaned forward to play the first notes. Pointing to the words, Mrs. Weekes sang:

> He has me singing a happy song
> He has me singing it all day long
> Though the days may be drear
> He'll always be near
> And that's why my heart
> Is always filled with song
> I'm singing, singing
> All day long.

The song had a swing to it that made Cassie think of something that Barbra Streisand might belt out, exaggerating the beat, improvising added syllables and notes.

When Mrs. Weekes said, "Let's try that again." The children sang, slurring word into word, line into line, lagging just a bit behind the organ.

The song ended, Mrs. Weekes put down her card and clasped her hands together on her bosom. "That's very good — *very good* — for the first try. Now, boys and girls, we're going to go to our classrooms with our teachers. Little ones first, and as we walk out we'll sing our theme song."

Above the noise of children shuffling to their feet, Mrs. Weekes's voice split the air: "Come let me tell / Great things the Lord has done."

The toddlers trooped out, looking bewildered. On Tracey's hip, Maybeth, mouth downturned in a pout, cheeks streaked with smudged tears, looked miserable.

Cassie glimpsed Andy, struggling to walk and sing at the same time. The oldest children filed out last, and the footsteps faded into the hall to the side of the foyer.

Cassie stared ahead into the empty church. The sun coming in the row of windows on the right fell like strips of wide masking tape along the tops and backs of the pews ahead of her, across the black rubber floor runner in the aisle, then part way up the sides of the pews in the center aisle, stopping just before it reached the crosses carved in the ends of the pews.

She closed her eyes and slouched down, leaning her head against the hard back of the pew, trying to picture what it must be like in this church on Sunday. The children off in the class-rooms while the parents gather here to worship. Women in their flowered cotton dresses and straw bonnets and open-toed summer pumps; men in starched white shirts and straight-legged pants with cuffs. Plain folk, rising to sing a hymn led by Mrs. Weekes. Perhaps Jim Brackett among the hymn-singers, holding the hymnal in one outstretched hand. His back straight, his blue eyes shifting now and then from his book to Mrs. Weekes.

Cassie pulled herself up, yawning and stretching, staring at the billowing curtains and the dust churning, suspended, in the sunlight. How far would her thoughts about Brackett go if she were to let them?

He was certainly not the sort she'd ever lusted after. When-ever she thought about making it with anyone other than Michael, it was usually with some gorgeous Israeli, perhaps the type you see in photos of troops taking a break from their tense forays along the Golan Heights. One of those magnifi-cent olive-skinned tall and lean guys with dark snappy eyes. A clean-shaven demi-god in army khakis with the sleeves rolled up, taking a year or so off from his advanced studies in archae-ology and literature and classical music to do a patriotic stint in the army. Oh yes, the men she fantasized about must be always educated liberally, unlike Michael.

Once she made a crack about most engineers being narrow, and Michael never let her forget it. In the heat of their battles he would frequently sneer, "*You*—you *never* think logically." One time he read her some garbled stuff about engineers and mathematicians having the corner on pure thinking, while the impractical ones, the dreamers, the ones with liberal arts backgrounds, go through life incapable of anything but shoddy reasoning. Cassie often wondered what she had in common with her husband. But then, what could she possibly have in common with Jim Brackett? Did compatibility have anything to do with either success or failure in a marriage?

There was no relief in the hot breezes. The quiet of the empty church and the muffled sounds of voices coming from the classrooms somewhere off to the side made her drowsy and she struggled to keep from lying down on the pew in the dusty sunlight.

Nine

Emma held open the screen door. "How did it go?"

"Just fine."

Cassie followed Emma into the kitchen and looked out the window over the sink. Andy and Dennis were crouched in the dirt under the swing set, poking at something with sticks.

"Come, have some coffee. Or would you rather have iced? It's so hot."

"Iced, please, thanks."

Esther was at the kitchen table, leaning on her elbows, doing a jigsaw puzzle. She looked up. "Hot 'nuff for ya?"

Cassie laughed.

Gordy was in a play pen near the fireplace. Cassie leaned over the pen, the old wooden kind with bars, a miniature jail cell.

In the pen with Gordy was a dirty yellow blanket, with the satin binding torn and frayed. A plastic baby bottle half full of milk lay on its side on the plywood floor of the pen, dripping milk from the nipple.

Cassie bent into the pen. "Hello, Gordy."

Gordy's nose was running; black grime lined the creases of his plump neck, arms, and legs, which splayed out from his body, balancing him. Cassie offered him a finger, but when he reached for it, she noticed the black under his fingernails, and pulled her finger back, leaving him teetering forward. Gordy, you are in need of a bath.

On one foot the baby was wearing a tiny red sneaker, re-minding Cassie of the almost-square, white cloth shoes on a doll she once had. Between his splayed legs Gordy had the other sneaker by the laces and was banging it on the floor of the pen.

"Cassie, cream and sugar in your iced coffee?"

"Both, thanks."

Gordy smelled of urine and something sour she couldn't identify. Where his diaper had come out of his plastic pants around one leg, it was soggy. Did Gordy have one of his little accidents? He looked at Cassie, the snot beneath his nose glistening. He picked up his sneaker and chewed on it.

Instinctively, Cassie reached for the sneaker, then drew her hand back.

"Esther, the baby's chewing on his sneaker. Should I take it from him?"

Without looking up from her puzzle, Esther said, "Nah. He can't hurt it."

"I didn't mean—what I meant was—"

Emma came over to the playpen. She shook her head at Gordy, feigning mock surprise. "Somethin' 'bout these Thurlows," she said, laughing. "Both my Esther and my Vernon were always takin' off their shoes and chewin' on 'em. And now Esther's own boy. Must be somethin' lackin' in their diets." She bent over the pen, cupped Gordy's chin in her hand and tipped his head up. "Suppose that's so, Gordy? Suppose you're lackin' somethin'?"

Spittle dribbled from the corner of Gordy's mouth.

"Come, sit, have your coffee," Emma said to Cassie. "How's that puzzle comin', Esther?"

"Pretty good. Ought to finish it by tomorrow."

"How long have you been working on it?" Cassie asked.

"Two days, not countin' today. Sometimes Ma helps me with it. Thousand pieces, and half of 'em sky. See?" She reached down beside her onto a chair and brought up a cardboard box with a picture of the Golden Gate Bridge on it. Except for where the bridge towers poked into the sky, the whole upper half of the picture was blue.

"Do you do many of these?" Cassie asked.

"'Bout all she does in the summer, isn't it, Esther," Emma said.

"Yup," Esther said, snapping two pieces of ground together.

"Might say she's a regular addict."

Esther's hands cradled the sides of her head. Skin sallow, forehead sprinkled with whiteheads. Did she ever get out outside, into the light of day?

Emma said, "So, you met Stacey and Midge."

"Well, only briefly. I thought Stacey looked awfully young to have kids that old."

"She is young. Esther's age. Isn't that right, Esther?"

"Uh huh."

"Stacey and Esther were in the same grade all through school. Well, *almost* all the way through school." She caught Esther's eye and the two of them smiled.

Esther said, "What Ma means is, Stacey *had* to get married."

"Ah," Cassie said.

"Yes," Emma said. "She and Earl had been goin' steady since she was thirteen and Earl was fifteen. You were in eighth grade, weren't you, Esther?"

"Uh huh."

"And when she was fifteen and he was senior in high school they wanted to get married in the worst way. But her father— he had a miserable temper. When he got drinkin', he beat Stacey and her mother somethin' awful. And he forbid Stacey and Earl to get married, sayin' he'd *shoot* Earl if he come round his daughter again." Emma leaned back in her chair and lowered her voice. "Course, there's always been a lot of talk about Stacey and her father."

Cassie frowned. "What?"

"Well, it warn't no secret the way Stacey's father was when he got drunk, and everybody knows what a pretty little thing Stacey was and—well, you can just imagine." She shook her head, eyes closed. "Tst tst."

"But *that* weren't goin' to stop Stacey," Esther said. "I mean, her father's threatenin' to shoot Earl."

"I *guess* it weren't," Emma said. " 'Cause Stacey told it all around — made it a *point* of tellin' it all around — that she'd find a way to get her father to let her marry Earl. Remember, Esther?"

"It's what she said to *me*, anyway."

"So. When her father found out she was pregnant — that was with Laura Ann — he was *all* bent out of shape and, well, there you have it. Stacey got what she wanted, all right."

"How many kids does she have, besides the two girls?" Cassie asked.

"Well, there's Laura Ann, she's ten, and Heather Jo, she's almost nine. Those are the two girls you're takin' to Bible School."

"Yes."

"And then there's the twins, Jonathan and Jason. Cutest little tykes. They're three. Well, almost four."

Emma snapped two pieces of blue sky together.

Cassie wondered what they did with the puzzle at mealtimes. Did they push it to the end of the table, taking care to keep the pieces together and the corners square? Did one of them put his plate on the bridge, or on the ground, where he could pretend he was picnicking by the bridge abutment, his water glass floating on the blue sky above?

Emma said, "And of course, you know all about Midge."

"Huh?"

"Midge Fecteau."

"Yes, I know who you mean. But no, I don't know about her."

Was Emma going to fill Cassie in on all the neighbors? When she finished telling about Midge, would she continue, house by house, all the way down the Otis Corner Road, ending with the church, saying, "Of course you know all about the Weekeses"?

"Well, Midge has had an *awful* hard time. When she was a baby — why, she weren't more than two years old — her father left her mother with six kids, all young ones. After that, Midge's mother had Lord knows how many men, not one of 'em ever offerin' to marry her. So, when Midge herself was fourteen, maybe fifteen, she took up with some man. No one knows for sure who it was, but, no sooner was the baby born than Midge took up with *another* man, Willy Hescock, from over Wilmot Falls way, and everybody knew *he* weren't no good. He married her, though, just before *their* first baby was born."

"First baby?"

"Oh, they had three, one right after another. Then, least this is what everybody says, Willy come home sick from work one day to find her with Bubba Wentworth and everybody knew *that* man weren't nothin' but trouble. So Willy left her, but not before he had an awful row with Bubba and called Midge everythin' you can think of. And to this day, nobody knows for sure whether little Jimmy belongs to Willy or to Bub."

Cassie remembered that Jimmy Fecteau was grinning when she picked him up, grinning when they left Bible School, and when he ran up the dusty path toward the house after Bible School, he turned to stare at the car, still grinning. Did he sleep with that grin?

Emma said, "Jimmy's dark, like Bubba, and Bubba's own mother was a Canuck Indian, and, well, you can tell poor little tyke's not too bright." She shrugged. "But I suppose it don't matter who little Jimmy belongs to, 'cause Willy left Midge and it weren't too long after little Jimmy was born that Bubba left her too."

Somewhere upstairs a child was crying, sounding cranky.

"Esther, there's April," Emma said.

"Wouldn't you know," Esther said crossly. "Guess I'd better get her up."

Emma explained, "Looks as if our April Dawn is about to

give up naps. Esther still puts her down, but at least half the time now she never goes to sleep. Now let's see, where was I. Oh yes. After Bubba Wentworth left Midge, she started goin' with Peter Fecteau. Thing about Peter, though, was he never did just move in with Midge, way the rest of 'em did. He was bound he was gonna do right by her. When they got married, Peter insisted it be a proper weddin', done by a minister."

"You mean he wanted to make an honest woman of her?"

"Exactly! Everybody said that very same thing: 'Got to hand it to Peter Fecteau', they said, 'bound he's gonna make an honest woman outa Midge.' Well he did, and after, when they had two kids of their own and it looked like Midge was finally settled down, he give his name to the rest of her kids. He give all those kids his name, and he give 'em a decent home, too."

Emma tipped her glass up to get the dregs of the iced coffee. She set her glass down and burped, mouth closed, chin pulling back against her neck. "Got to hand it to Midge, though. Can't really blame her for the way she was. After all, look how many men her mother had, and Midge, too. Course, I always did believe, really, that blood will tell. But since Peter Fecteau's made a home for her, everybody's surprised she's turned out to be a decent mother after all."

Esther came into the kitchen, leading a barefooted, pouting April Dawn by the hand.

"Look who's here, Nana," Esther said.

Still pouting, April Dawn snapped her hand from her mother's and padded over to Emma, who lifted her onto her lap. "Come heeyah, Nana's baby doll. Aren't you Nana's big girl?"

April stuck her thumb in her mouth and shook her head, her face shiny, her blond hair matted with sweat.

"You're *not*? You're *not* Nana's big girl?" Then she jiggled the child and said, teasingly, "I'm gonna steal some honey from you. Nana's gonna get right into your honey spot and steal some honey!" She tipped April back and buried her face in her neck, kissing her and growling, "Ruh ruh ruh." April squirmed and thrashed her head, half protesting, half laughing hysterically, as kids do when adults tickle the breath out of them.

By the end of the first week Andy was beginning to tire of Bible School, complaining, "All they do is color color color."

"What do they color?" Cassie asked.

"Jesus. Pictures of Jesus. Jesus holding a baby lamb, Jesus making a blind man see again. Can that really happen?"

"What?"

"Jesus making a blind man see."

"What do *you* think?"

"I don't know. It sounds pretty hard to do that."

Later, as Cassie was tucking him into bed, Andy said, "All this time I've been wondering about something."

"What's that."

Andy pulled his hand from under the covers and held it out, palm upturned, in a gesture of explanation. "Well, there's Jesus. Then there's God. He's the father, right?"

"Right."

"Well, I didn't know who the Lord was but I think I know now."

"Tell me."

"The Lord must be the grandfather."

"Ah. That makes sense."

Andy reached up and put his arms around his mother's neck. Cassie slipped her arms around him, her hands under his head, and squeezed him, pressing her cheek to his, savoring its smooth softness and sweet smell.

"Goodnight, honey."

Andy rolled over, reaching for his stuffed clown. "Good-night, Mum."

Later that night, for the third night in a row, Cassie got out of bed to shut the window. This time, seething, she slammed it shut, waking Michael, who asked, "What the hell are you doing?"

"Shutting the window."

"*Shutting* it! Christ, it must be ninety degrees in here! What the hell for?"

"For the dogs, that's what for. There must be a dozen out there and they're all barking their goddamn heads off."

"Jesus,."

"They're driving me fucking crazy and I can't sleep."

"I thought moving up here was supposed to make you happy. I thought life in the country was supposed to be pleasant, but all you do is bitch about the dogs. Or if it isn't the dogs, it's the neighbors, or what people like Skillin do with their land. Look, with that window shut it's hot as hell in here. I can hardly breathe."

Cassie lay back down and kicked the sheet to the bottom of the bed, thinking, Good. Maybe you'll bloody suffocate.

Mrs. Weekes held up the card. "That was very good. Let's try that again. Now that we've learned all our songs, we have another week to practice them so we can sing them real perfect." She nodded to the organist, and pointing to the words on the card, led the song:

> I thirsted in the barren land of sin and shame
> And nothing satisfying there I found ...

The song was rousing, evangelical. Cassie chimed in on the chorus:

Drinking at the springs of living wa-aw-ter
Happy now am I, my soul they satisfy
Drinking at the springs of living wa-aw-ter
O wonderful and bountiful supply!

"That's *good*. That's *very* good, boys and girls," Mrs. Weekes said. She cocked her head to one side, looking down at the children in the first few rows, like a robin looking down at the ground with one eye, listening for worms. "And we must remember that Lord Jesus doesn't *like* it when we are sinful, does he?"

In the last row, three girls were poking each other, giggling, chewing gum, one blowing bubbles and snapping her gum, all three rolling their eyes as if to say, "Dig her!"

Mrs. Weekes said. "Now before we go to our classrooms, let's sing 'There's Room at the Cross.' Because we must always remember, no matter how sinful we are, if we ask Lord Jesus to forgive us, there's a place for each and every one at His cross."

The children stirred. They liked the song. Sung in waltz time, it loped along like a country and western song.

Singing from her pew at the rear of the church, Cassie pictured Roy Rogers and Dale Evans, on horseback, in their ten-gallon hats and beaded shirts with string ties, cantering (Roy on Trigger, Dale on Buttermilk) toward the cross, joyful smiles on their shining faces as they sing:

Theyah's rewm at the cross for a-yew
Theyah's rewm at the cross for a-yew
Though mill-yuns may come
Theyah's still rewm for one
Yes theyah's rewm at the cross for a-yew.

And Christ hanging there, millions of the redeemed at the foot of the cross, elbowing one another, jockeying for the best spot. To the side of the cross, looking out over the heads of the mob at the people still coming, is Mrs. Weekes, beckoning, calling out, "Room for one more up here, folks. Step aside. *Please* make room, folks. Let that lady in the blue hat through. Make way. Always room for another one." Finally, despite the fact that every inch of available space at the foot of the cross is taken up, Mrs. Weekes rams in just one more, one more than the space can take, and that packed throng swells, perhaps a few too many inhale a trifle too deeply at the same time, and the cross wrenches loose from the pile of rocks in which it's anchored and falls over backwards, crashing to the ground with a sickening thud, like a felled tree. Then what? Would the millions scramble forward, vying with one another to help? "Jesus *Christ*," one might say. "Here, let me help." Or, "Hey buddy, can I lend you a hand?" Or maybe, "Jesus, you okay? You hurt, Jesus?"

Then, the children were tramping out, already into the last stanzas of their marching song which, after singing it twice a day for five days, they now sang with gusto:

> Come let me tell
> Great things the Lord has done
> Come let me tell
> Great things the Lord has done
> He made us all
> And loves us every one ...

Strapping the Dalpey girls into their seatbelts in the front seat, Cassie noticed the Bible on Heather Jo Dalpey's lap. On the front, a WASP Jesus with two blond WASP children at his feet, staring up at him adoringly. The Bible's pale blue cardboard cover reminded Cassie of the Trixie Belden books she used to read when she was Heather Jo's age. She would buy one whenever she saved up forty-nine cents, and devour it the same day.

Above the racket of the car bouncing along the rough road, Cassie asked, "Hey kids, did you have fun in Bible School today?"

Only Andy answered. "It was okay."

Cassie stretched up to look in the rear view mirror at Jimmy, who was in the middle of the back seat, staring straight ahead, grinning.

"Hey kids," she said. "Why don't we sing one of our Bible School songs?" No response. Determined, she said brightly, "C'mon, let's sing. 'Theyah's rewm at the cross for a-yew, Theyah's rewm at the cross for a-yew.' "

Laura Ann joined in obediently on the second line, barely audible.

Cassie smiled encouragingly at the girl, who blushed and looked out the window. Cassie sang, " 'Though mill-yuns may come, Theyah's steel rewm for one.' " Undaunted, she belted out the last line with abandon, yodeling on the last word. "Yes theyah's rewm at the cross for a-yew-hooo!"

Heather Jo looked up at Cassie, eyes round, lips pressed together.

Cassie smiled sweetly at Heather Jo. "There now, Heather Jo, wasn't that *fun*?"

Heather Jo stared at her Bible, as if Jesus might save her from this crazy woman.

"Hey everybody, wasn't that *fun*?"

No answer. She stretched her neck to look in the mirror. Jimmy again. She looked at the road, then back at Jimmy in the mirror.

"Hey Jimmy. Did *you* have fun today?"

Jimmy grinned.

Ah Jimmy, I knew I could count on you. Happy-as-a-lark Jimmy Fecteau. Perhaps Jimmy's problem was that he *couldn't* speak. She wanted to pry open his mouth to see if he had a tongue.

In high school, she was on her yearbook's biography committee, which had to come up with half a dozen nice things to say about every one of the 317 graduates in her class. What might they have said about Jimmy? "James Fecteau ... 'Little Jimmy.' Quiet yet pleasant manner ... always a ready smile ... paragon of cheerfulness ... nary a care nor a worry ... has an exceptionally dry wit ... goes through life unperturbed ... "

Then Andy was saying, "Okay everybody. I have an announcement to make. If you believe in God, raise your hand."

Shit. Cassie glanced over the back of the seat at Jimmy, whose hand was not up, and next to him, Andy, whose hand was, stretched straight up, arm rigid, fingers stiffly together. She couldn't see Dennis, seated directly behind her. The Dalpey girls squirmed, their hands down.

"Andy, maybe you —," Cassie said.

"Okay, then. If you *don't* believe in God raise your hand."

Again, silence, and again, Cassie felt Heather Jo wiggle against her.

Cassie slowed up to let Jimmy out, waiting to see that he got inside his house. Midge appeared in the doorway. Cassie imagined, beyond her, men draped about the place. A rheumy-eyed man in front of the tube, stocking feet up on a tattered plastic footstool, swilling beer in his t-shirt. A man stretched out on the couch, reading the *National Enquirer*, slathering over the headline, "Sex-Crazed Mother Dashes Out Infant Son's Brains on Cellar Floor." In the bathroom, a man in the shower, singing "There's Room at the Cross." And in the bedroom, still another one, waiting for Midge.

Enough, Cassie told herself, as she and Midge Fecteau exchanged waves.

Ten

That afternoon, to quiet Andy's cries of "But I'm *thirsty*!" before they went shopping at the First National, Cassie pushed open the door to Mary Ellen's restaurant.

She ordered a Coke for herself and a root beer for Andy, and while the girl was filling the glasses, she looked around.

It was the first time she'd been there. On the left, a counter with a half dozen chrome stools covered with red oilcloth. Opposite the counter, three high-backed oak booths with tables covered with dark green linoleum, trimmed on the edges with aluminum strips.

The first two booths were filled. Carrying her Coke, Cassie headed for the third booth. "Come on, Andy, and don't spill that root beer."

Not till she was alongside the third booth did she notice Jim Brackett sitting there. He was reading *The Boston Globe*.

"Oh! Sorry," Cassie apologized. "I couldn't see over the back of the booth."

"Please, sit down," Jim said, folding his paper.

Cassie slid into the booth and Andy followed.

"What brings you into town on such a hot day?" Jim asked.

"Shopping. Even with all the stuff from the garden, there's always bread and milk and meat."

"Mum," Andy whined. "I can't get the paper off this straw."

Cassie took the straw, ripped the end of the paper, and started to pull the straw out.

Andy grabbed at the straw. "Wait!" he ordered. "I want to blow it off."

"Andy, not today."

"But I *want* to. I *have* to blow it off."

"Not *now*, Andy."

Jim spooned the tea bag out of his cup and, holding onto the tag, he wound the string around the bag and spoon, pressing the liquid out of the bag into the cup. Cassie had watched her mother do that countless times.

She looked at Jim's hands, at the long slim fingers, noticing again how his thumbs angled out from his wrists. He shoved the bag onto the saucer next to the cup, pulled off the tag, read it, and passed it to Andy.

Salada Tag Lines. In college, when she was on a tea kick, she loved to read the tiny red words of advice as she sipped her tea. Corny aphorisms that told how one could change, could make problems vanish, could improve morally. Reading Tag Lines was like having Ben Franklin right at your elbow.

Andy read the tag. "What's *that* mean? I don't *get* it."

She read the tag. " 'With two eyes and one tongue, you should see twice as much as you say'. That means that it's better to do a lot of looking and noticing, which is the way you learn, instead of talking. That you don't learn much if your jaw's always flapping."

"I think that's *dumb*."

Cassie looked at Jim, shrugging.

"I didn't write it," he teased. "How is your garden coming?"

"Great, really, considering how dry it's been, and also that we can't spare the water for it."

"What do you mean, spare the water?"

"We're still waiting for Myron Ricker to drill. All we have is the old dug well."

"Ah, Ricker."

"He was supposed to come last May. Here it is almost the middle of July and we never have much more than a foot or so of water in the well. Once it was as low as eight inches."

"Ricker's got more important things on his mind. More profitable things."

"You mean houses? Developments?"

"The man's ruthless. Where there's a dollar to be made, Ricker'll do anything to make it." Jim turned his teaspoon over, resting the bowl of the spoon upside down on his saucer, the handle on the table, and repeated, "Anything."

Cassie wanted to reach across the table and slip her hand under his, to see what it would feel like. She turned to Andy. "Almost done, honey?"

Stupid question. His root beer was only half gone. She could feel Jim looking at her.

"I want to drink *all* of it," Andy said, slurping.

She glanced up at the overhead fan, which was humming quietly, its huge blades slowly chopping the air. She looked at Jim. If she could find something wrong with him, some gross physical imperfection, she would be safe. Safe from wanting to know more about him, from wanting to be with him, from wanting to touch his hand, his face.

Jim said, "I never did like air conditioning. I'm partial to fans myself." He looked at Andy. "Did you ever see such a big fan, Andy?"

"Um," Andy murmured, sucking up the last of the root beer.

Jim turned and looked at the clock on the wall behind the soda fountain counter, and Cassie studied his profile. She stared at his ear, half hoping to see a tuft of white hair there. If there was one thing that turned her off, it was tufts of hair in men's ears. No hair in Jim's.

The last time she had waited in the check-out line at the First National, she'd studied a photo on the cover of a movie magazine: Oona O'Neill pushing a haggard, wasted Charlie Chaplin, huddled in a wheelchair. Oona in a plain cloth coat, her bedraggled hair caught up in a wispy bun. Chaplin, bundled up in a coat, muffler, and fedora, looking half-crazed.

A spring-fall romance. And weren't there others? Jackie O

and Ari. Bing Crosby and his Kathy. Justice Douglas and *his* Cathy. Carlo and his Sophia. Jim and his Cassie.

Jim was staring at her, smiling.

She blushed. You don't want him, she told herself. And besides, even though he looks healthy now, with your luck, he'd probably get sick and linger on and you'd have to tend him on his death bed. For years and years, maybe. Still.

"Well," she said. "We've got to get to the First National before it closes. Andy, ready to go?"

For answer, Andy sucked on the straw, rattling the ice cubes in the bottom of the glass.

As she and Andy walked out of Mary Ellen's, Cassie knew Jim was staring at them. She straightened her back, hoping she didn't look too fat. And at the same time she was annoyed with herself for caring how she looked.

The next morning Cassie opened the carton of eggs she'd sent Michael to buy from Sally Wilkins. She hadn't bought eggs from Sally since the time she'd found the three cracked ones. Since then, to avoid Sally, Cassie had been buying eggs from the First National, but lately had begun to tire of them. They weren't fresh, and the yolks, unlike the rich orange of Sally's eggs, were a pallid yellow.

Andy was watching the Saturday morning cartoons. A rock group was singing, "Scooby Dooby Doo, Where Are You?"

Michael was out measuring the water in the well. She watched him through the kitchen window. The stone cover had been pulled aside to reveal the round opening, and on the larger well rock itself was a long tape measure with a weight on the end. Michael picked up the weight and dropped it into the well, letting the tape slide through his hand. The coils of tape flashed white in the sun, leaping up off the rock as if under the spell of a snake charmer. Holding onto the last few feet of tape, he knelt on the rock, peering into the well, and lowered the tape until the weight just touched the surface of the water. Then, reading the number on the tape that lined up with the top of the well rock, he could tell to the inch how much water was left in the well. There was something primitive about the process. It was as if Michael were fishing in the black bowels of the earth.

She opened the egg carton, blinking in disbelief. Six cracked eggs. She looked out the window. Michael had put the cover back over the hole and was coiling the tape, wrapping it around his hand and elbow.

"Michael!" Cassie called.

Michael looked up, scowling. "*What?*"

"Would you come in here?"

Michael came in. "Christ, can't you wait till I finish with the well."

"Look."

Michael looked at the eggs, frowning. "Hmph."

"Still think I'm paranoid?"

"So don't buy any more eggs from her."

"Don't you think it's screwy? I mean, is that the way you figure, just don't buy any more eggs from her?"

"What do you want me to do, go punch her husband out?"

Cassie glared at him. "How much water in the well?"

"Seven inches."

"Jesus. I don't know how I can use any *less* water."

For two weeks she'd been taking laundry to the Coggerton laundromat, sitting there with Andy in the grimy wooden chairs, watching their clothes churn away in the suds, hoping she hadn't picked a machine which had just had someone's pissy diapers run through it. And in order to use as little water as possible for shampoos, she'd got Andy's hair cut short, and her own as short as she felt she could stand it without looking freaky. She encouraged Andy to pee outside at the edge of the field, and every day admonished him, "Don't flush the toilet,

Andy. Let Mum do it." When she scrubbed the bathroom sink, she used, she complained to Michael, "only about two goddamn tablespoons of water."

"When did you last call Ricker?" Michael asked.

"A month ago."

"Didn't he say he'd be here by now?"

"Oh sure. Every time you talk to him he sounds like he's on his way tomorrow. Only tomorrow never comes. Name one, just one, of these locals who has shown up on time."

"Calm down. Why don't you call Ricker again. Try to pin him down."

From the living room came the melodramatic, agitated voice of the cartoon announcer: "And now, *The Secret Lives of Waldo Kitty!*"

Cassie cracked an egg in the bowl and turned to Michael.

"*You* call him. *You* try. Beside, I have to go into town Monday to see about the dogs. Maybe Ricker will pay more attention to a man."

"What can I do for you?" The secretary in the selectmen's office peered at Cassie from behind blue-framed eyeglasses.

"I'm Cassie Atwood. Out at the old Gilman place on Thurlow Hill?"

"Oh yes."

"I'm here to see if something can be done about the dogs out our way."

"Oh?"

"We hate to make a fuss, and I don't want to be unneighborly, but for weeks now it seems all we hear are dogs, day and night. It's especially annoying at night, when we're trying to sleep. You see, our bedroom window faces the direction where all the dogs seem to be barking, and it's just the way the house is situated that—"

"Whose dog is it that's barking?"

"*Dogs.* It's a lot of dogs. Sometimes it sounds as if there are at least a half a dozen barking all at once."

"*Whose* dogs, then?"

"I don't know *whose* dogs. What difference does it make *whose* dogs?"

"Well, have you ever seen this dog? I mean, is it running loose on your property?"

Her voice rising, Cassie said, "It isn't one dog, and no, it's not a matter of them running loose on our land. It's dogs *barking* that I'm talking about. Dogs barking for hours at a time so we have to shut our windows."

The secretary said, "Because if dogs run loose on someone's property, it's against the law, especially if they don't have collars. The dog officer is pretty fussy about unregistered dogs."

Cassie leaned over the desk, her face a foot from the secretary's face. She thought, I could reach right out and twist your mousy little nose. Or knock off those glasses and poke you in your beady green eyes. Or grab you by your frizzy red hair and pull pull pull.

"It seems I am not making myself clear. We are being driven half crazy, day and night — nights, mostly — by a bunch of barking dogs. I want to know what can be done about it. There must be some noise ordinance — some law against dogs disturbing the peace, keeping people awake all hours of the night."

"Well, Mrs. — uh, Atwood. Why don't you just talk to our dog officer. He can tell you —"

"Fine. Who is he? What's his name? What's his number?"

The secretary reached for a piece of cardboard near the phone and put it on the front of the desk, saying to Cassie, "Stanton Wormald." On the card was a list of names and phone numbers.

Stanton Wormald. Stanton Wormald. Cassie was shaking

so badly she had trouble finding the name on the list. She bit her lip. "Where? Where's his number?"

The secretary pointed to his name and Cassie saw, "Wormald, Stanton. 624-0455."

Cassie stood up between the two rows of late peas. Her back was stiff from picking, from kneeling between the rows. Squinting in the bright sunlight, she looked toward the hills of Wilmot Falls. Maybe she would visit Jim Brackett one of these days.

But what could she use as an excuse? Perhaps she would bring him some of these peas. Ridiculous. With practically everyone who lived in Coggerton growing his own garden, bringing Jim Brackett peas would be like bringing coals to Newcastle. More cookies?

Andy was standing at the end of the next row. He had begun by helping her, now and then tossing a pod into the basket. Then, as the hour wore on, he ate three for every one he dropped in the basket. Now he made no pretense of helping. At first he had picked the peas out of the pods, one by one. But he quickly learned how to strip the pod, gobbling up a fistful at a time.

Well into July, the summer was in full bloom. The wild strawberries they'd discovered at the edge of the field and turned Andy loose in were gone by, and the hawkweeds had gone to seed. Yellow-eyed daisies had yielded to black-eyed Susans, and everywhere were goldenrods, their tight yellow buds soon to burst into flower.

She thought of Jim Brackett. Why would he be interested in me? What makes me think that all older men wanted younger women? She never particularly fantasized about getting it on with younger men. Any fantasies she had were about older men.

So wasn't it possible Jim Brackett considered her a baby, an unformed adolescent? Who knew how he looked at a thirty-two year-old woman from his vantage point of—what? sixty years? Possibly he went for more mature women, never looking at anyone under fifty. Emma had said all kinds of women chased him. Maybe half the women in Coggerton, including Emma, still had designs on him.

Most of the birds, finished with mating, were less raucous these days. The bobolink's upward-spiraling song was now an occasional dull "chek" as he sat, swaying, on an iron bush or juniper.

In the heat (drought, the weather forecasters were saying), the grasses of the field were already turning yellow, and among the few rows of the garden where there was no mulch, the dirt was powdery dry.

Cassie knelt down to pick more peas, occasionally flicking a pod to see if it rattled and wanted more time.

She began to sing, "I thirsted in the barren land of sin and shame, And nothing satisfying there I found." Without looking up, intent on getting at the peas in the pod he was splitting open, Andy began to hum with her, and by the time she ended the first stanza, he was singing along, "Where springs of living water did abound."

Feeling perverse, Cassie sang her own version of the chorus: "Tinkling in the springs of living wa-aw-ter, Happy now am I, My bladder's satisfied. Tinkling in the springs of living wa-aw-ter, O wonderful and bountiful supply."

Hearing the "tinkling" in the first line, Andy looked up, and when he saw his mother smiling, he laughed in delight.

"Good sense of humor, my sweet." Then they both sang it, loud, louder still, so that by the time they reached the end of the chorus, they were belting it out.

"Let's do that again," Andy said, no longer interested in picking peas.

They sang it again, mother and son, reveling in their blasphemy.

"Hey listen, Andy. It's okay for *us* to sing it that way. But just don't pull that with the others, at Bible School I mean. Okay?"

"I know, Mum. I know, But I can *think* it that way, with the tinkling, can't I?"

Cassie laughed. "Sure. You can think anything you like."

She lifted a pea vine and flopped it over in order to get at more peas. A clutch of earwigs, deprived of the shade of the vine, scurried under the mulch. Cassie forced herself to watch them, fighting her revulsion. Scoot scoot scoot, little Jimmy Fecteau, scoot scoot scoot. God, was she losing her mind?

She remembered Emma telling her Peter Fecteau had given Midge's kids his name. She imagined Peter gathering the kids on the scruffy lawn, the plastic tulips stuck in the strip of pea stones in front of the trailer a backdrop for the festivities.

Peter presents each of Midge's darlings with a gift, silver wrapped, with a flashy red satin bow on top. The children tear open the packages, tossing paper and ribbons to the ground, while Midge darts around, salvaging the wrapping paper, shaking the dust off the bows. The children open the boxes. Inside each is a piece of paper on which is written, "FECTEAU." They run to Peter, throw their arms around his neck, and in the joyful confusion, one says timorously, seeing how it sounds, "Dad-dee." Then all of them call out "Dad-dee! Dad-dee!" as they shower him with kisses and tears of appreciation.

Sated, Andy tossed his last pea pod onto the mulch and galloped off to his sandbox.

Life in the hills of New Hampshire was not exactly what she thought it would be. When they were packing to move here, she imagined quilting bees, barn raisings, neighbors helping neighbors—perhaps even being invited to the neighbors' to share Thanksgiving dinner, served on generations-old brown and white ironstone platters and plates. Hayrides. Country auctions. And best of all, convivial Saturday night ham and bean suppers at the local churches—suppers with all manner of pies and endless cups of coffee.

"Hi!"

Cassie jumped. Halfway between the house and the garden, coming toward her, were Emma, leading April Dawn by the hand, and Esther, pushing a baby carriage. Gordy's head bobbed from side to side as the carriage bounced across the lawn.

"Hi," Cassie said. "So busy picking peas I didn't hear you coming."

April Dawn pulled her hand out of her grandmother's and ran to the sandbox.

"Don't let us stop you. Keep right on with your work," Emma said.

"I'm just about finished. I'll put these peas in the shade." Cassie pointed to two aluminum lawn chairs between the well rock and the sandbox. "Take a seat. I'll be right with you."

Esther pulled the baby out of the carriage by his upper arms and swung him onto her hip. "Wanna go play with the kids in the sandbox, Gordy?" She carried him to the sandbox, put him in it, and said, "Nuisance wants to bother you."

When April Dawn had climbed into the box, Andy had moved over to make room for her. Now, eyeing Gordy warily, he yielded still more territory, taking his Tiny Tonka cement mixer and a wooden spoon as he moved into a corner of the box.

Cassie sat on the well rock. Emma swung the foot of her lawn chair toward the well rock, in order to face Cassie. Esther moved her chair to face the hills of Wilmot Falls, cool-looking beyond the hot July haze. Emma settled into her chair, her elbows on the aluminum arms, her hands clasped across her middle, her big white calves with their varicose veins held together primly in front of her.

Emma said, "Did you know we have new neighbors?"

"Huh? Where?"

"Oh, up there. Lot number one." Emma tipped her head in the direction of the woods behind the house, towards Skillin's lots.

"Is somebody building a house up there?"

"Not a house. They've put in a mobile home. I didn't actually see it bein' moved onto the lot. It happened just after noontime, while Esther and I were grocery shoppin', but Sally Wilkins says it's a beautiful double-wide."

"But I thought you didn't like trailers."

"Did I say that? I suppose it depends on what kind of mobile home you're talkin' about. I don't like them if they're no better 'n *shacks*, but I think some of the new ones look very nice."

Cassie wanted to ask Emma what qualified as a "better" mobile home. Maybe one with a little peaked roof. Or maybe the kind with the faux brick siding and white vinyl window shutters—Early American. Or one with an attached carport, or a Custom Cabaña. Once she and Michael had been driving along Route 1 out of Boston, past all the honkey-tonk eateries and miniature golf ranges and moccasin stores. One sign had caught her eye. It was at the entrance of a big parking lot crammed with trailers. The sign screamed: "Stop In And See Our Latest Model, THE FRANK LLOYD WRIGHT."

She wondered how they'd got to use Frank Lloyd Wright's name on a trailer. And what in God's name could it be? All glass and wood, with a Custom Cabana cantilevered out over a phony waterfall whose water is recirculated by a Frank Lloyd Wright Accessory Waterfall Pump? Frank Lloyd Wright must be writhing in his grave. Or maybe not. Maybe he would love to see his ideas being used in house trailers, within the financial reach of the common man.

"People from downtown," Emma said. "They were rentin' from John Skillin, then I guess they heard about these lots up here. Probably Skillin told them himself. New people, up from

Massachusetts. Three children — one, three, and five, Sally says, and he works in that new Pizza Hut in Barchester."

"I didn't know Skillin had apartments."

"Oh my, yes. I *guess* so. Why, John Skillin owns pret' near all the rentals in town. But they're not bad little apartments, are they, Esther?"

"Suited me and Gordon fine."

Emma added, "Esther and Gordon lived in one of Skillin's apartments first two years they were married," Emma explained. "'Fore they built their own home in Marston Corners."

Gordy burst out crying. Esther snapped, "April — April Dawn! You give your brother back that spoon."

"No!"

Esther jumped up out of the lawn chair. "April Dawn, you give Gordy that spoon. Now!"

April tossed the spoon at Gordy. Pouting, she dragged the dry sand with her hands between her legs. Her sundress was hiked up in her lap and between her splayed legs Cassie could see her loose yellow cotton panties. Cassie cringed. All that gritty sand sifting into the child's crotch.

Andy had stopped whatever he was doing to watch the ruckus over the spoon, his eyes darting from Gordy as he bawled, to Esther as she yelled at April, to April as she defied her mother, to Esther as she started for April, and finally to April, who relented. Then, with his wooden spoon, he began pouring sand into the tiny hole in the back of his cement mixer, now and then glancing warily at Gordy and April Dawn.

"They're not wasting any time up there, I will say that," Emma said.

"What do you mean?" Cassie asked.

"The new people up there. They've already called my Vernon to ask him to do the leachin' bed, and they're getting their well drilled right now."

"*What?*"

"They're havin' their well drilled today. Can't you hear that?"

Cassie listened. From the direction of Skillin's lots came a steady dull pounding. "That banging? I wondered what that was."

"Yes, that's Ricker. Most well drillers nowadays use fancy rotary machines. They do a real fast job but bore so quick down into the ledge they seal the cracks. Seal the water veins right up, so you have to go deeper. Ricker still uses an old rig. Pounder, they call it, and you can tell from the noise why."

"You mean Ricker is up there *right now*, drilling a well?"

"Well, yes, either him or his son. His son does most of the work now, since Myron's so busy with the buildin' end of his business."

"Goddamn him. We called him months ago to drill our well. How do you suppose those people rate, getting Ricker so soon after they've just moved in?"

"Well, I'm not sure. I suppose this bein' a small town and all, and everybody knowin' everybody else, John Skillin and Myron Ricker—and everybody else in town for that matter—are always doin' favors for each other and—"

Esther said, "Sally told me those people said they'd buy the lot only if they could get water right away. So Skillin got in Ricker."

Cassie was livid. "So that's the way that goddamn Ricker operates, is it?"

Loud above the pounding of the well rig came the barking of dogs. Cassie recognized the dogs as two of the regulars. One was the dog with the deep, steady voice, the other one the yapper, its high hysterical barking touched off by any other dog that barked.

"And those goddamn dogs. All we get here, day and night, are those dogs. Jesus, don't they drive you crazy, Emma?"

"Frankly, Cassie, no they don't. I don't ever hear them, 'less they're pointed out to me."

"Do you know who owns that dog? The one with the deep voice?"

Emma listened. "Well, I guess that would be the Tremblays' dog. They live in the old house down on the Pickard Cross Road, at the bottom of the hill."

"I know where you mean."

"Well, Ida Tremblay told me they was gonna stake their dog at the upper end of the garden again 'cause last summer they had some deer get in and raise Cain."

"They have a dog *staked* there? Is that why the barking always seems to come from the same spot?"

Emma bristled. "Can't say the Tremblays abuse the dog or anythin'. Always up there feedin' it and all."

"But isn't it against the law to keep a dog staked?"

Esther said, "Long as a dog's on its own property and it ain't runnin' or botherin' anyone else, a person can do whatever he wants with it. Dogs is just part of livin' in the country. Most people have dogs and don't mind if their neighbors' dogs bark once in a while."

Michael sipped a glass of the dandelion wine Jim Brackett had bought.

Cassie asked, "Do you like it?"

"It's okay. Kind of woody-tasting. And I'm not sure I like drinking something that looks like piss."

Cassie held her glass up to the window. The wine was clear, golden, and once she'd got over her surprise at its unusual taste, she loved it. Liquid gold. Ambrosia.

She should have hidden the wine, kept it all for herself. Or at least insisted on not opening it till winter when, as Jim had said, the wine would be like a draught of summer sunshine.

Michael said, "I stopped on the way back home to speak with Ricker about the well." He set his glass down on the table.

"You did? And?"

"Mum?" Andy said. "Do I have to eat any more chard?"

"Finish it," Michael said.

"Just a little more," Cassie said.

Michael said, "Hey, you should see where the guy lives. He lives on one of those side streets behind the center of town. The yard is a real crap heap. All this equipment lying around — a couple of trucks and two big signs out front, the one for house lots bigger than the one for well drilling. You'd never guess that natty old fart we saw at town meeting lives in the middle of all that shit."

"The well, Michael. What about the well."

"I didn't see him. I figured for sure he'd be home by the time I got there."

"Jesus, Michael."

"Look, I did try. I did see the wife."

"And?"

"She said she'd tell him I came by."

"That's it? That's all?"

"What the hell more could I do?"

"Nothing. Not a thing, I guess. Especially since our pal Ricker is right this very minute drilling on Skillin's first lot, right up the hill behind our woods."

"Huh?"

"Doing Skillin a favor, according to Emma."

"No shit! Son of a bitch."

Andy poked at his chard. "Is it time for dessert yet?"

"In a minute, honey," Cassie said.

"Peas paw haw," he chanted. "Peas paw cole. Peas paw in—"

"What?" Michael looked at Andy. "Cassie, What the hell is that?"

"I don't know. Andy, what's that?"

"Peas paw haw, peas paw cole, peas paw in paw, nie day ole."

"I don't mean say it again, Andy. I mean what *is* it? Where'd you get that?"

"From April. She said it today. And she said another one, too. Wanna hear it?"

Michael rolled his eyes. "Christ. Go ahead."

"Pah cay pah cay bake-a man, bay me cay 's fas' you can. Row it, pah it, mar wi' B, an' pu' in' uvva faw bay an' me."

"Is he saying 'Pat-a-cake, pat-a-cake' — that thing?" Michael asked Cassie.

"Must be."

"Andy, for Chrissake, where the hell did you hear that?"

"I *told* you. From *April*. In the sandbox today."

Michael said, "Is that kid retarded? How old is she, anyway? You think he ought to be playing with her? I mean, the influence and all."

"Come on, Michael. Aren't you the one always complaining about me being a snob? About me thinking I'm better than all our neighbors? So now you *don't* think it's just wonderful our son has the opportunity to play with such a variety of children? And really, compared to some, April is advanced. Why, take little Jimmy Fecteau, for instance."

"What do you mean?"

"Well, at least April Dawn makes an effort at speech. But little Jimmy Fecteau. I've seen no sign that he even has a functioning voice box, let alone a functioning I.Q."

"Jesus."

Cassie said, "Little Jimmy Fecteau, one two three. The cat's in the cupboard and can't see me."

Andy burst out laughing, clapping his hands in delight.

"But that's our secret, Andy, okay?"

"Mr. Wormald? This is Cassie Atwood. Out on Thurlow Hill?"

"Oh yeah. On the old Gilman place."

"That's right. I'm calling to report some dogs that have been barking near us. Mostly down over the hill, along the Pickard Cross Road. You know where I mean?"

"Yeah, I know."

"Well, we kept hoping the barking would let up, but it hasn't, and in the town hall they told me—"

"They said down to town hall you was in."

"Then you have a pretty good idea of our problem out here."

"Well, can't say I do, exactly. Just what is it's botherin' you? Any dogs runnin' loose on your property?"

"No. Not running loose. *Barking*. Keeping us awake nights and making it unpleasant to be outside during the day."

"Well, how long they barkin'?"

"I don't know. I never timed them. One night a whole bunch of them kept it up for at least three hours, I figured, before they settled down. All I'm asking is to have the laws about barking dogs upheld."

"Course, the laws about barkin' dogs in Coggerton aren't—"

"Excuse me, Mr. Wormald. I have here in front of me the State Fish and Game laws, and it says right here on page sixty-four: "Under this section —that's Chapter 466:31 — 'a dog is causing a nuisance or is a menace to persons or property under any of the following conditions : a) if it barks continuously for sustained periods of time—' "

"Lady, you don't have to quote me the law. I know what the law is."

"Then, what do we do about the barking dogs, since we agree there's a law about them?"

"Well, I suppose it makes a difference how long they're barking. Just like you read—though I knew the law anyway— it says, 'sustained periods of time'."

"How long would sustained be?"

"Well, I guess eight or nine hours."

"Eight or nine hours?! Are you *serious*?"

"Sure I'm serious. Dogs gotta bark sometime, you'll agree to that, won't you?"

"Mr. Wormald, let's get back to the issue. There are dogs barking near us. They are disturbing the peace. Our peace. What are you going to do about it?"

Silence. Then, "Well, most I can do is talk to the people. Course, if you don't know who owns the dogs—"

"I know who owns two of them anyway. One belongs to the Tremblays. They have it staked near their garden. The other is at the trailer just as you turn the corner at the Cross Road, going the other way from Tremblays'. That one has a yappy bark."

"I gotta be honest with you, Mrs. Atwood. Tremblays don't have much, and I know in years past they've kept their dog hitched near the garden, and no one complained before. Least they got a reason, the Tremblays. I wouldn't feel exactly right tellin' 'em they can't use their dog to protect their vegetables if they have to. But the other dog. Must be new people. I'll get down there and see what they have to say about it. Cause one thing I've learned in this business, there're two sides to every story, and I just want to be fair."

Get *their* side of the story? The *dog's* side? "Now Mr. Dog. Someone says you been barkin' too much. (You know how it is. Some people always complainin'. You understand I'm just doin' my job.) But I want to be fair about this. What's your side of the story, Mr. Dog? You think you been barkin' too much?"

Cassie was livid, but she felt she could not push Wormald any further, that she'd better take what she could get.

Eleven

On the third Saturday in July Myron Ricker moved his well rig into Atwoods' yard. He climbed down out of the truck, followed by the driver, a pudgy blond boy with a shaggy mustache. "Guess you been 'spectin' me long 'bout now."

"Yes indeed. I've had barely enough water to make the soup." Last week there were six inches of water in the well, and even that had become murky, so they'd been hauling drinking water from Thurlows'.

"Well, you know how 'tis. I've been pretty much tied up with the buildin' end of things. My boy here, Erlon, he's pretty much in charge of the well drillin' end now."

"Hello, Erlon."

Erlon blushed and nodded, his chubby pink cheeks turning crimson.

Myron droned, "Can't really blame people for wantin' houses put up quick. People without a roof over their heads don't hardly worry about water. I ain't sayin' it's any picnic gettin' low on watcr, but least you folks got a roof over your head. And you're luckier than most folks. You got a pretty good parcel o' land heeyah."

"Yes."

"I don't suppose you'd ever consider puttin' some of into house lots, would you?"

"No. Never."

Ricker shrugged. "Too bad. Nice view of Wilmot Falls ovah theyah."

"I can assure you, the last thing we'd do is—"

"But then, now I consider it a bit closer, might not be the best land for house lots after all. Nope, wouldn't be the best, because you people're land-locked, aren't you?"

"Huh?"

"Land-locked. None of your property's got any road front-age, has it?"

"No."

"Well then, wouldn't hardly be worth a man's time to de-velop a piece like this. Too much of an investment to have to maintain that private road comin' in heeyah. Couldn't offer the people the services that come along with a town road. Well, better get the rig goin'. Make sure Erlon's all set up, then I'll be puttin' him in charge, since I'm pretty much tied up with the other end of my business ovah Wilmot Falls way."

Later, leaving Andy and Michael to gawk at Ricker's well rig gouging its way into the ground beside the house, Cassie walked up the lane for the mail.

Out of sight, just beyond the rise in Thurlows' field, a ma-chine was working, straining, shifting gears. Every so often there was a loud clash—metal striking something.

Haying? she wondered. Can't be, they've already hayed the field. Plowing? But what would the Thurlows be plowing now, with everything so dry?

She turned the corner and continued up Thurlow Hill to the two mailboxes, Thurlows' and theirs, opposite Thurlows' driveway. Now she could see beyond the rise of the field into the flat where the machine was working.

A man was riding a bulldozer. Here and there were up-turned boulders; on some were white marks where the blade of the bulldozer, in digging them up, had scraped their gray roughness. The man on the bulldozer was in the middle of a long strip of bare brown earth, shoving a heap of dirt into a pile at the edge of the strip. Other piles of earth had been pushed up along the edge of the strip, making a ridge between the brown scar and the sun-scorched grass.

The man looked up and saw Cassie. He pulled back on a lever, jumped down and headed toward her, leaving the bulldozer running.

Cassie tugged at the mailbox lid, and fished inside to get the mail. Then she got out Thurlows' mail.

As he came nearer, he reached into the pocket of his short-sleeved shirt. The shirt was unbuttoned and as he walked, the shirt fronts trailed out behind him under his arms. He pulled a cigarette pack from his shirt pocket, lifted the pack to his face and withdrew a cigarette with his lips, then fished in a pocket of his green work pants for matches.

"Saw you up here," he said, lighting his cigarette. "Thought I'd come up, introduce myself." He dragged on the cigarette, then, cigarette still in his mouth, he twisted his mouth to the side, blowing the match out as he exhaled. He flicked the match onto the road. "Name's Vernon Thurlow." He nodded over her shoulder at Thurlows' house. "Will's boy. My folks've told me about you." His eyes swept down her body, then back to her face.

"Nice to meet you."

"I see you got the folks' mail there."

"Yes. Sometimes I bring it over to your mother."

Vernon's open shirt hung down from his elbows, the bright daylight coming through the cloth — sails catching the sun. The triangle of hair on his chest tapered to a strip which ran down his stomach, then into his pants which hung low on his hips.

Cassie had never seen such a deep bellybutton. It looked black, whether from dirt or depth she couldn't tell. If she stuck her finger in there would it go in up to the hilt, or maybe beyond, till she hit his spine, catching her nail on a vertebra? Or would his bellybutton close on her finger like a steel trap, squeezing it, biting it right off?

"You likin' it out here, Mrs. Atwood?"

"Please, Cassie. Yes, we do."

"Quite a change from the city, huh?"

Her head barely came to the top of his shoulder. He was standing over her, not a foot from her, and she had to tip her head back to look at his face. Otherwise, she'd be staring at his chest, muscular, tanned, almost sexy, were it not for the grime and the greasy sweat and the sour smell.

"Gettin' your water today, I see."

"I certainly hope so. We've waited long enough."

"Well, Myron's pretty busy these days. Has a lot of buildin' over to Wilmot Falls. Matter of fact, he's got so much work piled up ahead of him over theyah, he asked me to help him out."

"What?" Cassie frowned. "I don't understand."

"Loom. Ricker needs loom. Lotta ledge where he's buildin' and he needs loom for the landscapin' around the houses he puts in."

"What do you mean, loom?"

Vernon was her age, Emma had said. Thirty-two. Did *she* look that old? His brown crew cut was graying. But that wasn't what made him look old. It was his skin. Weatherbeaten, with thick creases around the eyes.

Vernon frowned. "Loom. Topsoil."

"Oh—*loam*!"

Vernon shrugged. "Loam. Loom. Same thing."

Cassie looked at the chugging yellow bulldozer in the middle of the naked brown patch in the field, suddenly realizing what he was doing.

"Are you—do you mean you are taking the topsoil from the field to put it on someone's lawn?"

"Well, wouldn't exactly call 'em *lawns*. Not yet, anyway. Most of the houses aren't even built yet."

"That's not what I mean," Cassie said. "It looks like you are taking off almost a foot of topsoil."

" 'Bout that much."

"But what about the field? Isn't that a good field? Didn't you—didn't your father farm it?"

"And my grandfather, and his father, too."

"But the ground there. What will it be good for again?"

"That soil there was runnin' out anyway. Hay we got off it this year's only 'bout half as good as what we got last year. Weren't hardly worth the trouble. Couldn't sell more'n hundred bales. The rest my mother uses for the sheep. Can't use it for nothin'. Might's well get what we can out of the sod." He sniffed, hocked, and spat.

"How long do you figure it took your father and your grandfathers to build up that soil?"

"Oh, 'bout, let's see. Hundred years?" He dropped his cigarette, twisting it out with the toe of his brown work boot.

A hundred years. And in one afternoon, this Thurlow grandson comes along and rips away that hundred years to peddle it for lawns for Myron Ricker's new houses.

"Well, 'bout time I got back to work. Anyway, like I said, that field's just about run out. Ain't much good for nothin' else." Walking back toward the bulldozer, Vernon called over his shoulder, "Real nice meetin' you."

Cassie started down the hill, then remembered she had Thurlows' mail. She hesitated, thinking to put it back in their box, but then decided not to. If the Thurlows had seen her getting out their mail to take to them they'd wonder why she didn't deliver it.

As she crossed the road and headed up Thurlows' driveway, a sharp explosion cut through the drone of the bulldozer. She jumped, her heart thudding.

In the Thurlows' back yard, just behind the house, Esther was sitting crosslegged on the trunk of the purple car ("Give 'Em Hell, Vern!" emblazoned on the side) with a gun across her thighs.

The sun glared on the car, glinting off the chrome trim on

the fins and the shards of broken windshield glass scattered on the hood.

What the hell was she doing there, with that gun? Cassie made a wide sweep in front of Esther as she approached the car, hoping to catch Esther's eye, prepared to wave and yell, "Wait! Don't shoot!"

Esther saw Cassie and nodded.

"Hi," Cassie said, taking care not to lean against the hot metal.

Esther was sitting on a striped beach towel folded in half under her. Her feet were dirty, the pink nail polish on her toenails chipped.

"Whatcha huntin'?"

"Not huntin'. Preventin', you might say."

"Huh?"

"Goddamn grackles." She pointed to the field on the other side of a stone wall beyond the car. "First year in ages my folks've had a decent crop of blueberries and the goddamn grackles are eatin' 'em as fast as they ripen."

Cassie looked out across the wall into the field. She couldn't see berries. Must be low bush.

Esther raised the shotgun and pulled the trigger. Cassie flinched.

A flock of birds rose, squawking and screeching. Cassie saw starlings and redwing blackbirds, and among the last to fly up, a robin.

"Esther, you've got more than grackles in that field."

"Grackles is what we call 'em. Hogs for the berries, is what grackles are, and we call any bird that eats berries a grackle." On Esther's chin was a ring of whiteheads. Her dark brown eyebrows almost met in the middle.

Esther lowered the gun. She was chewing gum, open-mouthed, working the gum from side to side in her mouth with her tongue, snapping it noisily on almost every chew.

"Do you do this a lot, Esther?"

"Yup. Whenever we get a few minutes, we come out here and scare 'em up out of the berries."

"We?"

"Yup. Me, Vern, my father, and once in a while even my mother, when she's got the time."

Cassie thought of the leering hillbillies in the movie, *Deliverance*, standing on a bluff in the hot sun, guns at the ready, waiting for their prey to float by on the river below.

"Esther," Cassie said. "It's against the law to shoot songbirds."

Esther made no response.

"Isn't it against the law, Esther?"

"It's against *my* law for them to eat our berries. 'Sides, nobody ever complained before about me shootin' these grackles. Don't expect anybody ever will complain, neither. And whenever I get a minute, I figure to come out here, watch those grackles settle on the berries, and when they all get settled, I'm gonna shoot 'em. Make 'em think twice the next time."

Cassie put Thurlows' mail on the trunk next to Esther, saying, "Here's your parents' mail."

"I'll give it to 'em."

Walking down Thurlow's lane, Cassie wondered if Esther had her in the gun sights, ready to blast her in the back.

As she came to the end of Thurlows' driveway, she looked across the road at Vernon, eagerly stripping away the soil, and heard Esther shoot the gun again. Goddamn rednecks.

The heat of August was heavy and still. Andy was cooling off in his plastic pool. Around him floated Fisher Price people, a couple of Lego blocks he used for boats, a yellow plastic canoe with a yellow plastic Indian, kneeling, paddle dipping into the water.

Cassie came out of the house with a glass of iced tea and a newspaper. She stood over the pool.

"Look Mum. I can make this doll tinkle."

Andy was holding a naked plastic doll face up under water, squeezing it. The doll had thick hair strands, molded as part of its head and painted brown, eyes painted open, and a round red mouth designed to take a tiny baby bottle.

When the bubbles stopped coming out of the doll's mouth, Andy hauled the doll up out of the water and, holding it at arm's length, he squeezed it around its middle, staring at the thin steady stream coming straight down from the doll's crotch between its pudgy legs.

"Having fun?"

Andy held the doll under water again. "Yeah. I love to make it tinkle."

Cassie sat on the well rock and set her glass of tea down.

She unfolded the newspaper: *The Coggerton Free Press*. Under the logo, in Gothic-looking script, "All I Know Is What I Read in the Papers—Will Rogers."

The paper came in the mailbox, free, once a week. She always read "Local Lines," by Norma Cilley.

"Mr. and Mrs. Leston Hobbs motored to Lancaster over the weekend to visit her sister, Wilma Goodrow, and her husband. The Hobbses report it's a good deal cooler up in the north country than down here in the valley!

"Spec. 5 Carl Chagnon spent a week's leave from his duties at Portsmouth Naval Shipyard at the home of his parents, Mr. and Mrs. Fred Chagnon of Whispering Pines Mobile Homes Court. Carl graduated C.H.S., '74. We wish him well in his service to our country.

"Julia Eggers called to say the annual Women's Club Penny Sale for Thanksgiving baskets for our less fortunate citizens is underway again. Volunteers will be calling on you to sell chances for a beautiful afghan made at a 'bee' by the gals in the Women's Club. Let's all pitch in to help this worthy cause!

"Friends and neighbors are glad to see Mertie Apthorpe home from her stay at Concord Hospital. Mertie has asked me to thank all those who remembered her with cards and flowers. 'Your thoughtfulness will never be forgotten,' says Mertie.

"Mr. and Mrs. Walt McPherson were surprised by family and friends on their 60th (Imagine!) wedding anniversary on Sunday. As well as a money tree and a beautifully decorated cake, the McPhersons were presented with sixty dimes pressed under glass in a frame to hang on the wall. This correspondent was privileged to be a part of the festivities and she herself heard Walt say, 'How nice to have friends and relatives who care!' "

The garden had grown messy. Here and there persistent ragweed poked up where the mulch wasn't thick enough. The cucumber vines were shriveled, the tomatoes and winter squashes ripening.

Dogs were barking on the corner below their field. She'd given up trying to get anywhere with the dog officer.

The last time she'd called him he'd asked her if they barked at night.

"Yes," she'd answered. "We shut the window so we can get some sleep. I'm sure they don't stop the minute we shut the windows."

"But they aren't keeping you up at night, are they?"

"They *would* if we had the windows open. Listen. I just can't keep going through this, Mr. Wormald. There are laws about dogs barking, disturbing the—"

"Mrs. Atwood, if you want to file a complaint about some-body, you just come down to Chief Glidden's office and fill out a form."

"But isn't that your job?"

"Do you know what I get *paid* for this job?"

"I don't, but what's that got to do with—"

"Three hundred. That's all I get for this job."

"So is what you're saying you'd enforce the law if you got paid more?"

"Well, you just come into the chief's office and file a complaint."

So she'd given up, having to content herself with fantasies of some dread disease wiping out all the dogs. Sometimes she schemed and plotted to get rid of them, picturing herself sneaking around, tossing every dog she could find a piece of poisoned meat. But most of the time she fumed, trying, without much success, to block them out by day, and shutting windows and sweltering by night.

She fanned herself with the paper. "Local Lines." Maybe she'll gather tidbits and chitchat about her neighbors for *The Coggerton Free Press*. She would call her column "Here's What's Cookin' on Thurlow Hill."

"Esther Lessard, daughter of Will and Emma Thurlow, completed her forty-third 1,000-piece jigsaw puzzle at her mother's kitchen table last night. As all her friends know, Esther is a puzzle pro and we can only hope they don't stop making puzzles in her lifetime! Her other hobby is killing songbirds.

"Friends of Midge Fecteau (on the Otis Corner Road) will be heartened to know that Midge is feeling better after a three-week battle with constipation. We all say, "Hope everything is coming out (ha ha) all right now, Midge!

"This good news from Esther and Gordon Lessard: After many months of trying and a few accidents, their son, little Gordy, Jr., is finally toilet-trained, much to the delight of his parents and grandparents, Will and Emma Thurlow. Training Gordy, Jr., was a real family effort, and we can only say what a fine example for others the Thurlows and Lessards have set. Keep up the Good Work, Gordy, Jr.!"

Andy, humming absentmindedly, was still filling and squeezing the doll. He was wearing only a straw cowboy hat and a short-sleeved jersey, soaked almost to the shoulders.

Some days ago, Cassie had noticed that rather than birdsong, cricketsong filled the air. Summer was on the way out. Shorter days, cooler nights. Cassie looked out at the hills of Wilmot Falls. Not long from now, they would be covered in snow.

"Mum?"

"What, Andy."

"Lookit this. Lookit this doll tinkle."

"Andy, enough with the doll."

Andy tossed the doll down into the water. In the miniature waves, Andy's tiny pink penis bobbed in the water between his splayed legs.

"Okay, now play something else. I'm going to finish reading this paper."

The dogs were still barking. Cassie turned the paper over and skimmed the real estate ads on the back page.

"PEACE N' PRIVACY AT PARADISE ACRES" screamed at her. She read on: "CHOICE LOTS AT PARADISE ACRES (On the Pickard Road in Coggerton). DON'T give up your mobile home. At PARADISE ACRES we WELCOME mobile homes! DON'T give your children up for ADOPTION. At PARADISE ACRES we love children! (The school bus stops at your door.)

"DON'T give away your cat or dog. At PARADISE ACRES your PET (Moose excluded!) will have more than an acre to run free! Come to PARADISE ACRES, where the byword is 'Live and Let Live!' ONLY $800 cash down! Balance $50 Monthly (Interest Free!) for 60 months. Take possession of YOUR LAND immediately! If you've had financial problems in the past, Don't let it 'BUG YOU!' Your credit is GOOD WITH US! This is YOUR CHANCE for 'A New Start in Life!' COUNTRYSIDE REALTY, COGGERTON. Call 624-0455."

"Andy, I'm going in to make a phone call. You get out of the pool now and dry off."

Andy stood up, stepped over the rim of the pool, and skipped off to the rope swing, his wet jersey clinging, his buttocks and legs dripping with water.

❀   ❀   ❀

"Emma?" Cassie said. "Where exactly on the Pickard Road are Skillin's Paradise Acre lots?"

"Just as you turn the corner, down the foot of the hill."

"You mean right below us? Below our field?"

"That's right. Tremblays owned that strip there along the Cross Road, and Roland Tremblay said he had all the land he needed for himself and his kids on the other side of his house, and course, Roland and Ida don't have much, and everybody knows they haven't had an easy time of things lately."

"Is selling their land to some developer the only thing they can do? I mean, did you read the ad, Emma?"

"I looked at it."

"That damn Skillin is filling up this whole corner with trash. Above us first, and now on the other side of us. Whatever happened to his big five-acre lots?"

"What?"

"His big lots. His love of land and all that. His selling everybody a nice big piece of land."

"Well, land's goin' up in value so much these days, up's high as five, six hundred dollars an acre, even out heeyah. Fact, one-acre lots on main roads get as much as two thousand dollars, sometimes. I suppose John Skillin figures land's getting scarcer and he has to cut his lot size."

"You mean, ram them in, trash heaps and kids and packs of goddamn dogs."

Cassie had never spoken so bluntly to Emma before. Though Esther must have told Emma how she'd disapproved of shooting song birds. And she imagined Vernon reporting to his parents: "That Atwood woman sure has a lot to say 'bout what we do with the loom on that run-out field 'crost the road."

"*Really*, Cassie, people have a right to do what they want with their property. You can't expect to run the whole of Thurlow Hill, you know."

Silence. Cassie chewed on her lip.

"Besides, it's just as I said—Tremblays haven't had it easy lately."

"What do you mean?"

"Oh? Haven't you heard?"

"Heard what?"

"About their dog."

"Heard *what* about it? You mean the one they have hitched by their garden, down past the corner of our field here?"

"Yes. Well, *some*one got in there and shot it. Right in the head, poor thing. Ida Tremblay was *awful* upset. They can't imagine who would do a thing like that. Roland says they've kep' that dog staked out back there all this time, and no one ever complained before."

"Hey, hold on, Emma. Are you saying—I mean, do those people think *we* shot their dog?"

"Well."

"Is that it, Emma?"

"Well, Ida did mention it to me."

"Because we complained to the dog officer? Is that it? Wait a minute. Do *you* think we shot the dog?"

"Well really, no one else has ever complained before."

"Jesus, Emma, we don't even own a gun."

"Oh?"

"So do *you* think we shot the dog?"

"After Ida told me, Will and I talked it over, but Will said he didn't think you were the sort of people who would do a thing like that."

"Thank you for that."

"But you can't really blame the Tremblays."

"Do you suppose it'd help if I went to see Mrs. Tremblay? To tell her we didn't do it?"

"Why, you know, that might just be a good idea."

❀   ❀   ❀

"What do you figure you'll accomplish, going to see them?" Michael asked.

"I just don't want them thinking we did it."

"Let them think we did. Maybe then they'll think twice about staking another one out there. One less dog for you to bitch about."

"You haven't met some of these people around here. I wouldn't want to cross them. And I certainly don't want them spreading it around that we're dog killers. If they think that, who knows what they might do. Poison our well or something."

"Since when did you care about what the neighbors think?"

He was right. But she couldn't explain to Michael why she didn't want to antagonize the neighbors, because she wasn't sure herself what it was she feared. "I just don't know what they'll do. When I asked Emma about Skillin's lots on the Pickard Cross Road, she all but told me to mind my own business. You know, like nobody's going to tell *them* what to do."

Michael shrugged. "I still don't see what you think there is to be afraid of."

Twelve

Turning onto the Pickard Cross Road at the bottom of Thurlow Hill, Cassie said to Andy, reading in the back seat, "I won't be long, so you just stay in the car and read. All right?"

"What?"

"*Listen* to me, Andy. I said, you stay in the car and read while I go visit this lady whose house we're going to. Okay?"

"Okay."

Along the side of the road, strips of bright red surveyor's tape were knotted around trees. A pickup truck was parked at the end of the row of tapes. Cassie swung out to clear the truck and as she passed, she saw John Skillin in the window on the driver's side. She pulled ahead of the pickup, parked, and got out.

"What are we stopping here for?" Andy asked.

Cassie shut her door and leaned into the open window. "I want to talk to the man in the truck behind us."

"Who? Who is it?"

"It's okay, honey. Remember the man who sold us our house?"

"Oh," he said, returning to his book.

Seeing her get out of her car, Skillin walked toward her. In the passenger seat of the truck was a man Cassie hadn't noticed when she drove past.

"Hello, Cassie. What brings you down this way?" Skillin asked, as if she lived miles away and were in alien territory, his territory.

"I was on my way to the Tremblays' and—"

"Oh? Tremblays'?"

"Yes." Damned if she'd offer an explanation. "And I saw your truck there, and—"

"What can I do for you?"

"I saw your ad for these lots in the Coggerton paper."

"Well, no sense advertisin' in any of the big newspapers when we get all the response we want for lots like this right from the local papers. Fact, fella in the truck there's George Potter, from downtown. Lookin' over lot number six here. Thinkin' of movin' his family out from downtown. Course, in your case, place that big we put in the Boston papers. But what was it you wanted to talk to me about?"

"I was wondering why you're selling lots this small. I mean, those lots above us, that used to be the other half of the Gilman property you sold to us?"

Skillin nodded.

"We were told you kept your lot size big. So that people would have plenty of room, plenty of privacy. Remember all that?"

"Well, you know, things are changing. I have to pay more for land now, so I have to figure to make a decent profit on it. I gave the Tremblays a decent price for this piece along here. Wanted to do right by them. They need the money, as you likely know. But I've got to get my money back—plus a little, of course. And this whole piece is only ten, maybe eleven acres, so it wouldn't do now, would it, for me to split it into only two lots. You can understand that now, can't you?"

Cassie poked her sneaker in the dusty gravel of the road. Below his belt, Skillin's pants stretched tight in horizontal wrinkles across his wide thighs and his crotch. She remembered his big rump.

"But I keep my prices reasonable here, so young people, young workin' couples just like yourself can afford to have a place of their own."

Where did she hear that before? Oh, right. Ricker, at town meeting. Ricker, benefactor of young people. How'd he put it, that putty-faced slime? Something about young people wanting a place to live, something they can afford. Little place they can call their own, where they can bring up their families.

"How nice of you," Cassie said. "And the trailers and kids and the dogs too, right?"

Skillin, eyes narrowing, crossed his arms over his chest. "Seems to me you've got enough land so you shouldn't complain. Sixty-five acres ought to be more than enough for anybody."

"Yeah, well, I thought so, too. But what good's sixty-five acres if it's surrounded by trailers and trash and damn barking dogs?"

"Course, if you don't like it up there—"

"That's got nothing to do with it. We just feel cheated, that's all. We're already driven half crazy by barking dogs, and when I saw your ad practically inviting more, I—how many of these trailer lots do you have here, anyway?"

"Well, we've got eight. Though we're holding back lot number eight."

"What does that mean, 'holding back'?"

"Means we're not selling one of them."

"Why? What's it good for by itself? Once you get a pack of trailers in here—"

"Now hold on a minute. You can't say for sure everyone who buys here is goin' to put in a mobile home."

"Yeah, right."

"Well anyway, we're holdin' back number eight for now." He laughed. "Who knows? Maybe I'll move out here from town myself. The wife always said she wanted a little place in the country."

"You mean you'd move out here in the middle of all the trailers and squalling kids and bloody dogs?"

"Might. Never can tell."

"That's bullshit and you know it."

He looked at her, expressionless except for narrowed eyes, arms still folded defiantly across his chest.

"Well you know, Cassie, if you don't like it out here, maybe you want to consider lookin' for a place that's more to your likin'."

"Fuck it." Cassie turned and walked back to her car, her teeth clenched.

"Cassie?"

She opened the car door.

"Say, Cassie!"

She turned.

"Let us know if you ever do decide to look for somethin' more to your likin'."

Cassie stared at him, incredulous.

"I imagine you folks could get two, two-and-a-half times what you paid for your place."

Bugger you, Skillin, she thought. She remembered the last lines of Chaucer's "The Miller's Tale": "And Nicholas is branded on the bum, And God bring all of us to Kingdom Come," and imagined Skillin being hog-tied and branded on his big fat rump, smoke curling up around the sizzling branding iron. *Fuck* you, anyway, Skillin, you fat-assed bastard.

She got in the car, slammed the door and drove off, seeing, in the rear view mirror, Skillin staring after her, smiling.

"Be right back, Andy," Cassie said.

"Okay."

Tremblays' two-and-a-half story house, close to the road, was connected to a low-roofed barn by a shabby, sunken ell. Leaning against the barn was a cone-shaped manure pile. Tipped, bottom up, against the end of the barn, was an old Victorian bathtub, its feet gone, its bottom and the curved enamel rim rusting and chipped.

The house, an old center-chimney colonial, much like the Thurlows' in size and shape, must have been nice once. But unlike Thurlows' house which, though weathered gray, still had flecks of paint to show it had at one time been white, this house bore no trace of paint. The clapboards, a few of which were hanging loose, the corner posts, the window frames, even the muntins in the six-over-six windows were splintery dry, like kindling.

A porch ran along the front of the house, its sagging roof below the second story windows covered with rusted corrugated tin. On one end of the porch roof a shiny antenna dazzled, a silver tree against the drab house. Holding up the roof of the porch were four wooden posts resting on a wooden floor which in turn was held up by cement blocks, two under each post. The porch sagged so deeply it was almost on the ground. She stepped across the porch. The window pane in the top half of the door to the house had a triangular piece of glass missing in the lower left corner. A piece of cardboard was taped over the hole.

Cassie knocked on the door.

To the right of the door was a squat, round-cornered refrigerator, its old porcelain grainy, dull, pitted with rust. On its front was an oblong tin plate reading, "Matchless. Sold by Cumberland County Power and Light Company." A doll with a stuffed body and plaster head and limbs sat atop the refrigerator. Stuffing spilled out of a tear in the side of the body, and one leg hung down over the top of the refrigerator.

Cassie knocked again, louder. She turned to look at Andy, whose face she could see through the open car window. He was reading.

"Yes?" the deep voice boomed.

Cassie smiled at the woman peering out from behind the door.

"Mrs. Tremblay?"

"Yes."

"I'm Cassie Atwood. From the Gilman place?"

The woman offered no sign of recognition.

"Up on Thurlow Hill, across from Emma and Will?"

"Yes, I know where."

"I was talking with Emma the other day and she suggested I might talk with you. Do you have a few minutes?"

She opened the door; Cassie side-stepped by her into the cramped hall.

The stench that assaulted Cassie was so strong she nearly gagged.

Straight ahead was a door and on the wall to the left of the door a great jagged patch of plaster was missing, revealing old split laths.

God, what *was* that smell? It burned her nose.

Mrs. Tremblay pointed to a doorway. "Go in the parlor there."

Cassie obeyed, stepping into the room. On a low table under a curtainless window overlooking the porch was a color TV. On the screen, a white-haired woman was lying under white sheets in a hospital bed. The camera had her in profile, showing in closeup her blue-gray face and dark circles under her eyes, which were staring, presumably without seeing, straight ahead. Seated by her bed was a pretty young woman, facing the camera. Judging from her gorgeous hair and makeup job, she was clearly in the pink of health. She was talking with the old woman—or rather at her, since there was no response from the catatonic figure in the bed.

Cassie said, "The reason I wanted to talk with you, Mrs. Tremblay, was because Emma Thurlow said you thought we might have killed your dog."

Mrs. Tremblay's lower lip twitched. Frizzy red hair, pale skin with a greenish pallor, a large, blade-like nose.

"Well, I never 'zackly said that. Way me 'n' my husband Roland see it, coulda been couple folks 'round here's what shot our Prince."

"I see."

"No, I never said nothin' like gat."

"We're not the kind of folks who'd do such an awful thing."

The woman had something the matter with her eyes. They didn't line up, didn't look at Cassie at the same time. They were pale blue, and one, milky, drifted around.

"Seems it'd take a real mean person to kill a dog good as our Prince was. Likely Prince just stood up to see who was comin' to the garden. All full o' trust and waggin' his tail, that dog, and what he git for hisself but a bullet in his head."

Cassie said, "Awful." Then, "Mrs. Tremblay, if you don't mind me asking, where are you from? You don't sound like a New Englander."

"I come from Prince Edward Island. Been here only since Roland 'n' me was married, 'leven years ago."

"Ah."

"Oh Dr. Lacy," the dark-haired lady on the TV was saying. "Do you think Mother hears anything? Under*stands* anything?" The white-haired, white-frocked doctor soothed, "It's hard to say, Tiffany. We just have to wait." He shook his head. "These things take time." The camera zoomed in on Tiffany's anguished face. "Ba-da-da-a-a ... " the organ trilled.

Cassie looked out the window, explaining, "Just wanted to check on my son. He's in the car."

"No need to keep the boy waitin' out there in the car. You just have him come in here."

"Oh well, that's very nice of you. But Andy's had a cold," Cassie lied, "And I hate to drag his germs into anyone else's house."

"That don't matter none. Nobody here but me and the baby."

"The baby?"

"Erma. I put her down for a nap. You ever tried them Rawleigh products?"

"What are those?"

"Rawleigh products. I buy 'em from Roland's sister, downtown."

"I guess I haven't heard—"

"Well, when my Orville was sick with a real hard cold last spring, we was orful worried 'bout him, pore li'l feller."

"I can imagine." Cassie couldn't figure which of Ida's eyes was the stable one, which the walleye. Just when she thought the non-milky one was the fixed one, it floated off to the side, and the other rolled into the center of its socket, and Ida turned her head slightly as if to line Cassie up in that eye. She decided to look at a point between Ida's eyebrows.

"And Roland's sister, she give me some of that Rawleigh's mustert plaster, and I took gat and rub'n'rub it all over Orville's little chest, and next day that cold all broke up. And we was about to take him to be doctored!" A child cried. "That'll be Erma. I'll go git her."

Ida left the room. Cassie looked out the window. Andy was still reading.

She looked at the color TV. It wasn't adjusted properly. Too much blue, making the woman in the bed look even more dreadful than she was supposed to look. Dr. Lacy had apparently left. The fair Tiffany still sat by the bedside, staring, anguished, at Mother's blank face. Then, Mother stiffened, lifting her head off the pillow. Her lips opened, quivering. Tiffany's weepy look changed to one of wide-eyed astonishment. And Mother, still staring, never blinking, jerked upward like a zombie lurching out of its coffin. She croaked, "My. Poor. Tiffany," and fell back onto the pillow. And Tiffany, tears gushing, dropped her head onto Mother's arm, her shiny black mane to the camera, and sobbed, "*Oh Mother!*"

Cassie glanced out the window. Andy still okay.

In a corner near the door to the next room was a tall round parlor stove; on its front door: "Peninsular 418." The only chrome trim left on the stove was on the circular foot rest near the bottom. The walls of the room were gray, the ceiling yellow from wood smoke, the floor bare wood, dulled and soiled. The air, with its heavy fetid odor, was oppressive. Cassie tried to breathe short shallow breaths, thinking maybe her senses wouldn't register the stench. No good. It only made her dizzy, and finally she gasped, inhaled deeply, and almost puked.

Ida returned, holding a child whose head was lolling on her mother's shoulder.

Cassie said, "Why hello there. And what's your name, honey?"

Then she saw the child's eyes. They rolled in their sockets, resting on Cassie but registering nothing, then quivering before rolling off in another direction. Holy Jesus.

"This here's Erma. She don't talk much because she's mental retarded."

"Oh. I—I—"

"She can say a few words." Ida twitched her shoulder on which the child's head was resting, and shouted, "Say hello to the lady, Erma. You say hello to the lady." Ida joggled her shoulder again and the child's head bounced upright, then out toward the room.

Eyes rolling, her voice voice barely audible, Erma said, "Hi." Her head flopped back again onto her mother's shoulder.

"How old is Erma?"

"Three 'n' a half. Been this way since she was eight months old."

"Oh dear."

"She was creepin' 'round on the floor and she somehow got holt a hairpin and she took 'n poked that pin into one o' them light sockerts."

"You mean a plug? where you plug things in?"

"Yes. Them things down near the floor. We took the pore li'l thing all the way to Hanover and they all said wasn't nothin' they could do for her."

"Oh. I'm so sorry," Cassie said. She reached out and touched the child's cheek. "Hello, sweetheart."

Erma lifted her head. "Hi," she piped again. Her blue eyes crossed and drifted off. Head on, Erma was pretty. Her vacant eyes were big, round, and a heavenly sky-blue. Her face was heart-shaped, her nose, mouth, and chin delicate. But from the side, her head was flat on the back, and the top was bald. Wisps of straight blond hair grew in a tonsure-fringe around the back of her head from ear to ear. From the side, she looked like an old woman ravaged by some horrid disease. Cassie thought of Karen Ann Quinlan, whom the courts wouldn't let die. In arguing for pulling the plug, some doctor had said a light shined behind Karen's head would shine out through her eyes, proving that all there was left of her brain was watery jelly. Cassie wondered how Erma would look in a photograph. Maybe if she wore a sunbonnet and were photographed head on. Would the camera catch how pretty she was? Could it freeze her rolling eyes, make them look normal?

"Course, me 'n' Roland, we ain't never been completely cavinced it were the 'lectric sockert what made her this way," Ida said.

"Why is that?"

"Because all the trouble with Orville begun when I was pregnant with her."

"Orville?"

"Yes, my boy. You come on in here. I'll show you what I mean." Ida put Erma on the floor in front of the TV. She sat there, limp, head rolling, eyes drifting, mouth hanging open.

Cassie followed Ida into the kitchen, hesitating, as Ida disappeared into a room beyond the kitchen.

In the kitchen, an iron sink on legs, and next to it, a pitcher pump mounted on a counter covered with red linoleum. Along another wall, a black iron wood cook stove, its top a jumble of dented aluminum pots of various sizes. The ceiling over the stove was brown with wood smoke. Next to the stove was a table with a marbled Formica top and chrome legs, and matching chrome chairs with red plastic seats and backs.

Ida appeared in the doorway of the room off the kitchen. "You comin'?"

"Oh, yes, sorry." Cassie stepped into the room: only one piece of furniture—a metal-framed bed, its green paint blistered and flaking. On top of the black and white-striped mattress was a heap of twisted, filthy bedclothes. A pillow without a case was stuffed against the head of the bed. Ida was standing over the bed, riffling through the jumble of bedclothes. The smell was overpowering.

Ida turned. In her hand she held a bunched-up dirty gray rag. She held it out to Cassie. "See? This is what I was tellin' you about."

"I'm sorry. I don't understand. "

She poked the rag toward Cassie. "You don't *see*?"

All Cassie could see was that part of the rag looked a darker gray than the rest of it. It looked wet.

"Ever' mornin' I have to wash Orville's bed sheets." She tossed the rag into a corner of the room and wiped her hands across her stomach. Hands red and puffy, fingernails jagged and dirty.

Piss. So *that's* the stench. Pissy bedclothes, pissy mattress. Yesterday's piss. Last week's piss. Last night's piss.

"Ever' night, ever' single night since he started goin' to school."

"No."

"Yes. First, when Roland and me was told he was gonna git put off the school bus if he don't behave, we whup him good. But me 'n' Roland decided weren't nothin' Orville was doin' wrong, because if he was, we'd'a beat it right outa him. And when they come out here from school and tell us he was actin' bad down there, we whup him more. But then, we heard from someone that Orville wasn't doin' nothin' on that school bus. That bastard school bus driver, he was tellin' the other kids to be mean to Orville. And they did what he tell them to do. They pick on him orful, knockin' his schoolbooks down, pullin' his hair."

"Oh, dear."

"And all this commence' to happen when I was carryin' Erma. So me 'n' Roland, we figure the sockert might not be the whole reason. We even asked one of them doctors up to Hanover if it could be all the trouble with Orville what made Erma mental retarded. I tol' him all the grief we was havin' with Orville on the bus and at the school and how his wettin' the bed all started when I was carryin' the baby, and that doctor—you know what that doctor said?"

"What?"

"That doctor said, 'Lots of things can go wrong with a baby 'fore it's born.'" She stepped closer, pushing the thick stench in the air toward Cassie. Cassie backed into the kitchen. Ida was livid now, her face red, her walleyes squinting. "Well, weren't nothin' left for me 'n' Roland to think but that there was a 'speracy."

"Pardon?"

"'Speracy. I said *speracy*. You know, like everbody gangin' up on our Orville."

"Oh yes, a conspiracy."

"Sometimes me 'n' Roland say we'll sell this big house and move away. Roland says we can get a fortune for a antique house like this. That'll fix 'em all, if we sell for a lot of money and move where no one can bother us."

In the parlor, Erma was where Ida had left her on the floor, in front of the TV. Cassie inched her way to the door. Ida stepped out on the porch with her.

"Well Ida, I'm sorry about your dog, but I did feel I should—"

"Well, the way me 'n' Roland figure it, one who killed our Prince will get it hisself one day." She cocked her milky eye at Cassie. "God'll punish the one who shot our Prince. Me 'n' Roland know that."

Jesus. Did Ida still suspect they shot the dog, and was laying a curse on her? Be just her luck to get in the car now, drive off and slam into a tree. God's wrath upon the guilty.

Andy was in the front seat of the car, pretending to drive. Patient kid. Normal.

Ida followed Cassie off the porch onto the dusty lawn.

"Say, Ida," Cassie said. "Do you know who any of the new people are? On the lots next to you here?"

"No one's there yet. But that John Skillin. He tol' us—after he bought the land from me 'n' Roland—that he sold the lot nearest us to some hooknose Commanists." She tipped her head back, chortling. "And Roland said, his eyes just as big as that (she made a circle by joining the tips of her thumb and middle finger), Roland said, 'John Skillin, you sonofabitch, you better not o' sold no lots to no hooknose Jew Commanists.'" She laughed again, snorting, her mouth twisted to one side. "That John Skillin, he's always jokin' with Roland. Next he tell Roland, he says, no, he never'd do a thing like gat. Then after a minute he says to Roland, 'But there is gonna be some colored movin' in' and for a minute Roland, he got really scaret. Then Roland asked John Skillin was he jokin' again and he says he was." Ida sneered. "That'll be the day, when we let some hooknose Jew bastards into the neighborhood. Ain't havin' no colored, neither. Fact, one night Roland thought someone was messin' 'round on our porch here, and I bet you know first thing Roland does is reach for the shotgun."

The Tremblays have guns, ready to shoot Jews and blacks. Would they come shoot them, too? Cassie wondered what Ida and Roland would do if they were to take a notion that she and Michael were hooknoses. Her own nose wasn't exactly a button pug. She shuddered.

She felt an urgency—a necessity—to leave Ida with the impression that she and Michael had a gun. God, what a hell of a note. She couldn't shoot a gun, didn't even want to touch one.

"Well, can't say as I blame you, Ida, the way things are today. Anyone comes messin' round' *our* place better think twice, too. I mean, we're peaceable folks and we pretty much keep to ourselves but if anyone up to no good comes near us, well, you know what I mean." Christ, did she ever dream she'd be talking like this: Keep out or we'll kill you?

Ida was quiet, studying her.

Cassie walked around to the driver's side of the car and, anxious to get out before Ida struck up a new topic, she hissed at Andy, "Back seat. Now. Quick. And buckle your belt." Andy scrambled over the seat, his sneakered heels bouncing off the roof of the car. Something brushed her ankle and she jumped. A plastic Nissen's bread bag.

She opened the car door and called out, "Well, be seein' you, Ida. Thanks again."

Ida said, "You must git pretty lonely back down in there by yourself."

"Oh, I always have plenty to keep myself busy."

"Well, you just come by and set and talk anytime you git lonely."

Hands shaking, she raced past Skillin's lots and turned onto Thurlow Hill, her mind churning: Ida and her hatred of Jews, blacks, and anyone else she imagined were out to get her. And the stench, and the baby who stuck her finger in the light socket.

"What took you so long, Mum?"

"Mrs. Tremblay and I had a lot to talk about."

"But I finished my book and it was hot in the car."

"I know, honey. Sorry."

She ached with love for her child. Normal, bright, sunny. Her eyes filled, stung. Grateful. Grateful for Andy. Grateful for not being Ida Tremblay. Grateful for what? It didn't matter. Grateful, even, for being out of that awful place.

She turned into the lane. God, what was happening to her dream of the Good Life in the hills of New Hampshire?

Where were the healthy, wholesome farm folk? Where their children, whom Cassie had pictured running hand in hand with her son through fields of buttercups, their hair shining in the sun, lifted by summer breezes. Where, indeed. Playing with sticks in the dust at Sally Wilkins' house, sitting on the floor in Ida Tremblay's, grinning like tongue-tied idiots in front of Fecteaus' trailer. That's where.

At least in Boston, she could talk to the neighbors. But here, ye gods. Esther and her puzzles, massacring birds. Sally Wilkins. Discussing dirty books over the teacups with Sally Wilkins, with time out to wallop her kid. And now Ida. She thought of Edgar Allen Poe's "The Tell-tale Heart," about the guy with the funny eye that drove another guy nuts. "I think it was his eye! Yes, it was this! One of his eyes resembled that of a vulture—a pale blue eye, with a film over it."

She stopped the car in the yard and got out. Weeping, she opened Andy's door, so worked up she didn't try to hide her tears.

Andy looked frightened. "What's the matter?"

"Nothing, honey, it's okay. You just go in the house. It's almost time for *Robin Hood.* I'll be right in."

Usually Andy dawdled, marking the place in his book and taking forever to get out of the car. This time, confused and frightened, he left his book behind, slid out of the car and scrambled into the house.

Cassie went to the well rock and sat down. She faced the woods behind the house, her back to the garden and the Wilmot Falls hills. She thought of Skillin. Scrimy little mealy-mouthed prick. Vernon Thurlow, stripping loam. Esther blasting songbirds. "You can't expect to run the whole of Thurlow Hill, you know," she said out loud, mimicking Emma. Stanton Wormald, the dog officer. Fucking twerp. And Skillin, what was it he practically said to her today? Oh yeah, right: If you don't like it, get out.

She rubbed her eyes with the heels of her hands and

breathed deeply, glad that the air *was* air, and not the burning stench of Tremblays' house.

"Jesus loves me, yes I know." God, where'd that come from? Then she hummed, "Jesus loves the little children, All the children of the world ..." And then, thinking of Erma Tremblay, "Suffer the little children." Again, tears welled. She blinked against them, forcing from her mind all but the crickets, whose time it was, singing their evening song at the end of the late August day.

Andy was watching *Robin Hood* when she came in.

She lifted the phone, hesitated, then dialed. "Emma? This is Cassie. I saw Ida Tremblay."

"Oh? And how did it go?"

"I guess she believed me."

"Well, good. No sense havin' bad feelin's 'mongst neighbors. We like things to run smooth in the neighborhood."

"Where's Ida from?"

"Oh. Well, Roland lived with his parents for the first thirty years of his life, right there in that same house. He was the only son. A sister married real young and she's been livin' downtown ever since. After old man Tremblay died, that left just Roland to look after his mother, who was crippled up something awful with arthritis, and then she went funny in the head. After she died, Roland come into the farm. And he lived alone for three, maybe four years after that. Then he went away — no one ever noticed he was even gone — and when he come back, he come back with a wife. All in the same weekend, too. Story was, least everybody says, that Ida was a mail-order bride."

"Huh?"

"That's right. None of us ever heard of that before. Story was, Roland saw an ad somewhere and wrote to the place in

Canada and when he heard back he went right up there and married her, sight unseen."

"Wow!"

"But poor Roland. He's had a lot of trouble ever since. A *lot* of trouble."

"You mean the baby? Erma?"

"Yes. And Orville. And, well, other things, too. We've since heard Ida never knew her father. And then, she never went beyond the third grade herself. I don't mean there's anythin' *wrong* with that. I just mean Ida's background and not havin' much education and all. Well, I'm not a *snob* or — but, well, you know what I mean. But I suppose a body can't help but feel sorry for the Tremblays. It's been hard for them, real hard. Oh, I see Will comin' in, wantin' his supper."

"Okay, Emma, thanks." Cassie looked out at the field. Swallows were diving and gliding, gathering insects.

In bed that night, Cassie said to Michael, "I'm telling you, the place was a hovel."

"What?" Exasperated, Michael dropped his book (*Who the Hell is William Loeb?*) to his chest. "You want to talk, we'll talk."

"Forget it. You're not interested."

Michael marked his place in his book with an emery board. "Okay, okay, let's hear it."

She felt like punching him.

"I'm just trying to tell you, Tremblays' house is a hovel."

"Jesus. Aren't you exaggerating just a little? The place does look run down, but —"

"A hovel, Michael, no better than a *hovel*."

"Come on. Hovels are what the peasants lived in the dark ages. Huts, with chickens and hogs groveling about on the dirt floors. All smoky and smelly and —"

"Yeah, right. And that's what this place was. You have to see it—"

"Sure, Cassie, sure. Pigs and chickens on the dirt floor, right?"

Cassie thought of Erma sitting on the floor.

"Well, no, but the retard—well anyway, the place stunk so—"

"Stank."

"Oh for Chrissake. *Stank.* Jesus, Michael, I'm trying to tell you that every place I go to around here seems worse than the last."

He turned to look at her. He was running the tips of the fingers of his left hand lightly, slowly, up and down his breast-bone. He did that all the time when he lay in bed reading or talking. It drove her nuts.

"I told you going there wouldn't accomplish anything. So what did it get you?" How he loved to say "I told you so."

"Nothing, I guess. It's just depressing, meeting the neighbors and they keep getting worse. Oh, and you want something else?"

"Go on."

"Emma says Ida Tremblay is a mail order bride."

"*What?*"

"Seems Roland saw an ad in some paper and the next thing everybody knew he'd gone to Canada and when he came back he was married."

"No shit!" Michael laughed. "Different strokes for different folks, I guess."

Cassie imagined an ad for mail order brides:

"For Sale: Willing women of all types. Strong, obedient, ready to go now. Specify hair and eye color preference. Prices reasonable. (Note: We have a number of slightly defective women with walleyes, questionable teeth, and limited education. These minor impairments, however, should not affect the overall quality. Reduced prices on these women.) Money order or bank draft only. No personal checks, please. Shipped as freight."

Though Roland went to Canada to fetch his bride, he could have had her delivered. There's Roland on his porch, watching the two St. Johnsbury men heft it down off the truck, groaning, sweating. One says to the other, "Oomph. Wait a minute, willya? Set it down a minute, willya?" They lower the heavy box, balancing it on the tailgate of the truck. The veins in his temple bulging, one guy says to Roland, "Jesus, buddy, what the hell you got in here, rocks or somethin'?" Roland signs the delivery papers, and the men climb into the truck and drive off. He opens the box and there is Ida, curled up among the excelsior, smiling, looking demure, batting her milky eye coyly at her husband-to-be. Gloria in excelsior. Before he hauls her up out of the box, Roland removes the packing slip: "Please notify carrier if contents arrive damaged in any way ..."

"Michael?" But Cassie could tell from his breathing he was asleep, puffing on every exhalation, irking her. Jesus, not tonight, Michael. She reached over and lightly shoved his top lip against his teeth. Often that shut up the puffing long enough for her to get to sleep.

She wondered if you can sell spouses as well as buy them. Ship 'em out U.P.S. "For Sale: One slightly used husband. Good provider. Sound teeth. Current wife willing to sacrifice because unable to tolerate certain bodily habits that someone else might consider picayune. (One woman's meat, another woman's poison!) No reasonable offer refused ..." She turned over, bunched up the pillow, and in her sinking consciousness Andy, whom she loved fiercely, and the retard, Erma Tremblay, for whom her heart ached, fought for her attention.

Thirteen

By the end of the second week of school, Cassie was getting used to having whole days to herself.

On the first day of school, waiting in line with other mothers and their kids, she pointed out the balloons hanging from the fluorescent lights. "Hey Andy, doesn't this look like fun?" Apprehensive, Andy held onto her hand. As the day wore on, she wondered how Andy was doing. Was he was given enough chances to go to the bathroom? Was he able to manage wiping his butt properly with the stiff little folded sheets of institutional toilet paper? Could he work the water fountain? Did he manage to get his six cents into the right hands so he'd have milk with his peanut butter and jelly sandwich he'd carried in his Scooby-Doo lunchbox? And the unthinkable: was recess well-supervised, or would some dirty old pervert snatch her baby? In the week before school started, she'd told Andy so many times, *"Never never go with anybody, ever, for any reason!"* that he'd finally yelled one day, "I *know*, Mum, I *know* all that. How many times do you have to *tell* me?" Still.

At three o'clock that first day, she was at the end of the lane waiting for the bus. It droned up the hill, its square yellow face nosing into sight. Her son was safe. The bus hissed and groaned to a halt, its lights flashing, kids bouncing up and down in the windows. Andy trudged around the front of the bus, tired-looking, his hair sweaty. She held out her hand as he approached. As the bus lurched forward, she waved at the driver, smiling. Make friends with him. Smile, wave and he'll look out for the kid. The driver nodded, smiling.

"How'd it go, your first day as a big first grader?"

"I sat next to a girl named Michelle."

"Was she nice?"

"I guess so. But she kept trying to kiss me at recess."

"Maybe that means she likes you. How was the bus ride home? You said you couldn't wait to ride the bus."

"It was okay. But everybody jumps and yells a lot and there's too much rushing around."

The second day of school was drizzly. Andy wore his yellow slicker which hung below his knees, thwacking against his legs. With effort, he stretched up to the first step of the bus. She lost sight of him, then he reappeared in one of the windows, his round-eyed somber face cowled in his yellow slicker which matched the yellow of the bus.

While Cassie was getting accustomed to days without Andy, she felt at loose ends, telling herself, *Do* something. *Accomplish* something. But what?

Once, when Andy was around three or so, she'd complained to Michael that she felt herself coming unhinged, unable to concentrate, to read a book or to keep her mind on anything anymore. He'd said, "I don't know what all you women complain about. Sure, you get six years where you're maybe tied down, but once the kid's in school, you can do what you want."

She became compulsive about the garden, not wanting anything go to waste. All September she canned mountains of tomatoes, froze still more Swiss chard, and hung batches of basil and mint to dry from the beams in the kitchen. Fiddling with the vegetables kept her from thinking just what it was she wanted to do. At least, domesticity was a familiar, easy cop-out, keeping decisions at bay. As she frantically froze and canned, she became obsessed with the notion that maybe the time was soon coming when they would have to survive off the land.

She read things like *Survival with Style* and *Stalking the Wild Asparagus*, and articles in *The New Hampshire Times* about solar hot water heaters, and yurts, and other do-it-yourself shelters.

But by the end of summer, when the only wild things she had learned to recognize and eat with confidence were dandelions, pigweeds, milkweeds, and a few mushrooms, she knew they couldn't possibly hack it when the end times came, because everybody would then be in the same boat and the ones with the guns would rip off the food from the ones without the guns. Your food or your life. So what difference did it make?

On a warm, late-September morning, Cassie wandered through the brown field where here and there frost-flowers grew up among the grasses, celebrating their springtime now, in everything else's autumn.

At the brook, she sat on the stone bridge, dangling her feet over the edge, looking upstream. Along the banks, thickets of ferns, yellowing, dying. She remembered sitting here during black fly season, seeing these same ferns just sprouted, tightly-coiled fiddleheads. Overhead, yellow and brown leaves, only a few months ago a lacy chartreuse canopy. She inhaled, trying to recall the fresh, promising smell of the woods in spring. Now the air was dank, a mix of dying vegetation and leaf mold, of animals rooting and digging, searching for suitable winter dens.

And the brook: low, barely trickling, revealing moss-covered rocks, fallen leaves, and sticks and pine needles caught among the rocks, creating miniature dams. She looked upstream. Something white was coming down the brook. She squinted, trying to make it out. It came slowly toward her, gliding like a leaf on top of the slow-moving water, left, right, then sliding over tiny waterfalls. It came close enough so she could see it: a styrofoam coffee cup. What the hell? Were there picnickers upstream along the brook, on their property?

The cup glided into the darkness under the bridge.

Cassie looked under the bridge. The cup had disappeared. But there was something else: a string of white foam, clinging to the granite bridge abutment. She scrambled down the bank and reached under the bridge. The coldness of the water startled her. She expected it to be tepid because of the way it gathered in little pools, barely moving. She scooped up a piece of the foam and sniffed it. No odor she could identify. She rubbed it between her thumb and fingers. It felt slippery. What the *hell*—detergent? She peered upstream. She saw one, two, possibly three more clumps of the stuff. She rinsed her fingers in the brook, wiped them on the seat of her jeans.

The brook flowed through Skillin's lots before it cut across a corner of Thurlows' field and into their property. "Damnit!"

She drove up Thurlow Hill. Skillin's lots were filling up. Four trailers, and a cement-block cellar foundation, capped over with boards and tarpaper. Emma had said a family with nine kids lived in the cellar, planning to weather the winter in there, building a house over it next spring. Meanwhile, every time Cassie drove by, there was more junk in the yard: a couple of jalopies, an old rusting chest freezer, a slab pile for firewood, a faded, battered Big Wheel, a heap of rubber tires, stuffed plastic trash bags, propped against the foundation outside the door.

Then, they started cutting the trees, right to the side edges of their narrow lot, and back into the woods as far as one could see beyond the foundation. And somehow they'd managed to get rid of bushes and grass as well, so that the landscape around the foundation was all bare, peppered with the blond circles of tree stumps. The place looked ravaged, laid waste.

Once there were a couple of kids in the yard: a boy in too-large sneakers, clown shoes, and a girl about Andy's age who, just as Cassie drove by, lifted her shift and stood there by the house, bare-assed, her legs spread. She was urinating. Cassie stared, looked quickly at the road ahead, then looked back again. The child stood motionless, a wet streak down one leg, gawking at Cassie's car as she drove by. Later, when she told Michael what she'd seen, he laughed. "Nothing like a little local color."

Now, as Cassie approached Skillin's lots and remembered the girl peeing in the yard, she wondered what the cellar hole dwellers did for a toilet, where they dumped their wastes. The brook? What else other than coffee cups and detergent was at this very moment trickling down the brook? Raw sewage? Big brown turds drifting under the bridge?

She passed two trailers, each with its growing accumulation of trash and junk in the dooryard, then drove slowly by the cellar hole. No one in the yard. A donkey was hitched to a clothesline pole. But what would she have done if there had been someone there? Requested—demanded—that they stop polluting the brook, stop crapping in the brook, stop pissing in the yard which sloped toward the brook?

At the Otis Corner Road, she looked left and right. No one was coming. Her foot on the brake, she rested her forehead on the top of the steering wheel. "You bastard, Skillin."

She turned around, drove past the trailers, Wilkins's house on the left, the cellar hole, two more trailers, Thurlows' torn-up field on the right and their house and barn on the left. Then, driving by the lane to her own house, she headed for Coggerton.

At the town hall Cassie said to the red-haired secretary. "I want to see a selectman."

"May I ask what it is you want to see us about?"

"No. And it's not any 'us' I want to see. It's a selectman. Or all three. I don't care which."

The secretary slid back her chair. "Just a moment." She stepped across the office and stood in the doorway of another room, "It's Mrs. Atwood, from out on Thurlow Hill."

A man's voice mumbled something Cassie couldn't make out. Then, the secretary asked, "What should I tell her, then?"

Another pause. More low mumbling, a chair scraping. The secretary turned and said to Cassie, "Mr. Stiles will see you now."

Roger Stiles appeared in the doorway of his office, leaning against the jamb, natty in his cranberry-colored western shirt with maroon piping, matching maroon pants, brown cowboy boots, and a black string tie. A country and western singer. He had a toothpick sticking out from a corner of his mouth.

"What can I do for you, Mrs. Atwood?" He shuffled the toothpick to the other side of his mouth.

"I was just out in our woods, and one of those styrofoam coffee cups came floating down the brook. And then I noticed all this white frothy stuff along the sides of the brook."

Stiles nodded, flipping his toothpick, his jaw falling and rising.

"Someone above us on Thurlow Hill must be polluting the brook."

Stiles straightened up. The heels of his boots were on the threshold between the two offices, the pointed toes off the sill just onto the floor of the secretary's office. "Pollution? Hardly think you could call one paper cup pollution."

"But what about the detergent all along the banks?"

"Detergent?"

"Yes, the white slippery stuff. Foam."

"Mrs. Atwood, every bit of foam you see is not necessarily detergent. It would have to take an awful lot of detergent dumped upstream to still be suds by the time it got to you."

"But wouldn't the foam suggest some kind of pollution? Something that doesn't belong in the water?"

"Maybe. No way to tell for sure."

The secretary was hunched over a ledger, sliding her pencil down the vertical rows of numbers, bringing her pencil down with a little thump at the bottom of each column.

Cassie said, "You know all those new house lots up above us on Thurlow Hill? Skillin's lots?"

Stiles nodded, rocking back and forth, the heels of his boots tapping faintly. What a stud. Probably has a CB radio in his pickup, and a rifle rack in the rear window of the cab.

"Well, I couldn't say for sure about the trailers," Cassie said. "But I'm sure the cellar hole—do you know the place I mean?"

Stiles nodded. "Steadbacks. Moved here from Barchester."

"I'm sure they don't have a proper septic system. And that lot—all those lots, border the same brook before it comes onto our property."

Stiles nodded, flipping his toothpick.

"So—doesn't that say something? What about ordinances about septic systems? About polluting streams and rivers and all."

"Coggerton doesn't have any ordinances pertainin' to septic systems. That's the state's business."

"You mean the ones who came out and looked at our septic system before we could cover it?"

"Yup. Water Supply and Pollution Control."

"You mean I'd have to go to them to complain about this?"

"Well, you could try. Doubt if it'll get you anywhere, though. They're pretty busy over there. Understaffed. Pretty busy."

"But doesn't it bother you that there's this sort of thing going on? I mean, the brook getting polluted and the way those people are living out there?"

"Mis-sus At-wood. Coggerton's got plenty of room for

people to spread out in. One paper cup and a little bit of foam on one brook's hardly reason to get all excited, seems to me, and—"

"That's what you think," Cassie snapped.

Stiles stiffened. The secretary froze, her pencil stopping in mid-sweep down a column of numbers in the ledger. Stiles stepped just over the threshold into the secretary's office. "I suppose if you really feel you want to make a fuss about this, you can file a complaint with the health officer."

Health officer? She didn't know Coggerton had one. "Okay, sure. Where can I find him?"

Stiles said to the secretary, "Estelle, you got Stanton's number right there, haven't you?"

Estelle reached for something on the side of her desk.

"Wait a minute," Cassie said. "Stanton? You mean Stanton Wormald, the dog officer?"

"Yup," Stikes said. "Town this size can't afford to hire a whole other person for health officer, so we combine dog officer with health officer."

"Oh, that's just swell." Cassie looked at the secretary. "Gee, we're not going to get anywhere with Stanton, are we, Estelle?"

Estelle looked at Stiles, as if pleading for help.

Stiles said, "Well, if there's any other little thing we can help you with, Mrs. Atwood, someone's always here. Nice to meet you." He retreated into his office.

Cassie stared after him. Yes, there is one other little thing you can do, creep. You can choke to death on your goddamn fucking toothpick. To Estelle, feigning sweetness, she said, "I won't trouble you for Mr. Wormald's number, since I already have it, but perhaps you can help me with something else. Can tell me, please, how do I get to the Bracketts' place? I understand they live outside town?" It would be four hours before Andy got off the bus. She had to talk with someone in the whole stinking town who understood what she was talking about.

"Yes, out on the Wilmot Falls Road."

"And how do I get to that road?"

"Oh, well, that's easy. Just go down to Lower Main, turn left across from the Baptist church, and go about three, maybe four miles. You can't miss Bracketts' place. It's a big ole house set back from the road, on the right."

Driving through town, Cassie thought how unlike the stereotypical New England villages this town was. Villages with their snug white Capes and large white colonials with green shutters, and white clapboarded churches with plain spires and twelve over twelve wavy-paned windows, their solid front doors decorated with wrought-iron strap hinges, and all gathered genteelly around the village common. Lilacs and forsythia in the dooryards in spring and now, in autumn, century-old maples turning scarlet.

Lining both sides of Coggerton's main street were rows of buildings, mostly wooden, a few made of brick. Stores below, apartments above.

Cassie slowed at the overhead yellow blinker which divided one end of Main Street from what was called "Lower Main." On the right, a two-story gray wooden building with a sign on its side: "Laundercenter. Triple-Load Washers. Self-Service Dry Cleaning. 24-Hour Service." Opposite the laundromat was a drug store, a single story building, Woodard's Rexall Drugs.

Turning the corner, she glanced at Gilsum's Hardware Store with its small-paned windows newly painted white. ("Real colonial-looking," the woman at the town meeting had said.) Under the windows, boxes with petunias, the Women's Club's contribution for Coggerton's facelift for the Bicentennial Celebration.

She passed the Coggerton National Bank, Mary Ellen's Lunch with its "Waitress Wanted" sign in the window, Althea's Dress Shop on the left and, tucked in an alley between Althea's and the next building, a lunch wagon on whose side was written, in big red letters, "Here Cums Pete!" A side panel of the van, let down, served for the counter; just inside the van was a square cooler holding a swirling orange drink. Several people milled around the wagon.

Beyond "Here Cums Pete!" was a three-story brick block, letters above the second story saying "Hoffmann Building 1886." Once a factory, its ground floor now housed a barber shop and a junk store which called itself, in gold-colored Gothic script stenciled on the windows, "Ye Olde Thrift Shoppe."

Hoffmann. German name? But how could that be, here in WASP Coggerton? How could they have allowed any foreigner in? Was Ida Tremblay aware?

Cassie passed another brick building with cream-colored pilasters and a flagpole jutting out from the pediment on which was written, "Ethridge Memorial Library. 1882."

Then, wooden blocks on both sides again. More stores: "Lemieux Variety. Cold Beer. Cigarette's," and "Johnny-D's Pizza. Sub's. Belly-Buster's. Mile Long's." Ah, Coggerton's penchant for abusing apostrophes.

Gray and brown, brown and gray, the wooden buildings lining the treeless thoroughfare reminded Cassie of the false fronts on the lot of a western movie, propped from behind by diagonal posts, which a stiff wind could send clattering over backwards, one after the other, like cards in a card house.

Cassie recalled a scene from *Blazing Saddles*. The sheriff, a black guy, gallops across the desert into Coggerton. He clippety-clops along Lower Main Street, smiling confidently, a little dopily, as in the movie. Head cocked slightly, eyes half closed, languid. And then, people coming out of Woodard's Drugstore with their bottles of Rawleigh's Dyspepsia Remedy and Lydia Pinkham's Medicine. People on the library steps, nineteenth-century marbled-backed Bible tracts tucked under their arms. People at the "Here Cums Pete!" wagon, steamed hotdogs in hand, turning to stare. Whispers up and down the street, in the apartments over the stores, over the sloshing and vibrating Laundercenter, down the narrow alleys between the blocks. "Why it's a niggah!" the ugly whispers spread. "A niggah!! A niggah just rode into town!"

The road to Wilmot Falls rose and dipped and turned, and the houses gradually thinned out. A trailer here and there. A flat-roofed cement block building painted white with a sign out front, "Coggerton–Wilmot Falls Pentecostal Church."

And soon, Hog Hollow, with shacks close to the road, each with its own unique siding, extensions, ells, and assortment of junk in the yard. Shacks with travel-trailer extensions. Shacks not quite shacks, but almost proper houses, with foundations and cement-block chimneys coming out of the roof instead of tin pipes with tin-cone hats coming out of side walls. Past Hog Hollow, farmland spread out on both sides of the road.

Finally, a mailbox, with faded red letters on the side: "BRACKETT." She drove up the sloping gravel lane, got out of the car, listening, tensed against any dogs that might come charging out.

The gable end of the old Cape's peak end was broad, squat, lacking cornices. She tried, casually, to look inside the windows, but from where she stood and because of the way the light fell, all she could see in the panes were reflections of blue sky, and the swaying rusty leaves of a large oak.

A door slammed shut. A man appeared at the end of the porch along the front of the house. Cassie walked toward him. The sun, behind him, came down across his shoulder from the open side of the porch, and the front of him was in shadow. Because the sun struck Cassie full in the face, not until she was almost up to him did she see that it was Jim.

"Jim." She squinted up at him.

"Hello. What brings you out this way? Come sit down."
He turned and walked to the far end of the porch, where an old
man was sitting in a rocking chair. Jim nodded over Cassie's
shoulder and said, "Chair behind you. Sit down."

Cassie pulled a ladderback away from where it had been
placed against the house, and sat down, facing Brackett, who
then sat facing her. The three chairs formed a semi-circle: hers
and Jim's facing each other, the old man's in between, facing
the field in front of the house.

"This is my brother, Woodbury."

The old man nodded slowly, still looking ahead, out over
the field.

"And this is —" Jim looked at Cassie, his blue eyes smiling.
"*Cassie*. Cassie Atwood. People who bought Sam Gilman's
place."

Woodbury turned his head slowly toward Cassie. "Went
to school with Sam Gilman." He turned his gaze back to the
field, staring.

The old man, thin and wrinkled, was wearing old green
work pants, a faded blue flannel shirt, buttoned to the neck,
and a brown cardigan sweater that hung loosely, unbuttoned.
The cardigan had side pockets, and buttons that were not
plastic, but yellowed wood or, Cassie thought, possibly even
bone, and if bone, then the sweater might be as ancient as the
man himself. Maybe even his father's, or his grandfather's,
passed down to him, like a quilt from a grandmother to a
granddaughter. Here and there the sweater had been mended,
some repairs made with a darker brown yarn, one with green
yarn. His arms rested on the flat arms of the rocker, the fingers
of his hands curling over the ends of the arms. The knuckles
of his hands, high lumps, and the skin over them, shiny. On
his feet, brown leather slippers, placed squarely, several inches
apart, in front of his rocker. Everything about Woodbury was
bony, angular, fragile, except for the large round hump of his
back, so high it pushed his head forward, almost making it

seem to grow out of his chest, causing him to have to look up with his eyes when he wanted to stare straight ahead, as he did now, at the field.

The slanting sun fell on Jim's shoulders, onto his knees, onto Woodbury's knees and his slippered feet, onto Cassie's hands in her lap and down her shins, feeling warm through her dark jeans. The field, golden in the late September sun, swept upwards to two walls of woods, one behind the house and the other to the side, beyond the field. Dark evergreens, brightened at intervals with plumes of crimson and yellow and burgundy. The color was nearing its peak. In the field, crickets, their song persistent, but subdued compared to their raucous choruses of a month ago. Somewhere in the woods a chainsaw was howling, discordant and hurried above the steady, languid cricketsong.

Jim explained to his brother, "Cassie and I met at last town meeting."

Cassie said to Woodbury, "I remember what your brother said about development. About land being subdivided and sold for house lots all over town."

Eyes still on the field, Woodbury said, "You see what good it done him to talk about it. Ain't stopped 'em."

"But at least someone—" Cassie began.

Woodbury interrupted, louder, "Talk ain't never slowed 'em up one bit."

"Woodbury's right," Jim said. "As long as Ricker and the rest of them stand to make money cutting up land, one might as well be a voice in the wilderness, for all the good it does to question them."

"Ricker finally got around to drilling our well," Cassie said.

Jim asked, "What'd he charge you? If you don't mind me asking."

"Seven dollars a foot."

Woodbury snorted. "Figures, the bastard. Where are you from, anyway?"

"Massachusetts."

Jim said, "What Woodbury means is that Ricker has one price for people who've been here as long as he has, and another price for people from Massachusetts."

"What's the other price?" Cassie asked.

"Six a foot. Isn't that what Ricker charged Lonnie Vachon's boy, Woodbury?"

"It's what I heard."

Cassie said, "But that day in Mary Ellen's, when we talked about Ricker. Why didn't you tell me then that—"

"I suppose I should have warned you. But it wouldn't have mattered. Ricker's the only well driller for miles around. You needed water and you had no choice but to hire him, whatever his price."

"I'm sure my husband will be glad to hear about this."

"Ricker's not the only one. Ever since land prices started creeping up two, three years ago, just about everybody in Coggerton's has looked for a slice of the pie. There are hardly any exceptions. You see it going on out on Thurlow Hill."

"That's for sure. Skillin's got four trailers and a cellar hole above us, and the last time I went by along the Pickard Cross Road, there were already three trailers on his lots below us there. It seems all we hear is machines going and dogs barking and sometimes even kids and people hollering."

Jim nodded. "And Skillin's not the only one out your way."

"I know. Vernon Thurlow told me the loam he was stripping from the field next to us was for Ricker's lots on this road."

"Ah yes, Vernon. Vernon's dump truck rolls by here all the time, sometimes bringing in loam, sometimes taking out logs Ricker clears off the land before he sells the lots. And Vernon'll probably have a hand in Will's lots, too."

"Will's lots?"

"Will Thurlow, Vernon's father. I thought he already had them surveyed."

"Christ! Where do you mean, Will Thurlow's lots?"

"Why, practically under your nose out there on the hill. Between Thurlows' and that new house just past their field."

"Where Lester Wilkins's boy lives." Woodbury said.

"That's right," Jim said. "Lester, Jr. Last I heard Will Thurlow planned to put in two, maybe three lots between his house and where the Wilkinses live."

"You mean that lovely field, behind their barn, where they keep the sheep?" The first time she walked up the hill to Wilkins' to get eggs, she noticed the stone wall at the back of that field, and how carefully laid up it was.

"Same field," Jim said. "Will used to pasture cattle there because it was handy to the barn."

"Damn!" She bit her lip and blinked back tears, glad she was wearing sunglasses.

Jim leaned toward Cassie, sensing her distress. He patted her arm. "It's happening all over town. And I'm afraid there's not much we can do about it."

"Sonsabitches," Woodbury rasped. "Sonsabitches, out there waitin'."

Jim said, "He means Ricker. Ricker's bought up all the land on three sides of us. Those are his chainsaws you hear in the woods. He's got his crews up in there. They're at it all the time, bulldozing and digging and logging off every tree that's saleable."

"Is that why your brother keeps looking out there, at the woods?"

"Yes. Ricker has us penned in. He's been here half a dozen times, offering to buy us out, but he just doesn't get it. We were born here, Woodbury and I, and we plan to die here."

"Sonsabitches," Woodbury said. "Sonsabitches got roads right up to our property lines. Roads comin' in from everywhere like spokes on a wheel, squeezin' us in the middle."

"They'll have to drag us out of here," Jim said. "There's no other way we're going."

Woodbury lifted his left arm and with an index finger bent with arthritis, he pointed to the corner of the field where the two walls of woods met. "Six generations of Bracketts up in that old buryin' ground. I ain't gonna be the first to lie somewhere else."

Cassie looked to where Woodbury pointed, aware that Jim was watching her.

Beyond the yellow grasses, in the very corner of the field, were stone posts set at intervals. Connecting the posts, two rows of rusting iron rods, just visible through the grasses as the wind blew.

"Your family homesteaded this place."

Jim said, "Everybody that farmed here lies up there. My father, my grandfather. And it goes on, like that."

Woodbury dropped his hand to his lap, straight down, slowly. Then, with effort, he pulled his right hand toward his body and lowered it, robot-fashion, onto his lap. Both hands rested, curled, on his sunken thighs. He looked even smaller, more fragile. He said, "Tell her about the well." He appeared to have only one tooth in his lower jaw, a single spike behind his lower lip.

Jim shrugged. "I suppose there's no way to actually prove that."

A wasp hummed onto the porch, then drifted back out into the sunlight and disappeared over the porch roof. "About a month, almost two months ago now, I drew a pail of water in the kitchen, and I noticed right off the water wasn't right. So I took a sample to Concord for testing, and they found some kind of fuel oil in it. Gasoline, they guessed."

"In your *well*?"

"Gasoline." Their eyes locked. Her breathing quickened. God, what beautiful eyes.

"That well was dug by our great-grandfather. We've never had any trouble with it. Oh, once in a while something crawled in there and died, but we always knew what *that* was, and all we had to do was pour a little bleach into the well, and then wait till the water cleared itself."

"Tasted sweet, the berry pickers always said," Woodbury said.

His eyes still on hers, Jim said, "Woodbury means the blueberry pickers who work the low bushes on the mountain over the next ridge. They come down off the mountain with their jugs and buckets to get water. This well got itself a reputation as having the sweetest water around. Now Concord says there's no guarantee it'll ever be right again."

"Someone poured gasoline down your *well*?"

"Ricker," Woodbury said.

"Of course, we can't prove it. But Woodbury and I are satisfied we know who did it."

"Can't you *do* something? I can't believe it."

"We can't prove it. There's no *way* to prove it. And till it clears—if it ever does—we'll just have to keep hauling water from the fire station over town."

"Jesus."

Woodbury cleared his throat—a swirly, phlegmy sound. "Sonsabitches better not get into the oak piece."

Jim leaned forward in his chair. "Woodbury, Cassie has to leave now." Then, to Cassie, "Woodbury's going to have a little rest now."

Cassie was confused. Had she overstayed her welcome? And what was the oak piece? She could see Ricker in the Bracketts' house, perhaps in the dining room, eyeing the furniture, figuring how much he could get for—she imagined—the Bracketts' oak pedestal table and matching chairs, the rounded-front china cupboard, the sideboard.

"Yes, of course," she said. She stood and placed her hand on Woodbury's forearm, squeezing it gently. Beneath the sweater and flannel shirt, his arm was bony, blade-like. Woodbury turned his head to her. She sensed he was looking up at her, though from where she was standing, leaning over, she couldn't see his eyes. He lifted his right arm and suspended it over her hand. Then, as if he feared hurting her with the nails of his curled fingers, he turned his hand over, and lightly brushed the back of her hand with the back of his hand.

Cassie did not want to let go of his arm. If they could be frozen that way, her hand on his arm, his hand on her hand, perhaps he could rest, could relax his vigilance.

Woodbury moved his hand back to his lap. "You take care now. They'll wear you down for the money they can get."

"Thank you," she whispered. "Goodbye, Mr. Brackett."

Catching up with Jim at the end of the porch, she turned to look back at Woodbury, sunken into his chair. Only his head and hunched back were visible over the arm of the rocker, making him look as if he were resting his chin on the flat arm. The sun was creeping higher up his body now, washing in gold all of him except his head, gray in the shadow of the porch roof.

She followed Jim to the other side of the house. There the land sloped down and away, toward Coggerton. On the porch side the sun had fallen on the weathered clapboards, giving the house texture and warmth. Here, on the shady side, the house looked flat, cold, the field grass dull, lifeless.

All along the slope were trees of an old orchard, run down now, their leafless, twisted gray branches and trunks echoing the gray of the house.

They walked past the old orchard and a row of low sheds connected to the house, extending back from it, dilapidated, sinking, propping one another up. And at the end of the sheds they came to an old foundation. "The barn," Jim said. "Or where the barn used to be."

They stepped onto a top foundation rock, chosen for its flatness along one side in order to take the sill. They stood facing the cellar hole, side by side, almost touching, now looking down into the saplings growing up in it, now looking out across the field, and the woods beyond the field. Cassie's sneakers fit on the rock. The toes of Jim's boots, two brown half-circles, stuck out over the edge of the rock, over the cellar hole.

"The reason I ended things back there with Woodbury was because he started talking about the oak piece, and I couldn't bear to have him talk about it, knowing he'd take it hard if he knew what was really going on up in there."

Her eyes fixed on a rotting beam that stretched from top rock to top rock of the foundation, Cassie nodded, encouraging Jim to continue.

"Up beyond the cemetery, in the farthest corner of our land, is a six-acre piece of land we always called the oak piece. A neat little wedge, walls on all three sides. My grandfather used to take us up into the oak piece and tell us, 'Boys, these oak'll be your retirement some day'. Even then, when we were kids, the oaks were, as my grandfather said, respectable enough, having been there in my great-grandfather's time as well. Of course, Woodbury and I never figured to cut any of that oak, and now some of it's two, three feet across."

A crow flew overhead, cawing; Jim and Cassie looked up, following it as it swept out of sight westward, on the other side of the house.

"Ricker's land comes up to two sides of the oak piece. He's got the oaks surrounded, you might say. Lately, we've been hearing the bulldozers up in there, near that corner of the land. So yesterday morning, before Ricker's men got in there for the day, I went up to the farthest corner of the oak piece."

Cassie inhaled and held her breath, not moving, fixing her eyes on a row of rusted, twisted nails in one of the moss-covered beams.

"And sure enough, they've knocked through the wall up there. Knocked the stones right over, scraping up the forest floor that hasn't been touched for at least a hundred years. Maybe never."

"You mean Ricker's on your property?"

"He's on it all right." Jim brought his hand to his forehead, anchored his thumb on his temple, and rubbed his fingers back and forth, as if soothing out weariness. "Up in the oak piece."

In the foundation, some little animal was scratching around in a tangle of dying raspberry vines, an occasional rustling indicating its whereabouts.

"There must be something you can do. There are laws."

"Laws. Yes, there are laws. I spoke with a lawyer. As far as he can tell, from studying our deed, we own the oak piece, but it's not altogether clear. And to prove we own it, we'd have to get a survey done, and that costs money. Then, we'd likely have to go to court, and even if I were up to that, to fighting Ricker in court, my brother isn't. It would kill him." He shook his head. "So let the bastards have it."

Cassie wanted to reach out, to touch his arm, to pull on his arm and turn him toward her. She wanted him to stretch his arms toward her. To enfold her. It was not sexual desire, she told herself. Or damn, *was* it? She couldn't, *mustn't* allow herself to believe that.

She touched his arm with her fingertips, very lightly. Jim looked down at her, startled.

"I'm sorry," Cassie said. "About Ricker I mean."

Jim turned and started walking back, past the row of sheds, into the shadow of the Cape, and out into the sun by the oak tree. She followed and they stood by the tree together. A truck full of logs rumbled by.

"How old is your brother?" Cassie asked.

"Eighty-nine. Ninety this October twenty-three." And then, as if she'd asked, he said, "Sixty-one my last birthday."

"But the difference—that's quite a—" She stopped, embarrassed to be asking.

"We had different mothers."

Cassie walked around her car and reached in her windbreaker pocket for her keys. Jim followed, standing next to her.

"I have to meet my son at the bus now."

"Yes. Andrew."

He looked as if he didn't want her to go. And she, crazily, wanted to stay, to stay with these two men. After all, other women drop out, disappear. The only difference is, they leave home and husband and security and kids to look for love, for adventure, or to search for identity. But she would leave for none of those things. She would leave home to help Jim take care of Woodbury.

She could help Jim look after things. Could bring a shawl to Woodbury in his rocking chair as October came in crisp, then a blanket to wrap around his legs as it got colder still. And then, a couple of soap stones heated on the woodstove and wrapped in towels, one for under his feet, the other for him to hold in his hands in his lap as he sat there, watching the woods.

She turned to Jim to say goodbye.

Looking down at her, Jim raised his right hand to her face, suspending it next to her cheek. She could almost feel its warmth. If she tipped her head just slightly, his hand would be cradling her face, and she wanted to say, "Yes, *please.*"

But then he dropped his hand, frowning.

She said, "The bus drops Andy off at three-fifteen."

Jim nodded.

She opened the car door and Jim said, "Thank you for coming. It's nice to see you."

Driving down the lane, she looked in her rear view mirror. Jim was still under the oak, watching her go, his hand raised in the attitude of a policeman stopping traffic.

Fourteen

At the kitchen sink, Michael opened and drained a can of tuna, while Cassie scraped the strings from a stalk of celery.

She said, "And they're pretty sure the gasoline was dumped in there by Ricker."

"Can they prove it?"

"Jim said they can't."

"Shit. Poor old duffs."

"They're not duffs."

"You know, if you feel you have to get that involved in other people's business, you might as well spend the day in front of the soap operas. What's *with* you, anyway. Christ, do you get off on old men?"

Cassie slammed the celery stalk and knife on the counter, and went to the kitchen table, her back to him. If Michael looked at her now, could he tell she were blushing? She remembered a line from Milton: "The mind is its own place, and of itself can make a heaven of hell, a hell of heaven." My mind *is* my own place, and he can't get in there. He can't ever know what I'm thinking.

After all, how many times had she told Andy that no one could tell him what to think? If she were to let her mind run free with thoughts of Jim Brackett, Michael would never know. She shut her eyes, remembering the way Jim held his hand next to her face this afternoon, how he almost touched her. Wanted to touch her. There was nothing fatherly in that.

"You sick or something?" Michael asked.

She turned and looked at him. He had both hands on the tuna can and was holding it straight out, over an empty milk carton on the counter, pressing the lid with his thumbs, squeezing out the oil, looking as if he were strangling it. Which was what she would like to do to him right now.

"No. Don't worry yourself." She studied her husband. What would he look like as an old man? He was already losing hair at the crown of his head, the way his father had lost his hair. She had to pick hairs off his pillow when she made the bed each morning. His back was covered with freckles, probably a result of those summers he lay frying in the sun, tanning his studly body. Would he get what her grandmother called "liver spots" all over the back of his hands, which had always been a trifle too thickset to really turn her on? And the way his eyebrows almost met over his nose. Sometimes she thought that made him look like an ape. At sixty-one, Jim Brackett was still gorgeous.

Cut it out! she told herself. She returned to the sink and rubbed the celery stalk under the faucet. "Do you want to hear the rest?"

"Jesus, I thought we were through with that."

"Will you listen, please? They said our friend Ricker charged us a buck more per foot for the well than he charges the locals. We got the rate for the suckers from Massachusetts."

"*What?* That goddamn sonofabitch."

She knew that would get him. He couldn't stand being screwed.

Michael put the tuna on the counter and washed his hands. "That prick."

Cassie chopped the celery. Even if Michael knew the Bracketts, had sat with them as she had this afternoon, he'd still be more concerned about the money than about their poisoned well.

With Andy in school, Cassie established a routine of shopping in Barchester. There was nothing in particular about Barchester to recommend it over Coggerton, except its larger supermarkets and the relative anonymity it offered.

The first week she went to Barchester she'd found a Dunkin' Donuts. She hadn't been to one since she was a kid and lusted after the jelly donuts.

Now, at the Dunkin' Donuts counter, all but knocking elbows with a man on one side, and on the other a fat woman with body odor. She looked around. Was anyone here actually dunking a donut?

Then a gum-chewing waitress in a shiny pink dress was trading her a cup of coffee and a honey-dipped for forty-three cents, plunking the donut on a little sheet of waxy-looking tissue barely large enough to hold the donut. The donut squished flat and chewy between her teeth when she bit it, little flakes of the sugary coating falling onto her jersey, into her coffee, on the counter. She pulled out napkin after napkin from the black and silver holder, trying to contain the mess, to get the goddamn donut under control.

The thick-walled coffee cup looked as if it held more than it actually did, so she miscalculated and dumped in too much sugar, stirring with the tiny wooden paddle.

The way the counter curved around, she was sitting almost opposite a couple of burly, fifty-ish men in green work shirts, swilling coffee and smoking. She felt they were staring at her, noticing the mess she was making. She slid off her stool, leaving half her oversweet coffee and a bit of beat-up donut.

The next week, she explored the center of Barchester, looking for suspenders for a pair of Andy's trousers that flopped down around his narrow hips.

In the town center was a Woolworth's, which looked exactly like the Woolworth's in the town where she grew up, and where, for ten cents, she always bought a root beer float that came in a tall narrow glass with a straw, a long spoon with a round bowl, and a tiny scoop of vanilla ice cream pressed onto the rim of the glass and nestling on top of the root beer foam.

She loved sipping the tingly root beer, taking bits of the tiny scoop of ice cream onto the spoon. When the ice cream began to melt, she mixed the rest of it into the root beer, then finished off the pale brown stuff, always by the spoonful, never sucking it up through the straw. In the Barchester Woolworth's, everything glowed slightly orange, as it did in the Woolworth's of her childhood.

She walked along the familiar creaky wooden floor between two rows of counters, heading for the back of the store. Counters on either side, filled with Pond's face creams, Cutex Nail Polish Remover, Maybelline eye makeup, Cashmere Bouquet Powder. And something she did not remember from the Woolworth's where she grew up: Lashbrite Lush Lash Lash Thickening Sticks and Lashbrite Eye Shadow Sticks, which came in lavender and turquoise cardboard tubes. Then, scarves, a rack of manila envelopes, sorted according to size, two and three-ring notebooks with fake blue linen or maroon phony leather covers. Charles River writing tablets.

The two rows of counters were bisected by an aisle across the middle of the store. Against the ends of the counters were racks of Halloween costumes. A black piece of plastic, shaped like a headless body, with a white skeleton painted on. A cowboy outfit, brown, with stiff fringe. A ballerina costume with a pale blue top, designed for a flat-chested seven-year-old, thin sequined shoulder straps and a skimpy stiff circle of pink net around the hips. Pinned to the waist was a pair of cardboard-soled ballerina slippers and a tiara, a plastic circle of sequins topped with a star.

Cassie read the label on the ballerina costume: "Ballerina. Three Parts. Body Suit. Slippers. Tiara." She pictured Stacey Dalpey stuffing Heather Jo into the ballerina costume, helping her lace up the cardboard slippers, adjusting the sequined straps, bobby-pinning the sparkling tiara into her blond hair. Then, Stacey standing at the door of her mint green house, proudly waving Heather Jo off. And Heather Jo, melting into the night like a transformed Cinderella, dancing, executing leaps and spins, pirouetting and trick-or-treating her way through the dust along the Otis Corner Road.

Cassie passed a counter heaped with Whitman puzzles, one with a thatched-roof cottage and a pond with sheep grazing along its edges. (Does Esther have that one?) Coloring books, plastic bags of olive green soldiers or red and yellow Indians, cardboard cards of dinosaurs under a sheet of stiff see-through plastic molded to cover their bodies exactly as they lay there, trapped, in profile, eight to a card.

Next, a counter divided by glass partitions into compartments for the tiniest things: toy watches, plastic whistles, plastic rings with adjustable backs, tiny plastic boxes containing pairs (black and white) of magnetic Scottie dogs. She'd had a pair of those. Thought they were magic, the way they jumped away from one another if you held them one way, then sucked together with a small snap if you held them another way. She used to wander around the house, finding surfaces to stick them on. Testing, sometimes startled to find a surface that took the dogs, other times puzzled when another she thought should, didn't.

At the back of the store were sets of pink dishes with scalloped edges, shiny silver kitchen utensils, and rows of coffee mugs hanging from a pegboard on the wall.

In the Woolworth's of her childhood, the pet department was at the back of the store. Tanks of guppies, goldfish, angelfish, and smoky-gray fish with bulging eyes. Cages with hamsters hiding among the wood shavings. Hanging cages with parakeets, blue. Flea collars, rubber dog bones, catnip, and boxes of Hartz Mountain Bird Seed.

She walked along the back of the store, then headed up the side aisle to the lunch counter, with its round, backless stools. She sat, wedging her purse between her stomach and the chrome lip of the counter.

There were only two other people at the counter. Four seats

away, an old woman in a long gray overcoat and orange stockings, hunched over the counter. Her white hair, fastened by a red barrette over her ear, hung in thin wisps to her shoulders. Cassie, warm in her windbreaker and jersey, wondered how the woman could stand it in her winter overcoat, buttoned to the neck.

A couple of seats past the old woman slouched a ruddy-faced man with sunken lips, a red and black woolen hunting cap on his head, the visor tipped up. Though the two were facing straight ahead, they apparently knew one another, for they were talking in low tones.

The countertop was black Formica—shiny and scratched, with here and there a few jagged streaks of gray, imitating marble. In front of Cassie was a glass case with a six-tiered metal rack. On one shelf a lemon-meringue pie, two-thirds gone. On another, a squash pie, sectioned in six even pieces. The other four shelves were empty.

"May I help you?" the waitress asked, smiling, pencil poised over a tiny yellow pad. (The waitress in Dunkin' Donuts hadn't asked, "May I help you?" She had just stood there, not smiling, waiting for Cassie to say what she wanted, speaking only when she brought the donut and coffee. "Forty-three cents.")

"Coffee, please. And what do you have for donuts?"

The waitress pointed with the eraser of her pencil to a round glass dome covering a plate of plain donuts on a chrome pedestal. "Those are what we have."

"Oh. And who makes them?"

"Bakery upstreet. Blanchard's. Made fresh every day."

"One of those then, too, please, thanks."

Cassie was enjoying herself, enjoying being polite. Enjoying the pleases, the thankyous. Looking at the old woman in the gray overcoat, and the polite waitress behind the counter, hearing the wooden floor creaking behind her, she fancied herself in a world of shabby gentility, where people, no matter how down and out, maintained their dignity and respected one another. Where they exercised manners.

The waitress wrote on her pad, tucked it into the pocket of her white uniform, took a small plate from a stack on the counter behind her, lifted the glass dome and with a napkin, took out a donut. She put it before Cassie, who said, "Thank you."

"You're welcome." The waitress poured coffee from a round Silex pot and brought it to Cassie, reached into a small refrigerator below the sandwich counter and brought Cassie a tiny tub of Half 'n Half.

Cassie smiled up at her. "Thank you."

"You're welcome." The waitress fished in her pocket for her pad. "Will that be all?"

"Yes, thank you." Was she going a little heavy on the thankyous? Would the waitress think her insincere?

The waitress fished out her pad, tore off the page and placed it, face down, a few inches from Cassie's coffee. "Thank you," she said, smiling.

"Thank *you*," Cassie said again, unable, it seemed, to stop herself. She pictured herself saying "Thank you" as she broke the donut in half, "Thank you" as she stirred the sugar and Half 'n Half into the coffee, "Thank you" after each sip of coffee.

She studied the pictures of menu offerings tacked up on the wall behind the waitress. A picture of a golden-toasted sandwich, potato chips on the side, and one slice of ruffled pickle. "Grilled Cheese. Everybody's Favorite. $1.20." Another of an open-faced sandwich showing a hamburger, bacon, lettuce and tomato on a bun with chips and two ruffled pickle slices on the side. "Baconburger. $1.55." Then, "Shrimp Basket. $1.88," and a photo of a wedge of pie with a swirl of aerated cream on top. "Pumpkin Pie. $.45."

The waitress put another cup of coffee in front of the woman in the gray coat.

"I don't generally drink two cups," the woman said.

"I know you don't," the waitress said.

"It gives me indigestion if I ain't careful."

The waitress nodded.

"Don't know whether it's the coffee or the donuts."

"Uh huh," the waitress said, writing on her pad.

Then, raising her voice, the woman said, "Got to be at the Trailways terminal pretty soon. My Dorothy's gonna be on that bus, you know."

The man said, "Today's the day she comes, is it."

The woman nodded. "This time she's gonna stay over. Long enough to see Stanley and Madelyn."

"That's nice."

The waitress rang up "20" on the wooden cash register, then began to wash dishes, sliding into the steel sink cups and saucers and spoons which clinked softly as they disappeared down in the suds.

As she ate the last bit of her donut (Now *there's* a donut: firm, neat to eat, brown on the outside, yellow on the inside), and was finishing her coffee, Cassie watched the waitress, bent over the sink, the sleeves of her turquoise sweater pushed up past her elbows. White uniform, white shoes, white pop-bead earrings, short red-brown hair, gray wing-framed sequined eyeglasses. Pink lipstick. Rouge. Thin.

Cassie wondered how old she was, and where she lived, what she did when she wasn't working. Maybe she had a husband on the night shift at one of the shoe shops. Couple of kids, maybe high-schoolers, who don't appreciate the sacrifices their mother makes for them.

Cassie recalled how good she was at jerking sodas and making lunches in the local drugstore when she was in high school in the fifties. Getting so good at the cash register she knew instantly that two packs of regular cigarettes at twenty-seven cents apiece came to fifty-four cents, and two twenty-eight-cent king-size filtertips came to fifty-six cents. She remembered how tedious the drugstore work had become after three years.

She pictured this Woolworth's lunch counter from outside the store, through a plate glass window. Only a few people at the counter, backs to the window, staring straight ahead, like the woman in the coat and her friend several stools away. Like the people in Edward Hopper's painting, *Nighthawks*. Lonely people drinking coffee late at night in a corner drugstore.

Maybe the people who frequented Woolworth's are the Nighthawks of Barchester, who shun the cheek-by-jowl clatter and coldness of Dunkin' Donuts for the slower pace of Woolworth's, where manners still counted, and donuts still come on a plate and coffee in cups on saucers, and the donuts are firm, real, plain. And where, for only a coffee and a donut you get a tiny bill passed to you quietly, face down, just as if you were at the Ritz.

Maybe she would become a Barchester Nighthawk. Would come here once a week when she shopped, regularly, until the waitress recognized her and without asking, would automatically bring her coffee and a plain donut. No words would have to pass between them. Or she might come with Jim. The two of them sitting quietly at the end of the counter. Perhaps now and then they could bring Woodbury. She and Jim, one on each side of him, would lead him to the counter, where all three of them would receive the accepting smiles and nods of the rest of the Nighthawks, who would honor Woodbury, this elder among them.

She would tell no one, not Michael, not Andy. She would come to Woolworth's alone, or with the Bracketts, in communion with all the other Nighthawks. Her other life.

Fifteen

Cassie sat on the front step, looking out at the Wilmot Falls hills through the branches of the maple trees, bare now in early November except for a few rusty leaves which clung tenaciously, scratching and rustling against the gray branches and against one another when light breezes stirred them. The day was warm for November, reminding Cassie of an April day that had the warmth of summer to it. She had sat on this same step and watched Andy on his rope swing. The brook raucous, a partridge drumming.

Over the summer she had read to Andy Frances Hodgson Burnett's *The Secret Garden*, which she had loved and which Andy had liked well enough, once he accepted the fact that there were no villains to spice things up. Upon encountering Mrs. Medlock, who prowled the dark corridors of Misselthwaite Manor, refusing to answer Mistress Mary's questions about strange goings-on in the place, Andy—supersleuth hot on the trail of something big—said, "I think this Mrs. Medlock is acting might-y sus-pi-cious! We better keep an eye on her!"

Cassie had to keep explaining, "Well, it's not *that* kind of story, Andy. There aren't necessarily any good guys or bad guys. It's about gardens and secrets and growing things and a mysterious boy who's shut way off in another part of the huge house."

Now, on this still November day, she remembered that spring day in April, when, like the spring described in *The Secret Garden* over and over again, everything was coming to life. How did Burnett put it? Green spikes coming up everywhere through the earth. Things underground crowding one another out, scrabbling to push up out of the ground to get their share of light and sun and warmth. And, oh yes, a pale green mist spreading over everything. Burnett could have been writing about springtime on the old Gilman place in Coggerton.

Except for a hound dog baying at Christ knows what on the Pickard Cross Road, and a belated cricket which chirped from somewhere and from everywhere in the brown grasses of the field, this day in November was silent. Summer had packed it in.

On the power line which ran through the field, clutches of birds sat motionless except when now and then one would sidestep a few inches, as if to re-establish its balance, or perhaps to cozy up to the rest. Dark chunky outlines. Starlings.

A week ago a gang of robins — more than she'd seen together since the spring — landed on the lawn, hopping around, silent except for occasional nervous clucking. She wished she could fly south with them, could slip across the lawn into their company, her fingers tucked into her armpits, ready to flap her arms as the robins took flight. Autumn wanderlust, tinged with melancholy.

Now, the starlings on the wire. Must be fifty or more, conferring, planning departure times, flight patterns. A snatch of Handel's *Messiah* came to her, sung, urgently, by the bass: "The kings of the earth rise up, and the rulers take counsel together ..." That's what those starlings are doing, and the robins before them. Taking counsel together.

In a way she was glad summer was over. Until the first killing frost, it seemed the garden wouldn't quit. The tomatoes kept coming, and she kept canning. Just when she'd say, for the hundredth time, "Okay, that's it. I'm all done," she would hear about imminent, maybe catastrophic food shortages, and she'd harvest yet another batch of tomatoes.

By mid-August the garden had grown so lush she felt almost threatened by it. The winter squashes grew, their foliage a yard-high canopy of giant leaves on enormous, hairy, hollow stems — a tropical rain forest. She told Andy that the gentle Tasaday lived out there, under that great green tent of squash leaves, and if he looked really hard, he might see the smoke of their campfires curling up above the leafy roof. "There!" she would say, pointing. "There! Did you *see* it? Wasn't that a wisp of smoke coming up there?!"

Andy, not convinced, but wanting to believe, would circle the garden, edging up to the squash patch, peering in, leaning on his knees to see just under the leaf canopy, moving his head this way and that, never too close, always ready to pull back, to run, should there actually be any sign of life there. A few times he asked Cassie, "Are they *really* under there, the Tasaday?"

"What do you think?"

"*Really*, Mum!"

"Well, it's *exactly* the kind of place the Tasaday like to live in the jungle. And of course, those wisps of smoke ..."

And Andy would trot off, still neither convinced, nor quite disbelieving.

The foliage of October had been dazzling, but she preferred the softness of this time. Brown grasses, gray trees, gray stone walls. The distant hills already had about them a hint of the purple haze of winter. And though the day was warm for November, it had—unlike that day in April when she watched Andy on his rope swing, and listened to the brook sing and the partridge drum—no promise of increasing warmth in days to come.

Under the maple trees, leaves were ankle high. She thought of the Bracketts. Was Woodbury on the porch, watching the woods? Sitting there, huddled against the cold, eddies of dead leaves swirling up on the porch, settling by his feet, and under his rocker. Then, snow falling, covering him, the first big flakes landing atop his head, his thin thighs, in the valleys between his knuckles, filling the creases of his clothing. Smoothing over all the harsh angles of his body, covering his slippered feet, molding and forming itself to his body. Falling and covering, until only a soft outline of the man is there, a still white form against the white field beyond.

The dog on the Pickard Cross Road was howling again, and from the same direction came the racket of hammering, hollow-sounding in the still air, louder than it might have been a month ago, when there was foliage to muffle it. The hammering was coming from one of Skillin's lots below them. By the middle of October, all the lots but the eighth one had been sold, and as each lot was sold, a trailer sprung up on it.

Thurlows' sheep had been moved out of the pasture beyond the barn and enclosed in a small area behind the house, between the barn and the purple car Esther had been sitting on, shooting birds.

Along the road past the Thurlows' barn, red surveyor's tape marked off three house lots, carving up the pasture, ending forever the possibility of that particular field being used for farmland again. Red tape: red for rape. For prostitution, for blood money, for the Thurlows and Skillins and Rickers and the rest all selling their souls.

She hardly ever saw or spoke with Emma these days. Once she'd met her at the mailbox and Emma had told her they were selling a few lots.

"Course," Emma had explained, "I've always said to Will, I don't really mind what he sells as long's I don't have to see it from my kitchen window." And Emma wouldn't see the lots, and the trailers that would surely go on them, because the barn stood between them and her house.

Cassie had said nothing, and Emma, unable to bear any stretches of silence in the conversation, continued, "Well, we figured we just *had* to sell a few lots, taxes bein' what they are. And of course, we don't *need* all this land, and neither Vern nor Esther's husband, Gordon, wants to farm it. And it's just like Will says, we've struggled so long, we deserve to be comfortable in our last years."

Cassie had sensed that Emma wanted her approval, but probably didn't expect it, since Cassie had so often complained about Skillin and Ricker. But she also knew that Emma was telling her what they were going to do no matter what anyone said or thought. Cassie had learned that everyone in the neighborhood, probably in the whole town, believed that a person has the right to do whatever he wants with his own property. So if all the people felt that way — especially all the people who had lived here for generations — who cared what some outsider thought? Especially an outsider who'd been here less than a year.

So she had nothing to say to Emma that day at the mailbox, and had they not been neighbors, and had Emma not shown her certain courtesies, Cassie might have walked away without waiting for Emma to explain about the lots.

One of Thurlows' lots already showed signs of activity. The stone wall along the road had been bulldozed down to make room for a driveway, a culvert had been laid in the ditch along the road, and gravel had been dumped in the driveway and run over with a truck.

The hound had stopped howling, and now Cassie heard only the cricket and the hammering on the Pickard Cross Road, a curious combination.

She pulled herself up off the step because it was time to meet Andy at the bus. She headed up the lane, aware, as she walked, that her footsteps fell as the hammer fell, as if her feet were marching in time with it. She quickened her pace enough to be out of step, though the effort of doing so only made her more conscious of the hammering.

Thurlows' field to her left glowed, backlit by the low autumn sun. On her right, the wild apple trees of the old orchard were bare except for a few apples and yellow leaves.

Woodbury Brackett. There could be worse ways to die than being buried in snow, a long gentle snow that fills in all the spaces, smoothing the rough spots, chilling the man, numbing his body into the burning warmth of frostbite, and finally freezing his heart into slowing, slowing, stopping.

Sixteen

Snow held off until after hunting season, making it less easy for the hunters to track the deer. For the first three weeks of November, Cassie stayed out of the woods, going only as far as the clothesline beyond the well rock, wearing Michael's red windbreaker, hanging up clothes nervously, quickly, keeping her back to the house, her eyes on the woods. The day after hunting season ended, the woods were silent again, and by the end of the day, thick, low-hanging gray clouds had choked the sky.

The snow began the next day, after Cassie walked Andy to the school bus. Throughout the day, Cassie wandered from room to room, watching the snow pile up on the brown lawn and the garden, the well rock, the tops of the clothesline poles. In the woods, it transformed what had been a tangle of pines, bare hardwoods, dying brushy undergrowth, and fallen leaves, into a clean, uncluttered palette of black, white and gray.

When she went to meet the school bus that afternoon, Andy was already half way down the lane. Snowflakes drifted down in front of her face, dissolving in the distance into a gray-white curtain surrounding Andy, whose ruddy cheeks matched his brick-orange snowsuit which in turn echoed the few shriveled red-brown apples still clinging to the branches that arched, with their fresh veneer of snow, over the lane. The air was silent: no crack of hunters' rifles, no dogs barking, no chain-saws, no locals drag-racing up and down Thurlow Hill, no bulldozers knocking down stone walls and spreading gravel.

By late evening the snow stopped, the sky cleared and a three-quarter moon appeared halfway up the sky, illuminating the snow. Before going to bed, Cassie turned off the last light and stood in the kitchen, looking out across the snow, able to see all the way to the end of the field. A great smooth unbroken snow-sea stretching to a wall of trees dark against the blue-black sky.

❀   ❀   ❀

Sucked out of the fuzziness of sleep, Cassie squinted at the clock on the table beside the bed. One-thirty. Who the hell could be running a chainsaw at this unearthly hour? She lay there, listening. Then she realized: snowmobiles.

She tugged at the covers. "Michael? Michael!"

"Unph?"

"Listen to *that*. Snowmobiles. One-thirty in the morning and they're out riding around on snowmobiles."

Michael rose up on his elbow, lit by the moonlight that fell on him in rectangles from the six over six window at the head of the bed. "Is that what that is?"

"Listen!"

Michael sat up, as if in doing so he could hear better. "Where are they?"

"Sounds like Thurlows' field."

"The one right next to us?" He flipped back the covers and padded across the floor to the window. "Can't see anything from here. Let's go upstairs."

From the attic window, through the tops of the row of trees that ran along the stone wall separating their land from Thurlows' field, they watched lights moving in the field — detached, eerie, streaking to the side, flickering behind the trees, then disappearing, as the invisible snowmobiles dipped into one of several low spots of the field. The air was filled, the house invaded, by the drone—now steady, now a hysterical, high-pitched whine.

"Jeez," Michael said. "Those things really move."

Damn, he's enjoying this.

In bed again, they lay on their backs, listening.

Michael said, "Wouldn't Andy be bullshit about those things."

"You mean, wouldn't *you* love one. You like that racket?"

"Jesus. You expect dead silence all the time?" He rolled over, his back to her. "Why the hell are you always squawking about people having a little fun. God."

Cassie seethed. Fucking redneck.

The next day, as she was swiping snow from the mailbox, the drone of snowmobiles, muffled at first, became a roar as two of them appeared over the crest of the hill, their bullet noses pointed toward Cassie, swaying up and down on their front ski-runners.

Just as she was thinking they didn't see her, would run over her, or at the very least, chase her up onto the bank of snow the plow had pushed to the side of the road, they slowed. One of the snowmobiles was much smaller than the other, and on its black nose was written, in silver letters arranged in a hot pink triangle, "Kitty Cat." Under a chartreuse ski cap emblazoned with "Arctic Cat," was the brown, grinning face of little Jimmy Fecteau.

With a flourish, aware Cassie was watching, Jimmy turned the hand grips of the snowmobile, his elbows bouncing up and down. The Kitty Cat slowed to a purr and deftly, the boy nosed the machine over the snow bank into Thurlows' yard, his head turned toward Cassie, his foolish grin cocky.

Behind little Jimmy came the big one, blue-black, with "Arctic Cat" on the front and "el Tigre" on the side.

The man, in a puffy black snowmobile suit, a black crash helmet, and amber goggles, had one knee up on the seat. He nosed "el Tigre" onto the snow bank, twisting the handgrips. The beast gave a sudden lurch and charged up over the bank, its nose slanted, suspended out over the other side of the bank while its rear track crawled to catch up. The front tipped down, its ski runners slapping onto the driveway on the other side of the bank. For just a moment the thing seemed stuck, its rear end grinding away on the bank. But the man gave a few more twists of the hand grips and the thing was freed, and after a few left-to-right wiggles of its butt, it was off, up the driveway.

Cassie figured he must be Peter Fecteau, Midge's husband. Midge of the many men. Generous Peter, who gave all her kids his name. And the way he twisted the handgrips of the snowmobile, and how by doing so he could make the thing speed up, slow down, she wondered if that explained his success with Midge, whom at one time no man, or legions of men, could satisfy. Maybe Peter mounts Midge the way he mounts his snowmobile, twisting her nipples and revving her up the way he revs up his metal steed.

As the winter months passed, Cassie got used to the snow-mobiles, though she hated them. She lay awake listening, cursing, plotting ways to do in the bastards who rode them. She would give them all presents of long trailing scarves with the macho names of their snowmobiles knitted right in — el Tigre, Brut, Superstinger, Whip, Ski-doo TNT, Big John Cyclone, Cheetah — scarves that would catch in the tracks of the snowmobiles and strangle their wearers to death, the Isadora Duncans of the snow belt. Or she would set up competitions which featured daredevil stunts like twenty-foot snow banks to hurdle. Contests designed to crush the spines of anyone dumb enough to enter them.

The snowmobiles were just one more thing thrown at her. There was nothing she could do about the dogs, there was no one who cared about the scum on the brook. Even Michael didn't seem overly upset about the trailers as long as, like Emma, he couldn't see the things surrounding them, squeezing them all around. And if she didn't bitch so about the snowmobiles he would probably have one himself.

Cassie had asked Emma if it was necessary for the snow-mobilers to use the field next to them.

Emma had replied, "Well, it's an awful good place to ride. So handy to the barn, where Will works on the machines. And everybody has such fun on them."

"But that field is only about three hundred feet from our house. Couldn't they ride around on your side of the road?"

"Well, not really. We used to ride some in the sheep pasture, but now we've sold that land, it wouldn't hardly be right to ski-doo around on that now, would it?"

"But you've got 350 acres up behind you. Why does it have to be this field right here?"

"Well Cassie, we've always used that field for Ski-dooin'. Anyway, seems to me you oughtn't object to folks havin' a good time."

One day Stacey Dalpey called. "Wanna go snowmobilin'?"

"No thanks." Hadn't word got around how she felt about the things?

"We have a great time. Last year we started a club, The Cog-gerton Cadets. My Earl's president. We meet twice a month in a clubhouse some of us girls fixed up on the mountain road. We cut a trail going right to the top of Jackaway Mountain, and when you get to the top you can see all the way to Bourne. That's thirty miles away. Next year the club's gonna get a groomer in—"

"Groomer?"

"Yeah. It's this real neat machine cuts a eight-foot trail and smooths over the bumps too. The club's gonna hire it to cut trails from our clubhouse to the other clubhouses around. We're gonna be able to get on our machines at night and pick up riders in Marston Corners and all of us'll go together all the way to Hollett. They got a real nice log cabin clubhouse over to Hollett. They call it the Warmin' Hut and they always got a pot of coffee on. Sometimes they get as many as thirty-five, forty machines there a night."

Cassie pictured it: a big fluorescent yard light high up on a pole in the yard, shining down blue on the snow, matted down and packed hard from snowmobiles coming and going. Snowmobiles lined up like horses at a hitching rail, riders on some of them, adjusting their clothing, fiddling with something on their machines, calling out to one another, their breaths blue clouds. Teenagers, flirting. Girls doing their best to look alluring in their puffy suits. And the fellas, their goggles pulled rakishly up onto the tops of their helmets. Kneeling up on the seats of their snowmobiles, towering above the girls, revving their machines—vrum vrum varoooom—twisting, twisting as they yell above the din of idling machines, and machines coming and going, roaring at full tilt.

Inside the Warmin' Hut, a big aluminum coffee urn on a makeshift plywood counter littered with styrofoam cups, sugar packets torn open, sugar spills and coffee rings, and one common white plastic spoon for stirring. A juke box grinding out country and western music. Couples coming and going, stamping their fat-booted feet on the square of bright green indoor-outdoor carpet just inside the door. Couples flirting, fumbling for each other's waists and knees under the puffy suits. On the log walls of the Warmin' Hut, carved hearts with lovers' initials. And there, painstakingly-carved: "The Coggerton Cadets. Jan 1976."

Then Stacey was saying, "We took Jason and Jonathan— my twins—out the other night for the first time, and weren't they crazy about it, though! Bet your little boy'd love it."

Probably he would, Cassie thought.

"Want us to come ovah some night on our machines?"

"No!"

Stacey chirped, "Nevah know if you like it till you try it."

"Oh yes, yes I do know. And I can tell you right now, I not

only hate every goddamn snowmobile, but if any come onto our land, I'll shoot the bastards."

"What?"

"That's right. Shoot. And as a matter of fact, the lane in here is mined."

"Mine? Whadaya mean, mine?"

" 'Mined'. I said. I said 'mined'. Which means if I see a snowmobile coming down our lane onto our property, I press this little button right by the window here, and then that snowmobile'll get blown right the hell up to smithereens."

"Oh. Well. Well ah, well all I got to say is if — I mean, if you don't bother us, we — I mean, I guess everybody's got a right to their own opinion."

"You're absolutely right about that, Stacey. Goodbye." Fuck Stacey Dalpey and fuck her neat mint-green house and fuck her neat Barbie doll daughters and fuck her neat snowmobiles.

Seventeen

Cassie parked the car on Main Hill, locked it, flipped up her jacket hood and walked down the hill toward the town hall.

A year ago, when she and Michael, shy newcomers, had waited inside the foyer for the meeting to begin, she saw the people streaming in as sturdy, hard-working, plain-speaking country folk. True-blue yankees, salt of the earth. Now, bitter, she saw them another way. Saw them as having climbed down out of the trees, lumbering out of the alleyways between the drab wooden buildings downtown, talking gibberish, bananas in hand, knuckles dragging on the sidewalks.

This year Emma had not offered to babysit, and of course, Cassie wouldn't have asked her to. And since Cassie knew no one else she considered reliable, it was decided that Michael would stay home with Andy.

Inside the hall, she pulled back her hood and unzipped her jacket, feeling none of the pleasant anticipation she'd felt last year, about to experience her first New England town meeting, a meeting of people gathered together to decide their own destiny in the true spirit of democracy.

She was not sure why she'd come here tonight. She expected nothing, hoping only that there might prove to be something, someone, that might suggest their coming to Coggerton wasn't the dreadful mistake she'd come to think it was.

Just inside the hall, a boy was passing out flyers. Under his baseball cap, his hair stuck out in fuzzy red-brown clumps over his jug-ears. Bozo the Clown. His thick, round, rimless eyeglasses magnified his eyes, making them look blurry and distorted. Cassie took a flyer he held out. Grimy stubby fingers, chewed nails. He smelled like a kid who'd been sweating, rolling in dirt, put to bed unwashed only to get up to sweat and grub in the mud again the next day, and the next.

Cassie sat on the top row of the bleachers along the side wall and read the flyer: "IF YOU VOTE FOR ZONING, YOU LOOSE YOUR FREEDOM!!" She searched the hall for Jim. The last time she had seen him was in November when she had driven out to his house with a jar of tomato soup she'd made.

She had walked along the porch, surprised — disappointed — to see that Woodbury was not in his rocker, watching the woods.

At her knock, Jim opened the kitchen door, his electric-blue eyes meeting hers.

She handed him the soup. "It's kind of like V-8 juice, but better, I think."

"How nice. Thank you." He stepped out and took the soup from her.

"Your brother—?"

"He's doing poorly."

"I'm sorry to hear." Then, "Well, I won't keep you, I just—"

"Cassie."

"Yes?" There was an urgency in his tone that made her heart skip.

"Perhaps if things had been different—for you—for all of us."

"But why—why can't—"

He set the soup on the porch, reached out, cradling her face in his hands. For a long moment, he stared at her, saying nothing. Then, "We both know why."

Despite her efforts not to cry, tears welled.

He drew her toward him, enfolding her. He smelled faintly of wood smoke.

She said, "But things can change. They already have changed for me."

"No, dear." He released her and held her at arm's length, hands on her shoulders. "It will be all right. You have your life ahead of you. You have your son. Besides, you don't want to be saddled with an old man—and his even older brother."

"I don't think about that. I don't care about that. I don't—"

"Shh. It will be all right."

But she knew it wouldn't be.

After, driving down Bracketts' lane, she saw, in her rear-view mirror, blue-gray smoke drifting out of the chimney against the pale November sky. She had not seen him since that day.

Emma Thurlow had told her that people "Mainly keep pretty much to themselves in the dead of winter." She was right. Cassie hardly went anywhere herself since the first snow, and now she wondered if it were so with Jim, if he, too, had spent much of the winter at home.

Judge Parker, the moderator, was opening the meeting, and as she watched him do his odd little shuffle and deep knee bends, dipping down, left to right, peering out over his glasses as if peering under a fence, or perhaps peeping under someone's Venetian blinds, it seemed impossible that a whole year had passed since the last town meeting.

"Article One," Judge Parker said, reading from the warrant. "To see if the town will vote to authorize the see-lect-men to appoint a planning board to consider a zoning ordinance for the town of Coggerton. Roger, would you explain this one?"

At the front of the hall, Roger Stiles straightened his back and inhaled. "This article was put in the warrant by petition. Few folks got together and thought perhaps Coggerton ought to have some kinda zoning regulation." His good-natured smile suggested that since this is a free country, a free town, a democracy, people are entitled to have their say, however foolish their ideas.

Judge Parker said, "Perhaps one of the sponsors of the article would like to explain why they petitioned to have this put in the warrant." He looked around the hall, smiling.

The people rustled, turning their heads, waiting expectantly for one of the petitioners to stand up. Cassie got the feeling that if one did stand up, the crowd would be upon him, would lynch the fool, or tar and feather him.

"Here, Mr. Moderator." At the rear of the hall, standing, a tall, brown-haired woman, in a Black Watch tartan jacket and a white ruffled blouse. She spoke with confidence, hands by her side. "My name is Susan Oakley. My family and I came to Coggerton two years ago, and we have grown to like this town, but some of the things we came here for are disappearing. With all the development going on all over town, we petitioners think it would be to our advantage if Coggerton had a simple ordinance, one that would preserve what rural beauty we have left while maintaining the value of our properties."

From the way the woman pronounced her r's, Cassie figured she must be from New Jersey, or New York. An outsider.

People stared at her, letting her have her say. But it was clear they were also regarding her with a degree of suspicion, perhaps thinking her a bit haughty, a bit too urbane, to be telling them what to do.

Undaunted, Susan continued, "The time has come when we can no longer say, 'It's my property and I can do what I want with it.' We have to consider the rights of others, the rights of our neighbors, and what's good for the community as a whole."

From somewhere in the bleachers a man yelled, "Nobody tellin' *me* what to do with my property. An' anybody who don't like it can just go back where they come from!"

There was scattered chortling throughout the hall. Susan stared in the direction of the bleachers, looked down at someone next to her, shook her head, and sat down.

The man clambered to the floor with such force that Cassie felt the bleachers rumble beneath her. Big and burly, the man wore a knit cap, a dark brown crewneck sweater, too short in the sleeves and stretched tight above his hairy pot belly. Grimy work pants hung low on his hips, baggy in the seat and crotch.

He was bow-legged and hipless, like one of Andy's plastic cowboys fashioned to sit atop a plastic horse. He stomped toward Judge Parker, stopping several feet in front of him, asking, "What I want to know is what's gonna be next if we allow in this zoning thing? I ask you that!" He snapped his head up and down, challenging the moderator to answer his thorny question.

Parker nodded. "Thank you, Rod."

Around the hall people nodded their heads, murmuring in agreement. The man turned to face the people and, emboldened, said, "The way I see it, we let some outsider put in this zoning thing and next thing we're gonna see is them big shots in the govament ovah t' Concord tellin' us what kinda houses to build, or how we hafta raise owah kids. And seems to me, once them fat-cat people from the govament get nosin' around in owah business, why we might's well just invite in the Commies and let *them* take ovah. My feelin' is, we been gettin' along just fine here in Coggerton for almost two hunnert years, and I bet we can make it just fine through the next two hunnert if all these interferin' guardian angels'd just quit takin' it upon theirselves to keep watchin' over us, tellin' us how to run our affayahs." He stuck out his lower lip, nodding, indicating he was finished.

There was a brief moment of silence, as the people let the sense of his words—the brilliance—sink in. People began to clap, and within seconds the applause had spread throughout the hall. How lucky Coggerton was to have such a champion of freedom—someone who spoke their language—not that fancy woman with her highfalutin ways, coming into Coggerton, trying to tell people what to do with their property.

The man lumbered up the bleachers, crashing back down onto his flat bottom. Cassie caught a whiff of cow manure. A greasy-haired teenage boy grinned at the man and clapped him on the back. "Way to go, Rod!"

Cassie again searched the hall for Jim Brackett, but didn't

see him. She did spot Ricker and his son, Erlon. How alike they looked. Both had fleshy lips and bulbous noses. The only difference was that while Myron was gray-faced, his son's face was florid, as if in coming into existence he had had sucked up all the health, the color, from the father. As if there were only one body's worth of blood between the two of them, and the son had gotten it all.

Parker called for the vote, not a single hand in the hall was raised in favor of the zoning article, and Susan Oakley left the hall, likely recognizing the futility of her petition.

Cassie skimmed the twenty-two articles in the warrant. Most looked much like last year's articles about moneys to be raised for the fire and police departments and the ambulance corps, articles about street-lighting and street signs needing replacement, and new paint for crosswalks in the downtown area. There was article she didn't understand about revenue sharing, an article about a new sewer system and an article about the town dump. Nothing she needed to know about.

In need of a toilet, Cassie left the hall and followed the sign saying "Beano" and "Rest Rooms" down the stairs into the basement.

At the foot of the stairs, in a brightly-lit office, a man was talking, his voice loud above the garbled scratchy voices coming from some kind of radio. Curious, she stepped across the hall and looked in. Police Chief Paulin was talking on the telephone in front of a gray box from which were coming the garbled voices.

Seeing her, Paulin raised his eyebrows in question. Cassie pointed at the door marked "Ladies."

When she came out of the ladies room, Paulin was in the doorway, his blue shirt cool against the bright white light of the office behind him.

Had he been standing there all the time she was in the toilet, listening, wondering why she was in there so long?

And after she goes back upstairs, will he go into the Ladies' room, inspect the sink, the stalls, to see if she'd vandalized the place — ripped the toilet paper holder from the wall, carved graffiti in the oak stall, smeared obscenities in lipstick all over the mirror?

"Mrs. Atwood, how're things out your way?"

"I guess they could be better. But how do you know my name? We've never met."

Paulin laughed. "In a town the size o' Coggerton, ain't hardly no one I don't know. Everybody knows everybody else, and everybody else's business, too. Should think you've lived here long enough to find that out."

"Yes, of course. I remember you from last year's town meeting, when you tried to get more money for the Police Department."

"Ah. So you saw that, did you. Same every year. Never enough money to run the department the way it oughta be run. Don't know why I should bother about this town, 'cept I was born here and I hate to leave. But this town, you know what they did?"

"What?"

"A while back about fifteen of 'em, fifteen of the worst punks in town, got together a petition. They took it to Judge Parker, not that *he* coulda done anything with it. But you know what that petition said? It said town oughta cut back the Police Department to the chief and his assistant. Do away with all the specials, is what those punks wanted to do."

"Why?"

"Why? Because it was the town's best special, Ernie Levesque, who kicked a bunch of them punks off the library steps a couple months back. They decided they owned the library and took it over, drinkin' and tossin' the cans everywhere, swearin' and bad-mouthin' everybody what walked by." He shook his head. "And the town's growin', spreadin' out everywhere, and those fools up there" — he swept his hand up the stairway, indicating the people at the meeting—"every year wantin' to cut the police budget."

"Oh brother!"

"Things okay out your way?"

"Well, I don't know of any trouble out there. But there are a lot of houses going in, and noise—dogs barking all the time—so it's not exactly like living in the country anymore."

"You got locks on your doors?"

"Yes."

"Good. 'Cause there's been some things goin' on out your way lately."

"Like what."

"Well, one thing, anyway. Ovah beyond you, up the Otis Corner Road, just before you come to Pig Pen Corner in Marston Corners?"

"Yeah."

"You know that old white Cape just this side the Marston Corners line? The one the summer people from Connecticut come to on weekends?"

"Yes." Whenever she had driven by the lovely old Cape it had looked empty, though the lawn was always mowed.

"Week and a half ago, that place got broke into. They cleaned out the place, then stove up the place somethin' terrible. Cut up mattresses, busted glass all over the place, and even left messes on the floor, just like dogs."

"Jesus."

"Just plain mean punks is what they are. Always seems it's the summer people or new people they go after."

"Do they know who did it?"

"I got a pretty good idea. Course, I can't prove it enough for Judge Parker's satisfaction. *He* takes the attitude you gotta catch 'em red-handed, with fifty witnesses lookin' on. Even then, he'd likely give the punks suspended sentences. They don't call him Suspended Sentence Parker for nothin'. I'll just give you a piece of advice, Mrs. Atwood."

"Please."

"You keep your eye on those Steadbacks out your way."

"Steadbacks? You mean the ones in the cellar hole?"

"You got it. Ain't hardly a week goes by we don't have some trouble with them. Always some of the older ones runnin' up and down the hill in unregistered vehicles, or vehicles with bald tires, most of the time drunker 'n skunks."

"Can't the town *do* something about that? About them?"

"Just what do you think I been tellin' you? This town don't *want* to do nothin' about people the likes of Steadbacks. Half of 'em not any different themselves from the Steadbacks. And it's the same old story. Upstairs tonight, I bet you they've already raised their usual fuss about too many specials and how this town don't need no specials, anyway, 'specially out your way."

"Christ."

"Those Steadbacks. Suppose you know they got kicked outa Barchester."

"No, I didn't know."

"They was livin' in a cellar hole ovah t' Barchester. Livin' like pigs for years, till 'nough people complained, and the health authorities finally came and evicted them. Kicked 'em right outa Barchester and into Coggerton. We get 'em all, right here in Coggerton, all the ones no other town'll have."

"But what about the health authorities here? I should think — ah, I get it. Stanton Wormald. He's Coggerton's health—"

"You got it. And Stanton ain't *never* gonna kick no one out 'cause o' health reasons." Paulin, imitating Wormald, said, " 'After all, poor family like Steadbacks ain't botherin' nobody, health-wise.' Oh, and you shoulda seen the place in Barchester after the health department got them all outa there. I ain't seen it myself, but I heard about it. Heard it was the *nastiest* place. And this is what I'm gettin' to. When they went into that house, they found all kinds o' things other people had reported missin'. A coat some girl at the high school reported stolen. A hi-fi set from a house only three doors down. A wallet with half a dozen credit cards, and other things like that."

"Great. And now they're our neighbors."

"Just thought you'd a right to know, is all."

"I do want to know. Thank you."

"Well, been real nice talkin' with you, Mrs. Atwood. Just give us a yell if you need us out theyah."

Upstairs again, Cassie stood at the back of the hall, not wanting to draw attention to herself by returning to the bleachers.

The Bozo the Clown kid was still standing by the door to the hall with his anti-zoning flyers tucked under his arm. He reminded her of a joke she'd been told by the boy in the apartment block she lived in when she was a kid.

The boy was Dickie Inferarra. Dickie was eight, two years older than she, and there was something a little thrilling about him, the way he swaggered around, the way he'd sidle up to her with his jokes, with the stories he'd tell her about hanging around the dump behind the row of garages of the apartment block, and about throwing cats into the in-ground garbage pails beside the back doors of the apartments. Dickie would play with her, tell her jokes, hint at dark deeds, as long as there was no one else more interesting around, like Dickie's best friend, Donald Scammell. Whenever Donald would amble into the yard, he and Dickie would run off, usually to the mysterious territory behind the garages. They'd leave, with Dickie not even saying so much as goodbye, and Cassie, jealous, would watch them disappear into the tiny space between the row of garages and the chain link fence.

But the joke. It was Dickie's joke she now recalled. And in recalling it, she also remembered details surrounding the telling of the joke that had nothing to do with the joke itself. She and Dickie were in the back yard. She was straddling her Huffy Convertible bike which only recently she'd learned to ride without the training wheels. Her favorite possession, that bike. Blue fenders, blue handgrips, gleaming chrome handlebars. The sun was bright and the chrome handlebars were hot to the touch.

The joke Dickie told was about a traveling salesman — Dickie had a fund of traveling-salesman jokes — who'd come to a farm and asked for a place to sleep for the night. Uh-oh! Sorry! the farmer tells the salesman. No room at the inn. Unless, of course, you want to sleep with my daughter. Well, I guess I could put up with that, seeing it's only one night, replies the salesman. Fine, then, says the farmer, but I'll have to put a sheet between the two of you in bed. Sure, sure, anything you say, says the salesman. Some years later the salesman returns to the very same farm where he encounters a deformed idiot kid hanging around. Why son, says the salesman. What's the matter with you? You look all *funny*! And then, the punch line, which Cassie hadn't understood. (In fact, she rarely understood Dickie's jokes. She laughed at them because she knew from the way he told them that they were "dirty," which made them funny, even hilarious.) The punch line: The deformed idiot replies, "Hah, mister. You'd look funny, too, if you'd been strained through a sheet!"

Now, as Cassie stared at the Bozo kid at the rear of the hall, she heard Dickie deliver the punch line, heard him start to snicker before he finished it, and wondered, absurdly, if the sheet through which Bozo had been strained was muslin or percale, and how many threads it had to the inch. Was it clean or dirty, fitted or flat, plain or printed with tiny flowers?

Standing at the front of the hall, Myron Ricker was droning on, holding his soft gray hat close to his chest, reminding Cassie once again of an undertaker, shuffling and offering condolences to the bereaved, all the while sizing up what sort of funeral he can bleed out of them. He was saying, "... somethin' in reference to that in the paper the othah day bears out the same thing. I shoulda been smaht and cut it out. Bears out the same thing. A town violated what they agreed to do. Seems to me, when it comes to decidin' whether or not town should take ovah a road in a development, it shouldn't be left up to a few people to decide, 'cause that's where overlookin' the good of the people comes into bein' at times. Now, my way of thinkin' is, anybody objects to town takin' over a developer's road, why that party's calibratin' itself to the big developers, and ain't takin' into consideration the small developer like myself and some others in town heeyah who just want to put in a few houses now and then, with the idea of givin' owah young folks a decent place t' live."

Cassie gathered from what Ricker said that it had to do with the taxpayers footing the bill for the maintenance of a road in one of his developments.

Parker said. "Okay Myron. Any more discussion on this article?"

"Judge Parker?" A man in the bleachers stood. Green work pants, faded blue plain flannel shirt with the sleeves rolled up to the elbows. Light brown crew cut and square, horn-rimmed glasses. Two large front buck teeth and a receding chin. A woodchuck.

"Go ahead, Howie."

"Well, seems to me our taxes ain't gone up 'preciably like some says they was gonna since we took on Myron's road up there off the Province Road. So I say we oughta vote on this article the way we voted on the one like it last year."

Fuck! It's not just Bozo. It's the whole goddamn town. The whole goddamn town's been strained through a sheet.

She had to get out of there, before all these people read her mind, saw what she was thinking and came after her, chasing her into a corner of the hall where they'd push against her, push until they suffocated her, killed her. Or if she didn't get out of there, she might become one of them, seeing things their way, screaming about outsiders and Commies.

On the top step outside the town hall she paused to zip her
jacket, breathing deeply the cold night air.

"Cassie."

She jumped, her heart thudding. Jim.

"Sorry. Didn't mean to startle you."

"It's okay. I was jumpy anyway. I had to get out of there."

"I figured you might leave, once you heard Ricker pushing
for the town to take over another of his roads."

"I didn't see *you* in there."

"Your husband, he isn't with—"

"No. He's home watching some dumb—he's taking care
of Andy."

"Would you like a cup of coffee? Mary Ellen's is open till
eleven."

"Yes," Cassie said, her heart slamming, her hands sweating.

They stepped into the soft yellow light of Mary Ellen's
restaurant. *A clean, well-lighted place.* They ordered, and sat in
the same booth she and Andy had sat in with Jim last summer.

Cassie slipped off her jacket. She wished she were wearing
something other than her sweatshirt and jeans, wished she
looked *pretty* for him.

"Why do you bother going to town meeting?" she asked.

Jim raised his eyebrows and smiled. "Good question. Don't
really know why I bother anymore. Habit, I guess. I've been
coming to town meeting since I was a teenager, when my
grandfather and father would take me. A Brackett was at
Coggerton's first meeting, and I guess I feel kind of obligated
to be there."

Cassie watched his eyes look first at her eyes, then her
mouth, before returning to her eyes again. He asked, "How
have you been, your first winter out there?"

"All right. Getting cabin fever, though. I never did save
that dandelion wine for winter, as you suggested. And then

when the snow came, I wished I had."

"Why don't you make your own this year? Thurlows' field next to you is all dandelions in spring."

"I know. That's where I got the greens last year." If only his eyes weren't so blue. "How is your brother?"

"Fair. Better than he was a few months ago. Every year he seems to pick up when he smells spring in the air."

Jim's hands were folded loosely on the table in front of his cup of tea. Cassie's hands twisted an empty sugar packet in front of her coffee cup. She calculated: If she moved her hands three inches, their hands would be touching.

"I never did thank you properly for the soup you brought us that day. I hope you didn't think I was rude."

"Of course I didn't."

"I was preoccupied with Woodbury. I wished I could have spent more time with you."

Cassie dropped the sugar packet and slid her hand forward, touching his.

Jim lifted his hand and covered hers, squeezing it gently, barely perceptibly. For a few moments they sat that way, his hand motionless on hers, both she and he still, looking at their hands. Then Jim lifted his hand and with the tips of his fingers, he caressed the back of her hand, her knuckles, her fingers. Without lifting his gaze, he shook his head left, right, left again.

"What?"

No answer.

"What? Tell me. *Please.*"

Then, suddenly, Jim withdrew his hand and closed his eyes.

"Jim?"

He opened his eyes. They were moist, shining. He shook his head. "No, Cassie, there'd be no point. It can't happen. You know it as well."

"Damn!" she whispered. "Damn *damn.*" Her eyes stung. She looked at him, pleading, "Why *not?*"

Jim shook his head again, slowly, his eyes sad.

Eighteen

Early April. Morning.

"Cassie? Have you heard the news?"

"What news, Emma?"

"The Bracketts' place burned."

"What? When?"

"Three days ago. I would have let you know sooner but I was waitin' for all the details from my Vernon. He's on the volunteer fire department, you know. Fact, this is his seventh year and—"

"What about the men?—Jim and—"

"Well, I was about to tell you. Jim Brackett's all right, but the old man died in the fire."

"Jesus Christ!" She'd been leaning against the wall, and now she slid down along the wall, to sit on the floor. Woodbury in his chair on the porch, watching the field. Jim handing her the dandelion wine. And sitting with him in Mary Ellen's, their hands together on the table. Cassie's eyes stung. She shut them, listening to Emma.

"Course, Woodbury didn't *have* to die. It was just his stubbornness. Vern said when he got there, the old man was standin' on the porch, wavin' a shotgun, yellin' at all the men to stay back. Then, when Vern and a couple of the others tried to reach him, to talk him into comin' down off the porch, he pointed that gun right at them and told them he'd shoot for sure if they stepped onto the porch. And everybody *knows* you don't fool around with Woodbury. Everybody always said you could take Woodbury at his word. Finally, Vern says, Woodbury lowered his gun and when he did, a few of the men jumped up onto the porch. But the old man just stepped back into the door to the kitchen, and Vern says when they were almost to him again, he raised his gun again and started hollerin' and carryin' on somethin' dreadful. You know how these old farmhouses go, once they catch fire. Anyway, once the old man stepped back into that kitchen, Vern says, there wasn't any man there fool enough to risk his own life goin' in there. Anybody fool enough to try it would burn to death sure, if the old man's gun didn't kill him first."

"And his brother? Where was his brother?"

"Jim? Well, at first no one knew where he was, and some even thought he might be in there with the old man. But seems he was over town for somethin' 'cause he drove in right after the old man stepped back into the kitchen and disappeared. Vern says Jim took it *awful* hard. Just about went into shock, I should say, from the way Vern describes how he acted."

"What do you mean? How *did* he—"

"Well, Vern says when they told Jim his brother was in the house, all he did at first was to look up at the house, look right at the kitchen door. Then he nodded. Didn't say nothin', just stood there noddin' for the longest time—Vern says it seemed like forever. Then after a while, Vern says, Jim shut his eyes and said—barely loud nuff for Vern to hear—he said real slow, 'So they did it. They did it. They did it.' Vern says there was no question in his mind but what Jim Brackett'd gone clear crazy, 'cause no one could make a particle of sense outa what he was sayin'. Finally, Vern says, Jim Brackett walked right over to Erlon Ricker—Myron's boy—and said to him, in a quiet voice, just like he was askin' the time of day—that Jim says to Erlon, 'You goddamn sonofabitch. You and the rest of you greedy bastards.' "

Cassie remembered that Jim and Woodbury had told her how the Rickers had the Bracketts' place surrounded, how they kept pressuring the Bracketts to sell their land, and how, they suspected, the Rickers had poisoned their well.

"Why do you suppose Jim Brackett said that to the Ricker kid, Emma?"

"I'm sure I don't know. Course, that Jim Brackett's always been persnickety, always complainin' about Ricker buildin' houses here and there around town. But I must say, from what Vern tells us, Erlon Ricker took what Jim said to him real big. After Jim said what he did, he walked down the driveway to where he'd parked his pickup behind the fire trucks and other vehicles, and he climbed in the truck and just sat there, watchin' the fire, till every last man had gone home next mornin'. But—oh, I was sayin' about Erlon. He took it just fine, Vern says. After Jim Brackett walked away, Erlon just shrugged and stared after him, lookin' real sorry for him. Then he says to a few of the men that no one could really *blame* Jim Brackett for what he said, it bein' such a terrible shock to come home and hear his brother's still in the house."

"Do they know what caused the fire?"

"Well, no, though everybody knew the old man was careless when he lit the stoves. Will once saw him throw a cupful kerosene on the kitchen stove fire to get it goin'. Saw him just lay down some paper and then some logs on top, without botherin' to build a proper fire with kindlin', and then just toss that kerosene on top. Nearly singed Will's eyebrows."

"Do they all think that's the way it happened?" Cassie covered the mouthpiece of the phone to keep Emma from knowing she was crying.

"I guess most of the men figured that's how it coulda happened, especially since the old man's been crazy-actin' this past year or so, sittin' on the porch all day long, starin' out over the fields at the woods, seein' God knows what. Kept sayin' Ricker was gonna steal his land. Got so he'd even taken to sittin' there with the shotgun 'crost his knees. Someone said once it was so cold, barely above freezin' and a raw wind blowin' too, that his brother practically had to drag him inside, off that porch. Why, sounds to me like old Woodbury was downright touched. I can't imagine Myron Ricker with all *his* money needin' to steal anythin'. Turns out, Myron offered Jim

Brackett a pretty handsome price for that land of his. Nobody could hardly call that stealin'. Not only that, it was Ricker himself, or rather, him and his boy Erlon, what took up a collection for flowers for the old man. Pretty generous, when you figure what Jim Brackett said to young Erlon the very night before."

"Ricker bought Bracketts' land? Already? Where's Jim, now?"

"Well, no one's entirely sure about that. Vern says for the longest time — fact, all night — he just sat there leanin' on the steerin' wheel of his pickup truck starin' at the fire. Next day, he drove off and no one can say for sure where he went. Downtown they're sayin' he went to stay with a cousin of his in Chichester — that's over Concord way you know?"

"Yeah."

"But then, Bertha Corson, who lives just this side of Hog Holler, says she knows for sure that not long after he drove away from the fire, Jim Brackett saw Ricker and agreed to sell him the land. Then, Bertha says, after they closed the deal, he was seen getting on a bus to Boston." After a pause Emma added, "Suppose Bertha should know. She lives out that way, after all."

Cassie wanted no more. "Thanks for telling me, Emma."

"Oh, that's all right. I'll let you know if there's any more news."

Sobbing, Cassie wanted to stay on the floor forever, her back against the cool plaster wall.

Cassie was surprised to see still there on the corner the big aluminum mailbox with its faded red letters: "Brackett."

It was mudseason. She held tight to the steering wheel, concentrating on keeping the car moving in the ruts of the lane. She stopped her car in front of where the Bracketts' house had been. The only thing that rose above the granite top rocks of the foundation was the central chimney. Several courses of bricks had been knocked off its top, leaving it jagged against the sky.

Underfoot, her boots crunched on black cinders and larger bits of charred wood as she picked her way through rusty nails and shards of window glass everywhere on the ground. In the cellar hole, more broken glass, some in huge, jagged, blade-like pieces which glinted in the sun, some of it smashed white into small pieces. In a corner of the cellar hole, a bedspring leaned against the foundation wall, its mattress folded in half and leaning against it, looking oddly unharmed except for a long slash in the ticking, oozing stuffing.

She headed for the orchard where she and Jim had walked last summer. Her eyes swept up the trunk into the still-bare branches of the huge oak tree. The branches nearest to the fire were singed. Nailed to the tree was a cardboard sign, crudely lettered: "No Trespassing. Police Take Notice." And then, the signature, "Myron Ricker." Fucking bastard. She reached up and curled her fingers behind the top of the sign, paused, then loosened her grip. Stepping around the tree, she went over to the barn foundation and stood on the top rock where she and Jim had stood together. She looked down into the foundation. The raspberry bushes there last autumn, dying, would soon come to life, filling and choking the foundation with a dense tangle of vines.

She walked around to the front of the house, where the porch had been. Patches of snow lingered in the dead grasses of the field. On that September day when she was here, the grasses, glowing golden, had been alive with crickets. This April day had the feel of winter about it. Cassie looked up. It could snow. The sunlight was weak, thin; clouds were thickening in the gray-blue sky. Turning, she realized she was standing just about where she'd sat that afternoon with Jim and Woodbury.

She pictured how it must have been, the night of the fire.

Clouds of smoke billowing up, layering themselves in thick black rolls, rolling and churning upward, higher and higher, until they dissolve into the deep night sky.

And there! Woodbury on the porch, lit from behind by the flames, the curve of his humped back silhouetted against the blinding light of the kitchen doorway. Vernon Thurlow steps onto the porch, then pulls back as Woodbury pushes the shotgun to within inches of his face.

Now Woodbury staggers back into the kitchen, only the tip of his gun barrel sticking out onto the porch. The fire gains momentum, feeding itself, surrounding Woodbury, until he is enfolded, his face white, whiter, blinding white, as he becomes one with the fire and disappears.

Cassie knelt and scooped up a fistful of charred bits. She crumbled a piece between her thumb and fingers, then quickly shook off the crumbs and wiped her hands on her jeans, shuddering, remembering an episode in the television series *The Ascent of Man*.

In that episode, Jacob Bronowski, the narrator, after giving a tour of Auschwitz, stood on the edge of a swamp, talking about man's inhumanity to man. Cassie had practically come out of her chair as Bronowski, in his dark blue suit, light glinting off his rimless round eyeglasses, waded into that swamp right up to his ankles, squatted down and scooped up a handful of mud and water—slime dripping down the sleeve of his suit jacket—all the while talking about the ashes of his relatives being there in that swamp, perhaps in that very handful of muck he'd just dredged up.

But how absurd, to think she might be sifting through the ashes of Woodbury himself. Still, he was in there, wasn't he, somewhere down among the black rubble of that cellar hole?

Feeling jittery, morbid, she stood up. Enough. She walked quickly along the front of the house, along where the porch had been, stepping around a refrigerator lying on its side, its door open.

She came to the oak tree, and this time, not looking around, not caring whether anyone saw her or not, she yanked the No Trespassing sign off the tree, ripped it in half, and threw the pieces into the foundation, thinking at the same instant it was wrong to throw them there, that she should've thrown them somewhere off the property, off this property Ricker had no right to. She closed her eyes. Her breath came in short gasps, her face contorted, her eyes spilled. "Jim," she whispered.

She drove down the lane too fast, not watching the ruts, not taking care to keep out of the ditch, not minding that the car was dragging and bumping along the high spots all the way to the Wilmot Falls Road.

Nineteen

Except when she met Andy at the bus, Cassie seldom left the house now. The spring before she had delighted in the partridge's drumming, noted the date the robins arrived, and been eager for any chance to walk in the woods, to sit, content, on the stone bridge listening to the brook make the same sounds again and again as it passed over and around the same rocks.

Now the partridge drummed, and she did not delight in its drumming. The robins came and began nesting before she took notice of them. The few times she walked to the brook or through the field, she heard not the brook or the songs of birds, but a dog barking there, a bulldozer droning there, a chainsaw growling off that way. Even the old lilac bush in the corner of the house annoyed her as it scraped its budding branches along the living room window, clawing on the glass.

The bulldozing in Thurlows' field next to them began in early May. One afternoon, on her way to meet Andy at the bus, Cassie detoured off the lane and climbed the slope where, from the top of the ridge, she could look down onto the broad flat sweep of field.

It was Vernon Thurlow, working his bulldozer, shoving the dark brown earth up in a long snake-mound at the edge of the field near the road.

Cassie did not have to climb the slope to see what was going on. She could have seen from the mailbox, but she rarely went to the mailbox now, letting Michael pick up the mail instead, because she wanted to avoid any encounter with Emma.

And there was another reason she didn't go to the mailbox anymore, a reason which Michael dismissed as irrational. One day she'd opened the box to find a notice from the Post Office: "Due to the many new residents who have moved into the rural area of Coggerton, New Hampshire, the Postal Service is now required to renumber certain boxes. It will now be necessary for you to use your street number in your mailing address. Your mailing address will now be: 44A Thurlow Road." No more RFD 2. 44A was not much different, really, from their old apartment address.

This time, she was not surprised to see Vernon Thurlow stripping loam. She had learned that the locals looked upon their land as something to be exploited.

From the top of the slope she could see Thurlows' barn, and beyond it, the field where only last spring, sheep grazed. Now there were three house lots. On one was a double-wide olive-green trailer with phony half-timbering on its ends. English Tudor. And on the second lot, a small box of a house, partly sided with mud-red asphalt shingles. Already in the front yard were a couple of junk cars, a dog house, a stack of cordwood. What was in store for the third lot?

The school bus groaned up the hill, then hissed to a halt. When Andy appeared in front of the bus, crossed the road, and headed down the lane, she angled down the slope to meet him.

A few days later, when Cassie stepped into the yard to meet Andy at the bus, an acrid odor assaulted her. Halfway up the lane the odor intensified. It was familiar; she'd smelled it somewhere before. Sulphur? Did it have something to do with Vernon's bulldozer chewing away on the other side of the slope?

Andy came around the front of the bus frowning. "Jeesh," he scowled. "What's that *smell? Yuck!*"

"I think it's coming from where the Thurlows are bulldozing in the field over there. Let's go look."

Andy zigzagged up the slope, stopping now and then to pull up dandelions, his hair shiny in the sun.

This would be the time to gather the blossoms to make dandelion wine. She had planned to, until the Bracketts' fire. She had planned to make some and surprise Jim with a bottle. But now she didn't even know where he was, or how to locate him. And anyway, it was clear he didn't want to see her. Maybe she'd make the wine anyway, as a kind of testimonial to Jim. Do this in remembrance.

She caught up to Andy, who was half humming, half singing a TV commercial, "Take a walk, take a walk, walk on over to Wyler's." At the top of the slope they looked down. At first, Cassie couldn't make out what they were looking at. Vernon was riding a machine which was hauling a green box, out of which flowed a wet black ribbon steaming blue smoke. Will Thurlow and Peter Fecteau followed Vernon, smoothing the black band with rakes.

It hit her: asphalt. Jesus fucking Christ, asphalt!

"What are they doing down there, huh Mum? What's that black stuff? Is that what the smell is?"

"What they are doing, Andy, is paving."

"But that's not a road."

"No, that's not a road."

"Then what are they doing that for?"

"I don't know. I'll be goddamned if I know. Jesus Christ. Let's go." She grabbed Andy by the arm, almost dragging him down the slope.

Skipping the amenities, Cassie said, "Emma?"

"Yes."

"What are they doing in the field next to us?"

Silence. Then Emma oozed, "Oh, haven't you heard?"

"No. Heard what."

"My Vern is building a racetrack."

"*What?!*"

"A racetrack. Course, I think I've told you Vern was awful fond of stock car racing when he was in high school, but since then he's been so busy, first helping his father, then paving and hauling and what not for Myron Ricker. And this is somethin' he's always dreamed of doin', you know — givin' young folks some kind of clean recreation. And you know my Vern, he don't tolerate any bums, any *bad* types, so you needn't worry about what *sort* of young folks'll be comin' to run their cars there."

"*What?*"

Emma repeated, louder, "I said you needn't worry 'bout what *sort* of young folks'll be comin' to use the track, 'cause—"

"What are you *saying*? They're gonna race *cars* out there? In the middle of the *field*?"

"Well, yes. Course, mostly it'll be just weekends when Vern holds the races. 'Cept once in a while during the week some young fellas might want to practice a little."

"*Jesus Christ!*"

"I don't see how you can possibly object to young people havin' a good time now and then. And Vernon stands to make a steady livin' from this. Really, Cassie, all of us who've been here any length of time believe a person has a right to do what he wants with his own land."

"So that's it again, is it."

"What?"

"The old crap about doing what you want with your own land. The same old crap about not being allowed to say anything unless you've lived here three hundred goddamn years. What about *our* right to peace and quiet on *our* land? In *our air space*?

"Well *really*, Cassie, we *have* been gettin' along perfectly well all these years."

"Yeah, I believe that."

"Besides, it's not like Vernon's gonna do anythin' that's not right. It's good clean fun for the young folks."

"Emma, you know what? I would rather Vernon built a whorehouse in that field. A hundred room, ten-story whorehouse covering the whole goddamn field rather than a goddamn racetrack. And you know why?"

No answer.

"You know *why*?"

"Well! Really, Cassie, I—"

"Because a whorehouse would be quiet. Not a sound. Quiet. No noise."

"Really—"

"Yes, really. Anything but one more goddamn fucking goddamn bunch of noise heaped on us."

"Well! Perhaps if you don't like the way we—"

Cassie slammed down the phone, pulling down on the receiver, pulling, gripping tight, wanting to rip the phone from the wall.

Michael, home from work, burst into the kitchen. "What the hell are they doing in the field?"

"You're the engineer, my love. Can't you tell? They're paving."

"Oh for Chrissake, I know *that*. But what are they paving for, in the goddamn field for Chrissake?"

"They are building a racetrack."

"Are you shittin' me? Who told you?"

"Emma."

Michael went to the living-room window and leaned against the frame, arms up and to the sides, forming a cross.

Silhouetted against the light, he reminded her of the way the tormented father in Bergman's movie *Through a Glass Darkly* had looked, photographed from behind. Michael inhaled and exhaled, deeply, his shoulders rising and falling. "That's it, then, isn't it."

"Yes. So much for the Good Life."

Michael dropped his arms and turned to face her. "Now what?"

"The sooner the better, I think."

"Who do we get?"

"Skillin."

"Why *that* sonofabitch?"

"Because he *is* a sonofabitch, and he'll get us the most money, that's why. Oh, and you know how we joked about him not selling lot number eight on the Pickard Road below us there? How we said that gave the bastard access to this property? Doesn't seem so funny now, does it? See how easy it'll be for him now."

"That bastard. What a lousy fucking shame."

Cassie looked at him, then beyond him, past the lilac bush, past the garden at the hill beyond the field. She stepped forward and stood next to him, not touching, he looking one way, she looking out the window.

"Yes."

"Skillin?"

"Yes."

"Cassie Atwood."

"Oh. Cassie! How are you? Howah things out your way? How you folks doin'? Got your garden in yet?"

"Cut the crap, Skillin. You've won."

"What?"

"I said you've won. You can have the place. Put it on the market. Just hurry up about it and don't bother us any more than you have to about anything. All we care about now is that you do it fast and get the most money you can for us."

"Well, Cassie. I, uh—if you really want—"

"*Yes!*" she hissed. "Just do it. No more of your slimy bull-shit. Save it for your next sucker."

"Ah, well, there will be papers. Should I bring them out?"

"*No!* No, we'll come down there. We don't want you on this land until you have to be."

"Well then, whenever it's convenient for you."

"We'll be down."

She hung up the phone. She opened the kitchen window, breathing deeply, inhaling the perfume of the lilacs. Her eyes filled. She blinked, then closed her eyes to shut out the view. The spring morning was too beautiful.

That night, after Andy and Michael were asleep, Cassie stepped outside. Though the air was balmy for May, the dewy grass chilled her bare feet. She walked past the well rock and the clothesline—both sharp in the light of the full moon—to the front of the house. Beyond the maples rose the hills of Wilmot Falls, three black humps against the blue-black sky. The brook was rushing; the ground-water table was high this spring.

Below the hills, the lights of Coggerton, nestled in the valley. Silent night, unholy night. Wee Willie Winkie runs through the town. Wee Willie Winkie in his red and white-striped nightgown and elf's cap, flying up the dark wooden stairways to the apartments over the stores in the town, calling out, his twinkling voice reverberating off the drab wooden buildings on Lower Main, "Time for be-ed, little sleepy heads of Coggerton."

What an easy target the rows of lights looked. She imagined planes screaming overhead in the night sky, open bellies raining bombs. Or just one bomb — a nuke that wipes out the whole town and everything in it. The mushroom growing, arching over the town, frying all the unsuspecting innocents in their sleep.

She slipped around to the gable end of the house that faced the lane, standing on the lawn in a triangle of shadow. She looked up at the four-over-four attic window. In the distance a dog was howling, sounding more like a coyote, or a wolf. Sounding lonely, that far away.

And then she pictured herself up in that attic. Now, at night. Up there because Michael, unable to get to her, had called to warn her. To warn her that they were coming down the lane. Coming in a mob, a pack, to get her, to get the child.

She had barricaded the doors, shaken Andy from his sleep: "Wake up Andy! Move! Hurry! We're in trouble!" she screamed at him as she dragged him from his bed.

Upstairs, in the attic, she tucks Andy under the eaves. "Stay *down*, Andy. *Don't move!* Whatever happens, *don't move, don't make a sound!"*

She crouches by the window, hearing only her own breathing at first, and then she hears them. Hears the swelling roar of the mob, urged on by a voice or voices which now and then rise above the din.

Soon the glow of their torches appears in the lane, brightening as they get closer.

Now! Now — it's time! With the butt of the shotgun she smashes out a pane of glass. The glass tinkles onto the attic floorboards and falls muffled to the lawn below. She points the gun out the window, at the lane, resting the butt on her shoulder, the barrel on the muntin, just as they surge around the corner into view.

They are all there. Those in front with torches, others carrying sticks. Ricker in his gray suit and tie on a bulldozer, the torchlight glinting off the steel blade. Stanton Wormald, tugged and jerked toward the house by a pack of leaping, snarling dogs fanning out at the ends of their leashes. Esther Lessard, lugging a jigsaw. Sally Wilkins, in her blue terry-cloth bathrobe, her hair in pink rollers, holding high a stick, grinning, her lower lip pulled tight against her bottom teeth.

And look — there — along the side — the Dalpeys, all of them, on snowmobiles, zigzagging back and forth from the lane where their machines churn up gravel, to the field and lawn around the house, where the tracks chew up the grass, throw up loam.

Clutches of children, brandishing sticks and picking up rocks along the lane as they come, like the children in "The Lottery." Little Jimmy Fecteau leading the way, grinning, teeth glinting and brown skin gleaming in the moonlight.

And then Cassie shoots, and for a moment the mob hesitates, falling back with their torches, like the enraged mobs surging through the street of Paris in *The Phantom of the Opera*, faltering now and then for an instant as the pursued Phantom turns and leers or gestures maniacally at them.

Cassie blinked and dropped her gaze from the attic window. No dogs were barking. The air was still. Everything was silent.